Roman
Folktales

Roman
Folktales

Edited and Introduced by
Cristina Mazzoni

General Editor: Jake Jackson

**FLAME TREE
PUBLISHING**

This is a FLAME TREE Book

FLAME TREE PUBLISHING
6 Melbray Mews
Fulham, London SW6 3NS
United Kingdom
www.flametreepublishing.com

First published 2024
Copyright © 2024 Flame Tree Publishing Ltd

24 26 28 27 25
1 3 5 7 9 8 6 4 2

ISBN: 978-1-80417-814-0
ebook ISBN: 978-1-80417-958-1

The cover design is © copyright 2024 Flame Tree Publishing Ltd, featuring
Narrators of the Decameron, by the Master of the Rouen Échevinage, 1400s,
and decoration courtesy of Shutterstock.com/Anastasiia Veretennikova.

All inside images courtesy of Shutterstock.com and the following:
Kristina Birukova, paprika, a Sk and Kotkoa.

The text in this book is selected and edited from *Roman Legends: A Collection of
the Fables and Folk-Lore of Rome* by Rachel Harriette Busk, 1877 (Boston: Estes
and Laurita) as well as the following additional original sources: *Evenings with
the Old Story Tellers: Selected Tales from the Gesta Romanorum* by Anonymous,
1845 (London: Burns); *A Hand-book of Mythology: The Myths and Legends of
Ancient Greece and Rome* by E.M. Berens, 1894 (New York: Maynard, Merrill,
& Co.); Valerius Maximus, *The Acts and Sayings of the Romans*, translated by
Samuel Speed (London, 1678); *Letters* by Pliny the Younger, translated by William
Melmoth. Revised by F.C.T. Bosanquet, 1909–1914 (Harvard Classics. New York:
Collier & Son); and a translation of 'Cupid and Psyche' by John Cirignano.

Designed and created in the UK | Printed and bound in China

Contents

Series Foreword

STRETCHING BACK to the oral traditions of thousands of years ago, tales of heroes and disaster, creation and conquest have been told by many different civilizations in many different ways. Their impact sits deep within our culture even though the detail in the tales themselves are a loose mix of historical record, transformed narrative and the distortions of hundreds of storytellers.

Today the language of mythology lives with us: our mood is jovial, our countenance is saturnine, we are narcissistic and our modern life is hermetically sealed from others. The nuances of myths and legends form part of our daily routines and help us navigate the world around us, with its half truths and biased reported facts.

The nature of a myth is that its story is already known by most of those who hear it, or read it. Every generation brings a new emphasis, but the fundamentals remain the same: a desire to understand and describe the events and relationships of the world. Many of the great stories are archetypes that help us find our own place, equipping us with tools for self-understanding, both individually and as part of a broader culture.

For Western societies it is Greek mythology that speaks to us most clearly. It greatly influenced the mythological heritage of the ancient Roman civilization and is the lens through which we still see the Celts, the Norse and many of the other great peoples and religions. The Greeks themselves learned much from their neighbours, the Egyptians, an older culture that became weak with age and incestuous leadership.

It is important to understand that what we perceive now as mythology had its own origins in perceptions of the divine and the rituals of the sacred. The earliest civilizations, in the crucible of the Middle East, in the Sumer of the third millennium BC, are the source to which many of the mythic archetypes can be traced. As humankind collected together in cities for the first time, developed writing and industrial scale agriculture, started to irrigate the rivers and attempted to control rather than be at the mercy of its environment, humanity began to write down its tentative explanations of natural events, of floods and plagues, of disease.

Early stories tell of Gods (or god-like animals in the case of tribal societies such as African, Native American or Aboriginal cultures) who are crafty and use their wits to survive, and it is reasonable to suggest that these were the first rulers of the gathering peoples of the earth, later elevated to god-like status with the distance of time. Such tales became more political as cities vied with each other for supremacy, creating new Gods, new hierarchies for their pantheons. The older Gods took on primordial roles and became the preserve of creation and destruction, leaving the new gods to deal with more current, everyday affairs. Empires rose and fell, with Babylon assuming the mantle from Sumeria in the 1800s BC, then in turn to be swept away by the Assyrians of the 1200s BC; then the Assyrians and the Egyptians were subjugated by the Greeks, the Greeks by the Romans and so on, leading to the spread and assimilation of common themes, ideas and stories throughout the world.

The survival of history is dependent on the telling of good tales, but each one must have the 'feeling' of truth, otherwise it will be ignored. Around the firesides, or embedded in a book or a computer, the myths and legends of the past are still the living materials of retold myth, not restricted to an exploration of origins. Now we have devices and global communications that give us unparalleled access to a diversity of traditions. We can find out about Native American, Indian, Chinese and tribal African mythology in a way that was denied to our ancestors, we can find connections, match the archaeology, religion and the mythologies of the world to build a comprehensive image of the human experience that is endlessly fascinating.

The stories in this book provide an introduction to the themes and concerns of the myths and legends of their respective cultures, with a short introduction to provide a linguistic, geographic and political context. This is where the myths have arrived today, but undoubtedly over the next millennia, they will transform again whilst retaining their essential truths and signs.

Jake Jackson
General Editor

Introduction to
Roman Folktales

PROFESSIONAL STORYTELLERS have all but disappeared in contemporary Italy. Even in the late nineteenth century, those who made a living telling tales were already regarded as quaint and a thing of the past. About the Roman raconteur Cecingulo, for example, we read that, 'In days gone by, he used to sit in Piazza Navona of an evening when people had left work and had time to listen, and he would pour stories out by the hour. Now and then he stopped, and went round with his hat, and there were few who did not spare him a *bajocco*....There was no end to the number of stories he could tell.' The memory of Cecingulo is preserved in R.H. Busk's *The Folk-Lore of Rome, Collected by Word of Mouth of the People*. First published in London in 1874, the collection was published again in Boston in 1877 with the more accurate title *Roman Legends: A Collection of the Fables and Folk-Lore of Rome*. It is the source of all of the stories featured in this book, except those in the 'Classical Tales' section, which draw on a range of ancient texts.

Busk's work brings together tales from the city of Rome and the former Papal States around it, retelling stories that the author heard from local oral informants, whom she calls 'narrators', during her sojourn in the Eternal City. The narratives include the adventures of simpletons and tricksters such as abound in cultures around the world; tales of wild and domestic animals, both imaginary and real; stories centred on food that, by turns, serves to heal, poison, satiate or kill; accounts of love and marriage, Roman style – some are happy, most not so much; and the doings of supernatural creatures, both good and evil, including saints and devils, fairies, witches and ghosts. Some of the narratives in Busk's book rely on magic for their unfolding, and readers will recognize variations of classic fairy tales such as 'Rapunzel', 'Cinderella', 'Hansel and Gretel' and more. Many are steeped in Catholicism and often blur the line between religion and magic. There are also plenty of realistic stories, both comic and tragic, typical of the Italian novella tradition made famous by Boccaccio's *Decameron*. Busk transcribed and translated into English the spoken words of the Roman women and men around her because she could find no such stories in libraries and bookshops. Fortunately her knowledge of Italian and her participation in local daily life and religious practices led people to trust and talk to her.

R.H. Busk, an Englishwoman in the Eternal City

Rachel Harriette Busk was born in London in 1831. She was the youngest of six surviving children and one of five daughters; the travel writer and memoirist Julia Clara Byrne was one of her sisters. The Busk children were all brought up in the Anglican Church, but in 1858 Rachel converted to Catholicism; her example was soon followed by several of her siblings. Sometime after 1862 Busk moved to Rome permanently to be with her sister Frances Rosalie, who had separated from her abusive husband. In Rome, Busk worked as a correspondent for British periodicals on Italian and papal matters, in addition to producing her collection of local folktales. We do not know exactly where in Rome she lived (probably in the area around the Spanish Steps, where most British expatriates in Rome resided), nor when she left that city. She died in England in 1907.

When Busk published her research on Roman legends, she had already written about European and Asian folklore, including books on the oral traditions of Spain, the Tyrol and Mongolia. In the 1880s and 1890s her work also appeared regularly in the folklore journal *Notes & Queries*, founded in 1849 by William John Thoms – the man credited with inventing in 1846 the word 'Folk-Lore' (as it was then spelled), derived from 'lore', instruction, and 'folk'. In the early decades of the discipline, the term 'folk' was used to describe almost exclusively the uneducated and mainly rural poor. Today folklore no longer routinely involves this level of class bias. However, it does still encompass now, as it did then, subjects as varied as verbal lore, or the things people say – including folktales, legends and, more controversially, myths, as well as jokes, anecdotes and proverbs; material lore, or the things people *make*, not only tangible objects such as handicrafts, tools and clothing, but also foods, buildings and more; and customary lore, or the things people *do*, such as performances, traditions, superstitions and folk medicine, even the prayerful dusting of the altar at the Holy House in Loreto at 11 p.m. described by Busk in her Preface. Her work was dedicated to verbal lore, but her numerous notes present the reader with much information about material and customary lore as well. Busk believed such details provided some 'local colour' to folktales that often also exist in other places and may not seem properly 'Roman' without these culture-specific details. The favourite dishes of the Roman middle class, for example, are described in a note to 'The Enchanted Rose Tree' as including the still very popular 'supplì di riso', or fried rice balls, stuffed at the time with 'rigaglie' (poultry organ meat) and today with mozzarella; and capon with 'contorni', which Busk describes for the English reader as 'something more than "garnish", being something put round the dish, not merely for ornament, but more or less substantial, to be eaten with it, as sausages round a turkey'. The contemporary meaning is important, as today *contorni* normally refers to vegetable side dishes. Thanks to details such as these, this version of the French tale 'Beauty and the Beast' acquires a distinctively Roman flavour.

Folklore, Rome and the Unification of Italy

Although she received no formal academic training, in the 1880s Busk was an active member of the Folklore Society founded by Thoms, despite the Society's avowed materialism and anticlericalism. Busk was a vocal supporter of the Pope's political primacy over his territory, publicly opposing the newly founded Italian nation, unified in 1861 under King Victor Emmanuel II of Savoy. In particular she bemoaned Italy's incorporation of Rome and the Papal States following the Breach of Porta

Pia and the entry of the Italian troops into Rome on 20 September 1870. The following year Rome became Italy's official capital city. Busk calls the event that led to the deposition of the Pope 'the invasion of September 20, 1870'. She sees the date when the new government started 'to incite the people against the religious orders, but to no avail' as marking the start of a superstitious quest for the supernatural through mediums and spiritualist seances. Forbidden under papal rule, these activities became, after the events of September 1870, a means for Romans 'of gratifying that craving after the supernatural' otherwise denied them by the new secular regime.

Ironically, the unification of Italy that Busk so deplored was at the heart of the boom in folklore collecting and publishing that characterized late nineteenth-century Italy – in which Busk was an enthusiastic participant. Although Italy was 'united' by 1870 (even if some cities, such as Trento and Trieste, were to remain under foreign occupation for several decades longer), 'Italians' were not yet made – to paraphrase a famous dictum attributed to writer and politician Massimo d'Azeglio. In other words, there was not yet a pervasive sense of Italian identity. This cultural unification was encouraged, among other ways, through exposure to regional cultures other than one's own. This in turn prompted folklore scholars and amateurs alike to collect and publish folktales and other oral texts. Their effort was double-pronged. It aimed not only to spread information about each region across the country, but also to preserve in print vulnerable regional identities now believed to be at risk of being incorporated into a new, homogenized nation. Despite Busk's opposition to the unification of the country, her work thus fits perfectly into the wave of folklore collection that was impelled in large part by the process of Italian nation-building. The Sicilian Giuseppe Pitrè, widely considered the most important folklorist of nineteenth-century Italy, had been a Garibaldian volunteer who fought for the country's unification. Busk admired and corresponded with Pitrè, who respected and mentored her. Pitrè also published some of the tales Busk collected in his ground-breaking publication *Archivio per lo studio delle tradizioni popolari*.

Like Pitrè, most of Busk's fellow folklorists in nineteenth-century Italy were Italian men. However, she was not alone in her efforts and there were important foreign women collectors as well. The best-known among these was the Swiss German Laura Gonzenbach, who gathered tales from peasant women in Sicily and published them in 1870, a few years before Busk's own book. Like Busk, Gonzenbach collected tales in the informants' local language, then published them in her own native tongue. Less known but important British collectors of Italian tales around Busk's time included Evelyn Martinengo-Cesaresco, Francesca Alexander, Louise Hamilton and Isabella Anderton.

Collecting 'Traditionary Tales'

Busk opens her Preface to *Roman Legends* by saying she often heard that Italy did not have its own 'Traditionary Tales', as she calls them, to offer the world. She realizes that this is not true, however, when 'a certain humble friend' tells her that she has accumulated an entire book's worth of such stories in her own memory alone. Although most of the tales told by this friend did not make it to Busk's published book, it is thanks to her that Busk realized the existence of 'a vein of legendary lore underlying the classic soil of Rome'. Busk's search for published texts on this subject in bookshops and libraries, the method she had used in her previous collections of folklore, yielded nothing, which she explained was because 'no Italian Grimm had yet arisen to collect and organize them'. Busk therefore decided to source her own materials ('I was thus thrown back on my own powers of collecting'), since only some cheap editions of legends sold by itinerant vendors were available to her – and none of the stories she heard first-hand appeared in even these pamphlets. Instead, she chose to listen to 'the Roman poor', whom she saw as the vestiges of the descendants of ancient Romans, following centuries of increasing ignorance and decay.

The very traits of contemporary Romans that were criticized by so many foreign visitors to Rome at that time – ignorance, superstition and narrowmindedness, among others – confirmed for Busk that her narrators were indeed genuine 'folk', investing their stories with indisputable authority. Unlike many of her contemporaries, she saw her informants' ignorance as innocence, their superstition as part and parcel of their piety and the narrowness of their experience as evidence of a perspective that was exquisitely local. Through her practice of cultural sensitivity and local know-how, Busk treated her sources with tact and skill. She knew how to compensate them without offending them, and how to show politeness in the ways they expected, however peculiar that may have seemed to someone of her own nationality and social class. Above all, she knew that 'If you want to learn anything from them, you must submit to become one of them'. First of all, she explains, you have to be willing to converse on what interests your interlocutors most, be it the price of bread or the political situation, before you can expect them to talk about what interests you. She describes how to draw out a story that may have been dormant for decades, and the need to understand that often the tales have no clear development, may lack a beginning or an end or consist merely of fragments – perhaps only a title. In addition, she learned to accept that some stories were simply lost: 'Ah! I knew so many of those things once, but now they are all gone, all gone', one of her narrators laments. She even tells us about an old woman who refused to share her stories for fear of misfortune, leading Busk to express, with an evident sense of frustration, that, 'It is vexatious to think that a vast store is going to the grave with her under one's very eyes and that one cannot touch it'.

Busk's reference to the Grimm brothers, who founded German folklore with *Children's and Household Tales*, their renowned annotated collection of 1812–1857, accompanies her insistence on the authenticity of the oral tradition she collects directly – or, as the subtitle to the first edition announces: 'by word of mouth of the people'. Through both practice ('By word of mouth') and precedent (none other than the Brothers Grimm themselves), Busk gives a folklorist's authority to her book, which was after all the work of an amateur rather than a trained professional. She acknowledges some of her contemporary folklorists in northern Italy, such as Cesare Cantù and Angelo de Gubernatis, and states that no such work has been undertaken for central and southern Italy (despite the fact that Pitrè had already been publishing his multi-volume Sicilian oeuvre). Busk's *Roman Legends* is indeed acknowledged as the earliest printed collection of Roman folktales. But although she compares the tales in her book frequently, and at some length, to those from other countries, Busk mentions but does not appear to be acquainted with the early modern Italian fairy tales of Giovan Francesco Straparola in Venice and Giambattista Basile in Naples. These were the earliest in Europe, published in the 1550s and 1630s respectively. Even more surprisingly, with the exception of Tyrol (a borderland between Italy and Austria, about which Busk also published a book in 1874), she does not refer to any of the folklore of the rest of Italy. When discussing 'Cenriontola', for example (her Roman 'Cinderella'), she describes the German, Hungarian, Spanish and even Mongolian versions, but the only culturally connected one is from the North Tyrol – even though Basile's version, to name one, has so much in common with the one Busk collected in Rome.

Still, some of Busk's methods are certainly ahead of her time: she incorporates the storyteller's presence in the tale and acknowledges her own position as fieldworker, along with her role as both the initiator of the event and a participant in it. Some legends even start with a slightly derisive observation addressed to Busk herself: 'You know, of course, about St. Peter…'; 'What! Never heard of Pietro Bailliardo! Surely you must, if you ever heard anything at all'; 'There was Padre Fontanarosa too. Did you never hear of him?' And after the end of the fairy tale titled 'The Pot of Marjoram', we read an exchange between Busk and her informant: 'How well I remember," added the narrator, "the way my mother used always to end that story when she told it to me." "And how was that?" asked I eagerly, not at all sorry to come across some local addition at last. "But it has nothing to do with the tale, really," she replied, as deeming it too unimportant to trouble me with. "Never mind, I should like to hear it," said I.' Some narrators link their own tale to the preceding one, which they clearly listened to along with Busk: 'My story is also of a husband and wife, but they were peasants, and lived outside the gates,' begins 'The White Serpent'.

The Shape of Busk's Book

As the only one of her books to be written entirely as the result of her own fieldwork, *Roman Legends* remains Busk's most valuable contribution to folklore studies. The collection is divided into four narrative categories, the names of which Busk gives in a mix of Italian and English: *Favole; Legendary Tales and Esempj; Short and Treasure Stories and Family and Local Traditions; and Ciarpe*. The first section, titled *Favole*, fairy tales, is by far the largest grouping and contains some of the longest and most complex tales in the book. Although the word *Favole* in modern Italian also means fables (both words derive from the Latin *fabula*), Busk clearly states that no actual 'fable' was ever related to her when she asked for a *favola*. Instead, these are tales of magic filled with wondrous transformations and other familiar fairy-tale motifs, including envious sisters, evil stepmothers, magical objects and animal spouses. The narratives in the second section, *Legendary Tales and Esempj*, are mostly religious in content. The section includes stories from the time 'When Jesus Christ Wandered on Earth' and highlights from the lives of beloved saints such as Anthony and Francis of Assisi – who miraculously brings fish that had already been fried back to life! – as well as lesser-known ones such as Verdana and Theodora who, upon repenting of her sinful life, puts on male attire and joins a monastery of friars.

Busk tells us that her informants were far more willing to tell her legends than *favole* because the moral teachings of legends made them worth remembering and repeating, far more so than fairy tales. The Romans she spoke with were downright embarrassed to know and to tell her any *favole*, considering them nonsense only appropriate for a 'creatura' (a delightful word that, as we read in a note, is 'Roman vernacular for a child of either sex'). Busk then cleverly decided to tell her informants: 'Imagine that I am the *creatura*, and tell me one of your tales. I want something about transformations, fairy gifts and marvels of all sorts.' After the *Legendary Tales and Esempj* comes the third section of the book, *Ghost and Treasure Stories and Legendary and Local Traditions*. These are, as the first part of the title suggests, tales of ghosts and revenants, but also of historical and legendary figures such as the Pope killer Sciarra Colonna, the generous and forgiving Prince Borghese and the mythical female Pope, Pope Joan – as well as local narratives of love and death worthy of opera librettos like the Roman *Tosca*. The final section, *Ciarpe*, i.e. nonsense or gossip, brings together miscellaneous stories about loose devils and killer cats, clever friars and bad-tempered queens, beggars, misers and more.

The four categories into which Busk organizes her narratives, she states in the Preface, were provided by the informants themselves, through their spontaneous titling of each story. The names of each section are thus given as 'natural', as labels devised by the tellers themselves rather than imposed by Busk. This of course confirms the genuineness of the narratives and their right to appear in a folklore collection.

Yet the categories in *Roman Legends* are neither natural nor obvious, and noticeably present a falling hierarchy in terms of prestige. The first section includes the longer and more complex fairy tales – very demanding of their oral narrators due to their abundance of details and the surprising twists and turns of their narrative. Legends are shorter and more diverse forms of narration, but they are instructive and more or less historical, while ghost stories, although arguably less edifying than legends, are still meaningfully anchored to real life. At the bottom of the tale pile we have stories explicitly labelled simply as 'nonsense'. These categories, however necessary and even desirable, are hardly objective or value-free.

Furthermore, many of the tales in *Roman Legends* could easily fall into more than one category. What is a Roman-inflected rendering of the Genesis story of Joseph – surely a religious tale – doing among the *Favole*? Why does the Madonna in 'Nun Beatrice', listed among the *Legendary Tales*, act more like a fairy godmother than as the Queen of Heaven? What is 'Don Giovanni', a ghost story, doing among *Legendary Tales*? In turn, the heading *Ghost and Treasure Stories and Family and Local Traditions* is far too broad. The genres it contains include, in addition to the expected accounts of personal meetings with the spirits of the dead, the legends of an innkeeper who turns out to be Mary herself and that of a luxury-loving nun who converts to a life of poverty (both of which would fit better in the previous section of *Legendary Tales*), as well as the tale of a prince whom a fairy turns into a beast and the tale of a woman kidnapped by a wild creature (both easily identifiable as fairy tales and better suited for the *Favole* section). The contents of *Ciarpe* are likewise exceedingly diverse: there are lucky simpletons, such as are found in many fairy tales, and fairies who determine the fate of human protagonists in 'The Queen and the Tripe-seller' and 'The Gluttonous Girl'.

Notes on this Edition

The stories contained in Busk's *Roman Legends* are abundant and diverse. Spanning several genres and engaging with multiple topics, they could be grouped in a variety of ways. The present edition assembles a selection of the original tales rearranged for the contemporary reader according to themes rather than genres, well knowing that many if not most tales could have easily been placed in more than one category. It is often Love and Marriage that make Simpletons and Tricksters act the way they do, and, in turn, Love and Marriage – in these tales as in Italian culture more generally – are often at the heart of Food Stories: delicious fruits hide potential brides, a rich man learns how to fry while courting a beautiful fryer (*friggitora*), the ability to prepare a delicious dinner allows an impoverished young woman to marry a king.

Nineteenth-century versions of Classical Tales, dating from Greco-Roman antiquity and the Latin Middle Ages, appear under several headings. 'Twelve Feet of Nose', the story of a trickster, retells an earlier tale from the medieval collection *Gesta Romanorum*; 'The Enchanted Rose Tree' and 'The Dark King' rely on the second-century Latin tale of 'Cupid and Psyche'; 'The King of Portugal' is an example of the ancient *Caritas Romana* imagery. As the name suggests, and her brutal killing of her own children and herself confirms, 'Amadea' is clearly a Roman Medea, while the ghost in 'The Procession of Velletri' is related to the older one described by Pliny the Younger in ancient Rome's most famous ghost story.

Religion and Magic appear in every section because Simpletons and Tricksters frequently rely on them. About half of the Animal Tales are concerned with enchanted beasts, and what would Love and Marriage be without the presence of magic? Two of the Animal Tales are fairy tales and predictably end in marriage. Both are local varieties of a better-known story. 'Cenorientola' is clearly a version of 'Cinderella', even in the absence of a stepmother or a fairy, and even if her slipper is golden rather than crystal; likewise 'Vaccarella', another Roman 'Cinderella', features a stepmother crueller than most, but it is a cow, rather than a fairy godmother, who aids the protagonist in seducing the prince. The Roman Rapunzel's mother craves parsley – for Romans did not know the herb called rapunzel, i.e., rampion – and the protagonist knows what she is doing when she invites the prince into her tower and when she uses the magic she learned from her captor in order to obtain her freedom. She is no passive Grimm heroine.

However one may group Busk's tales – and the ways are various and endless – they remain rooted in the daily life of nineteenth-century Rome. Their characters frequent the Campagna and the streets of the *centro storico*; they eat chicory, tripe and codfish, according to availability and the religious calendar; they perform magic with figs and, less effectively, with chickpeas; they rely on donkeys and cats for work and protection from vermin; they invoke local saints such as Philip Neri for help and fear the capricious local justice even more than the Devil himself. These characters are deeply, entirely Roman – even as they retain a universal appeal in their relatable human foibles and charms, and the difficult situations in which they often find themselves.

Likewise, many of the tales these folks inhabit and animate remain recognizably themselves despite their Roman attributes: we can predict the outcome of fairy tales, the failures of the Devil's tricks, the rewards for the simpleton's kindness. In and outside of Rome, folktales transform themselves and each other variously and endlessly across time and space, shapeshifting to interact better with their tellers and their audience – pleasing, challenging, instructing, distracting. May this selection of nineteenth-century folktales, collected a century and a half ago in Rome by an Englishwoman with devoted attention and infinite care, and now gathered once again in admiration and respect, provide the twenty-first-century reader with similar opportunities to remember and learn, and to be entertained and inspired.

Cristina Mazzoni (Volume editor and Introduction) is the Wolfgang and Barbara Mieder Green and Gold Professor of Romance Languages and Cultures at the University of Vermont. Her expertise lies in European fairy tales, literature and spirituality, and food culture. Her many books include *Golden Fruit: A Cultural History of Oranges in Italy, She-Wolf: The Story of a Roman Icon* and *The Pomegranates and Other Modern Italian Fairy Tales*.

Tricksters & Simpletons

THESE STOCK CHARACTERS in world folklore old and new appear frequently in Busk's tales, as they do in the Italian literary fairy tales from the early modern period – the very first printed in Europe. Busk's 'Scioccolone', for example, is the Roman retelling of the story of the foolish but kind youngest brother who becomes king. Versions of this story appear in Giovan Francesco Straparola's sixteenth-century *The Pleasant Nights*, where his name is Pietro Pazzo, i.e., Peter the Fool, and in Giambattista Basile's seventeenth-century *Tale of Tales*, where he is named Peruonto. Both men, like Scioccolone, start out ugly, stupid and poor, but end up handsome, smart and wealthy kings.

In folk and fairy tales such as these, simpletons are usually redeemed by kindness – or, on occasion, by sheer luck. The related figure of the trickster, clever and mischievous, typically succeeds against individuals more powerful than he: a tailor gets the better of a sultan, for example, in that Roman incarnation of Aladdin titled 'How Cajusse Was Married'. Although tricksters are usually male, it is a young woman, considerably smarter and wealthier than her beloved, yet determined to marry him against her father's wishes, who teaches that other Cajusse everything he has to do to win her hand, in 'The Marriage of Signor Cajusse'.

Scioccolone

ONCE UPON A TIME there were three brothers, who were woodmen; their employment was not one which required great skill, and they were none of them very clever, but the youngest was the least brilliant of all. So simple was he that all the neighbours, and his very brothers – albeit they were not so very superior in intelligence themselves – gave him the nickname of 'Scioccolone,' the great simpleton, and accordingly Scioccolone he was called wherever he went.

Every day these three brothers went out into the woods to their work, and every evening they all came home, each staggering under his load of wood, which he carried to the dealer who paid them for their toil: thus one day of labour passed away just like another in all respects. So it went on for years.

Nevertheless, one day came at last which was not at all like the others, and if all days were like it the world would be quite upside down, or be at least a very different world from what it is. *Oimè!* that such days never occur now at all! *Basta*, this is what happened. It was in the noontide heat of a very hot day, the three simple brothers committed the imprudence of going out of the shelter of the woods into the world beyond, and there, lying on the grass in the severest blaze of the burning sun, they saw three beautiful peasant girls lying fast asleep.

"Only look at those silly girls sleeping in the full blaze of the sun!" cried the eldest brother.

"They'll get bad in their heads in this heat," said the second.

But Scioccolone said: "Shall we not get some sticks and boughs, and make a little shed to shelter them?"

"Just like one of Scioccolone's fine ideas!" laughed the eldest brother scornfully.

"Well done, Scioccolone! That's the best thing you've thought of this long while. And who will build a shed over us while we're building a shed for the girls, I should like to know?" said the second.

But Scioccolone said: "We can't leave them there like that; they will be burnt to death. If you won't help me I must build the shed alone."

"A wise resolve, and worthy of Scioccolone!" scoffed the eldest brother.

"Goodbye, Scioccolone!" cried the second, as the two elder brothers walked away together. "Goodbye for ever! I don't expect ever to see you alive again, of course."

And they never did see him again, but what it was that happened to him you shall hear.

Without waiting to find a retort to his brothers' gibes, Scioccolone set to work to fell four stout young saplings, and to set them up as supports of his shed in four holes he had previously scooped with the aid of his bill-hook; then he rammed them in with wedges, which he also had to cut and shape. After this he cut four large bushy branches, which he tied to the uprights with the cord he used for tying up his fagots of logs; and as the shade of these was scarcely close enough to keep out all the fierce rays of the sun, he went back to the wood and collected all the large broad leaves he could find, and came back and spread them out over his leafy roof. All this was very hard labour indeed when performed under the dreaded sun, and just in the hours when men do no work; yet so beautiful were the three maidens that, when at last he had completed his task, he could not tear himself away from them to go and seek repose in the shade of the wood, but he must needs continue standing in the full sun gazing at them open-mouthed.

At last the three beautiful maidens awoke, and when they saw what a fragrant shade had refreshed their slumbers they began pouring out their gratitude to their devoted benefactor.

Do not run at hasty conclusions, however, and imagine that of course the three beautiful maidens fell in love on the spot with Scioccolone, and he had only to pick and choose which of them he would have to make him happy as his wife. A very proper ending, you say, for a fairy tale. It was not so, however. Scioccolone looked anything but attractive just then. His meaningless features and uncouth, clownish gait were never at any time likely to inspire the fair maidens with sudden affection; but just then, after his running hither and thither, his felling, digging and hammering in the heat of the day, his face had acquired a tint which made it look rougher and redder and more repulsive than anyone ever wore before.

Besides this, the three maidens were fairies, who had taken the form of beautiful peasant girls for some reason of their own.

But neither did they leave his good deed unrewarded. By no means. Each of the three declared she would give him such a precious gift that he should own to his last hour that they were not ungrateful. So they sat and thought what great gift they could think of which should be calculated to make him very happy indeed.

At last the first of the three got up and exclaimed that she had thought of her gift, and she did not think anyone could give him a greater one; for she would promise him he should one day be a king.

Wasn't that a fine gift!

Scioccolone, however, did not think so. The idea of *his* being a king! Simple as he was, he could see the incongruity of the idea, and the embarrassment of the situation. How should he the poor clown, everybody's laughing-stock, become a king? And if he did, kingship had no attractions for him.

He was too kind-hearted, however, to say anything in disparagement of the well-meant promise, and too straightforward to assume a show of gratitude he did not feel; so after the first little burst of hilarity which he was not sufficiently master of himself to suppress, he remained standing open-mouthed after his awkward manner.

Then the second fairy addressed him and said:

"I see you don't quite like my sister's gift; but you may be sure she would not have promised it if it had not been a good gift, after you have been so kind to us; and when it comes true, it will somehow all turn out very nice and right. But now, meantime, that I may not similarly disappoint you with my gift by choosing it for you, I shall let you choose it for yourself; so say, what shall it be?"

Scioccolone was almost as much embarrassed with the second fairy's permission of choosing for himself as he had been with the first fairy's choice for him. First he grinned, and then he twisted his great awkward mouth about, and then he grinned again, till, at last, ashamed of keeping the fairies waiting so long for his answer, he said, with another grin:

"Well, to tell you what I should *really* like, it would be that when I have finished making up my fagot of logs this evening, instead of having to stagger home carrying it, it should roll along by itself, and then I get astride of *it*, and that it should carry *me*.

"That *would* be fine!" he added, and he grinned again as he thought of the fun it would be to be carried home by the load of logs instead of carrying the load as he had been wont.

"Certainly! That wish is granted," replied the second fairy readily. "You will find it all happens just as you have described."

Then the third fairy came forward and said:

"And now choose; what shall *my* gift be? You have only to ask for whatever you like and you shall have it."

Such a heap of wishes rose up in Scioccolone's imagination at this announcement that he could not make up his mind which to select; as fast as he fixed on one thing, he remembered it would be incomplete without some other gift, and as he went on trying to find someone wish that should be as comprehensive as possible, he suddenly blurted out:

"Promise me that *whatever* I wish may come true; that'll be the best gift; and so if I forget a thing one moment I can wish for it the next. That'll be the best gift, to be sure!"

"Granted!" said the third fairy. "You have only to wish for anything and you will find you get it immediately, whatever it is."

The fairies then took leave and went their way, and Scioccolone was reminded by the lengthening shades that it was time he betook himself to complete his day's work. Scarcely succeeding in collecting his thoughts, so dazzled and bewildered was he by the late supernatural conversation, he yet found his way back to the spot where he had been felling wood.

"Oh, dear! how tired I am!" he said within himself as he walked along. "How I wish the wood was all felled and the fagots tied up!" and though he said this mechanically as he might have said it any other day of his life, without thinking of the fairy's promise, which was, indeed, too vast for him to put it consciously to such a practical test then, full of astonishment as he was, yet when he got back to his working-place the wood was felled and laid in order, and tied into a fagot in the best manner.

"Well, to be sure!" soliloquized Scioccolone. "The girls have kept their promise indeed! This is just exactly what I wished. And now, let's see what else did I wish? Oh, yes; that if I got astride on the fagot it should roll along by itself and carry me with it; let's see if that'll come true too!"

With that he got astride on the fagot, and sure enough the fagot moved on all by itself, and carried Scioccolone along with it pleasantly enough.

Only there was one thing Scioccolone had forgotten to ask for, and that was power to guide the fagot; and now, though it took a direction quite contrary to that of his homeward way, he had no means of inducing it to change its tack. After some time spent in fruitless efforts in schooling his unruly mount, Scioccolone began to reason with himself.

"After all, it does not much matter about going home. I only get laughed at and called "Scioccolone." Maybe in some other place they may be better, and as the fagot is acting under the orders of my benefactress, it will doubtless all be for the best."

So he committed himself to the fagot to take him wherever it would. On went the fagot surely and steadily, as if quite conscious where it had to go; and thus, before nightfall, it came to a great city where were many people, who all came out to see the wonder of the fagot of logs moving along by itself, and a man riding on it.

In this city was a king, who lived in a palace with an only daughter. Now this daughter had never been known to laugh. What pains soever the king her father took to divert her were all unavailing; nothing brought a smile to her lips.

Now, however, when all the people ran to the windows to see a man riding on a fagot, the king's daughter ran to look out too; and when she saw the fagot moving by itself, and the uncouth figure of Scioccolone sitting on it, and heard all the people laughing at the sight, then the king's daughter laughed too; laughed for the first time in her life.

But Scioccolone, passing under the palace, heard her clear and merry laugh resounding above the laughter of all the people. He looked up and saw her, and when he saw her looking so bright and fair he said within himself:

"Now, if ever the fairy's power of wishing is to be of use to me, I wish that I might have a little son, and that the beautiful princess should be the mother." But he did not think of wishing to stop there that he might look at her, so the fagot carried him past the palace and past all the houses into the outskirts of the city, till he got tired and weary, and just then passing a wood merchant's yard, the thought rose to his lips,

"I wish that wood merchant would buy this fagot of me!"

Immediately the wood merchant came out and offered to buy the fagot, and as it was such a wonderful fagot that he thought Scioccolone would never consent to sell it, he offered him such a high price that Scioccolone had enough to live on like a prince for a year.

After a time there was again a great stir in the city, everyone was abroad in the streets whispering and consulting. To the king's daughter was born a little son, and no one knew who the father was, not even the princess herself. Then the king sent for all the men in the city, and brought them to the infant, and said, "Is this your father?" but the babe said, "No!" to them all.

Last of all, Scioccolone was brought, and when the king took him up to the babe and said, "Is this your father?" the babe rose joyfully from its cradle and said, "Yes; that is my father!" When the king heard this and saw what a rough ugly clown Scioccolone was, he was very angry with his daughter, and said she must marry him and go away for ever from the palace. It was all in vain that the princess protested she had never seen him but for one moment from the top of the palace. The babe protested quite positively that he was his father; so the king had them married, and sent them away from the palace for ever; and the babe was right, for though Scioccolone and the princess had never met, Scioccolone had wished that he might have a son, of whom she should be the mother, and by the power of the spell the child was born.

Scioccolone was only too delighted with the king's angry decree. He felt quite out of place in the palace, and was glad enough to be sent away from it. All he wanted was to have such a beautiful wife, and he willingly obeyed the king's command to take her away, a long, long way off.

The princess, however, was quite of a different mind. She could not cease from crying, because she was given to such an uncouth, clownish husband that no tidy peasant wench would have married.

When, therefore, Scioccolone saw his beautiful bride so unhappy and distressed, he grew distressed himself; and in his distress he remembered once more the promise of the fairy, that whatever he wished he might have, and he began wishing away at once. First he wished for a pleasant villa, prettily laid-out, and planted, and walled; then, a casino in the midst of it, prettily furnished, and having plenty of pastimes and diversions; then for a farm, well-stocked with beasts for all kinds of uses; for carriages and servants, for fruits and flowers, and all that can make life pleasant. And when he found that with all these things the princess did not seem much happier than before, he bethought himself of wishing that he might be furnished with a handsome person, polished manners and an educated mind, altogether such as the princess wished. All his wishes were fulfilled, and the princess now loved him very much, and they lived very happily together.

After they had been living thus some time, it happened one day that the king, going out hunting, observed this pleasant villa on the wold, where heretofore all had been bare, unplanted and unbuilt.

"How is this?" cried the king; and he drew rein, and went into the villa intending to enquire how the change had come about.

Scioccolone came out to meet him, not only so transformed that the king never recognized him, but so distinguished by courtesy and urbanity that the king himself felt ashamed to question him as to how the villa had grown up so suddenly. He accepted his invitation to come and rest in the casino, however; and there they fell to conversing on a variety of subjects, till the king was so struck with the sagacity and prudence of Scioccolone's talk that when he rose to take leave, he said:

"Such a man as you I have long sought to succeed me in the government of the kingdom. I am growing old and have no children, and you are worthy in all ways to wear the crown. Come up, therefore, if you will, to the palace and live with me, and when I die you shall be king."

Scioccolone, now no longer feeling himself so ill-adapted to live in a palace, willingly consented, and a few days after, with his wife and his little son, he went up to the palace to live with the king.

But the king's delight can scarcely be imagined when he found that the wife of the polished stranger was indeed his very own daughter.

After a few years the old king died, and Scioccolone reigned in his stead. And thus the promises of all the three fairies were fulfilled.

Twelve Feet of Nose

THERE WAS A POOR old father, who was very poor indeed, and very old. When he came to die, he called his three sons round his bed, and said they must summon a notary to make his will. The sons looked at each other, and thought he was doating. He repeated his desire, and then one of them ventured to say:

"But Father, dear, why should we go to the expense of calling in a notary; there is not a single thing on earth you have to leave us!"

But the old man told them again to call a notary, and still they hesitated, because they thought the notary would say they were making game of him.

At last the old man began to get angry when he found they would not do as he said, and, just not to vex him in his last moments, they called the notary, and the notary brought his witnesses.

Then the father was content, and called them all to his bedside.

"Now, pull out the old case under the bed, and take out what you find there."

They found an old broken hat, without a brim, a ragged purse that was so worn you could not have trusted any money in its keeping, and a horn.

These three things he bequeathed in due form of law, one to each of his sons; and it was only because they saw that the man was in his death agony that those who were called to act as witnesses could keep from laughing. To the notary, of course, it was all one whether it was an old hat or a new one, his part was the same, and when he had done what was needful, he went his way, and the witnesses went with him; but as they went out, they said one to another:

"Poor old man! perhaps it is a comfort to him in his last moments to fancy he has got something to leave."

When they were all gone, as the three sons were standing by, very sad, and looking at each other, not knowing what to make of the strange scene, he called the eldest, to whose portion the hat had fallen, and said:

"See what I've given you."

"Why, Father!" answered he, "it isn't even good enough to bind round one's knee when one goes out hoeing!"

But the father answered:

"I wouldn't let you know its value till those people were gone, lest any should take it from you; this is its value, that if you put it on, you can go in to dine at whatever inn you please, or sit down to drink at what wine shop you please, and take what you like and drink what you like, for no one will see you while you have it on."

Then he called his second son, to whose lot the purse had fallen, and he said:

"See what I have given you."

"Why, Father!" answered the son, "it isn't even good enough to keep a little tobacco in, if I could afford to buy any!"

But the father answered:

"I wouldn't tell you its value till those people were gone, lest any should take it from you; but this is its value; if you put your fingers in, you'll find a scudo there, and after that another, and another, as many as ever you will; there will always be one."

Then he called his youngest son, and said:

"See what I have given you."

And he answered:

"Yes, Father, it's a very nice horn; and when I am starving hungry I can cheat myself into being content by playing on it."

"Silly boy!" answered the father; "that is not its use. I wouldn't tell you its value while those people were here, lest they should take it from you. Its value is this, that whenever you want anything you have only to sound it, and one will come who will bring whatever you want, be it a dinner, a suit of clothes, a palace or an army."

After this the father died, and each found himself well provided with the legacy he had given him.

It happened that one day as the second son was passing under the window of the palace a waiting-maid looked out and said: "Can you play at cards?"

"As well as most," answered the youth.

"Very well, then; come up," answered the waiting-maid; "for the queen wants someone to play with her."

Very readily he went up, therefore, and played at cards with the queen, and when he had played all the evening he had lost fifty scudi.

"Never mind about paying the fifty scudi," said the queen, as he rose to leave. "We only played to pass away the time, and you don't look by your dress as if you could afford fifty scudi."

"Not at all!" replied the youth. "I will certainly bring the fifty scudi in the morning."

And in the morning, by putting his fingers fifty times into the ragged purse, he had the required sum, and went back with it to the palace and paid the queen.

The queen was very much astonished that such a shabby-looking fellow should have such command of money, and determined to find out how it was; so she made him stay and dine. After dinner she took him into her private room and said to him:

"Tell me, how comes it that you, who are but a shabby-looking fellow, have such command of money?"

"Oh!" answered he quite unsuspectingly, "because my father left me a wonderful purse, in which is always a scudo."

"Nonsense!" answered the queen. "That is a very pretty fable, but such purses don't exist."

"Oh, but it is so indeed," answered the youth.

"Quite impossible," persisted the queen.

"But here it is; you can see for yourself!" pursued the incautious youth, taking it out.

The queen took it from him as if to try its powers, but no sooner was she in possession of it than she called in the guard to turn out a fellow who was trying to rob her, and give him a good beating.

Indignant at such treatment, the youth went to his eldest brother and begged his hat of him that he might, by its means, go and punish the queen.

Putting on the hat he went back to the palace at the hour of dinner and sat down to table. As soon as the queen was served he took her plate and ate up all that was in it one course after another, so that the queen got nothing, and finding it useless to call for more dishes, she gave it up as a bad job, and went into her room. The youth followed her in and demanded the return of his wonderful purse.

"How can I know it is you if I don't see you?" said the queen.

"Never mind about seeing me. Put the purse out on the table for me and I will take it."

"No, I can't if I don't see you," replied the queen. "I can't believe it is you unless I see you."

The youth fell into the snare and took off his hat.

"How did you manage to make yourself invisible?" asked the queen.

"Just by putting on this old hat."

"I don't believe that could make you invisible," exclaimed the queen. "Let me try."

And she snatched the hat out of his hand and put it on. Of course she was now in turn invisible, and he sought her in vain; but worse than that, she rang the bell for the guard and bade them turn the shabby youth out and give him a *bastonata*.

Full of fresh indignation he ran to his youngest brother and told him all his story, begging the loan of his horn, that he might punish the queen by its means; and the brother lent it him.

He sounds the horn and one comes.

"I want an army with cannons to throw down the palace," said the youth; and instantly there was a tramp of armed men, and a rumble of artillery wagons.

The queen was sitting at dinner, but when she heard all the noise she came to the window; meantime the soldiers had surrounded the palace and pointed their guns.

"What's all this about! What's the matter!" cried the queen out of the window.

"The matter is, that I want my purse and my hat back," answered the youth.

"To be sure, you are right; here they are. I don't want my palace battered down, so I will give them to you."

The youth went up to receive them; but when he got upstairs he found the queen sunk half fainting in a chair.

"Oh! I'm so frightened; I can't think where I put the things. Only send away that army and I'll look for them immediately."

The youth sent away the army, and the queen got up and began looking about for the things.

"Tell me," she said, as she wandered from one cupboard to another, "how did you, who are such a shabby-looking fellow, manage to call together such an army?"

"Because I've got this horn," answered the youth. "And with it I can call up whatever I want, and if you don't make haste and find the purse and the hat, I'll call up the army again and batter down the palace in right earnest."

"You won't make me believe that!" replied the queen. "That sorry horn can't work such wonders as that: let me try." And she took the horn out of his hands and sounded it and One appeared. "Two stout men!" she commanded quickly; and when they came she bade them drive the shabby-looking youth out of the palace and give him a *bastonata*.

He was now quite undone, and was ashamed to go back to his brothers. So he wandered away outside the town. After much walking he came to a vineyard, where he strolled in; and what struck him was, that though it was January, there was a fine fig tree covered with ripe luscious figs.

"This is a godsend indeed," he said, "to a hungry man," and he began plucking and eating the figs. Before he had eaten many, however, he found his nose had begun to grow to a terrible size; a foot for every fig.

"That'll never do!" he cried, and left off eating the figs and wandered on. Presently he came to another vineyard, where he also strolled in: there, though it was January, he saw a tree all covered with ripe red cherries. "I wonder what calamity will pursue me for eating them," he said, as he gathered them. But when he had eaten a good many he perceived that at last his luck had turned, for in proportion as he ate his nose grew less and less, till at last it was just the right size again.

"Now I know how to punish the queen," he said, and he filled a bottle with the juice of the cherries, and went back and gathered a basketful of figs.

These figs he cried under the palace window, and as he had got more dusty and threadbare with his late wanderings no one recognized him. "Figs in January! That is a treat!" and they bought up the whole basketful. Then as they ate, their noses all began to grow, but the queen, as she was very greedy, ate twelve for her share, so that she had twelve feet of nose added to the length of hers. It was so long that it trailed behind her on the ground as she walked along.

Then there was a hue and cry! All the surgeons and physicians in the kingdom were sent for, but could do no good. They were all in despair, when our youth came up disguised as a foreign doctor.

"Noses! I can heal noses! Whoever has got too much nose let him come to me!"

All the inhabitants gathered round him, and the queen called to him loudest of all.

"The medicine I have to give is necessarily a very strong one to effect so extraordinary a cure; therefore I won't give it to the queen's majesty till she has seen it used on all her servants, beginning with the lowest."

Taking them all in order, beginning with the lowest, he gave a few drops of cherry-juice to each, and all their noses came right.

Last of all the queen remained.

"The queen can't be treated like common people," he said; "she must be treated by herself. I must go into her room with her, and I can cure her with one drop of my cordial."

"You think yourself very clever that you talk of curing with one drop of your cordial, but you're not the only person who can work wonders. I've got greater wonders than yours. I've got a hat which makes you invisible, a purse that never is empty, and a horn that gives you everything you call for."

"Very pretty things to talk about," answered the pretended doctor, "but such things don't exist."

"Don't they!" said the queen. "There they are!"

And she laid them all out on the table.

This was enough for him. Taking advantage of the lesson she had given him by her example, he quickly put on the hat, making himself invisible; after that it was easy to snatch up the other things and escape; nor could anyone follow him. He lived very comfortably for the rest of his life, taking a scudo out of his purse for whatever he had to pay, and his brothers likewise got on very well with their legacies, for he restored them as soon as he had rescued them from the queen. But the queen remained for the rest of her life with TWELVE FEET OF NOSE.

How Cajusse Was Married

♒

THERE WAS A POOR TAILOR starving for poverty because he
could get no work. One day there knocked at his door a good-
natured-looking old man; the tailor's son opened the door,
and he won the boy's confidence immediately, saying he was his
uncle. He also gave him a piastre to buy a good dinner. When the
father came home and found him installed, and heard that he
called himself his son's uncle, and would, therefore, be his own
brother, he was much surprised; but as he found he was so rich
and so generous, he thought it better not to dispute his word. The
visitor stayed a whole month, providing all expenses so freely
all the time that everyone was delighted with him, and when at
last he came to take leave, and proposed that the tailor's boy
should go with him and learn some business at his expense, the
son himself was all eagerness to go, and the father, too, willingly
gave his consent.

As soon as they had gone a good way outside the gates the stranger said
to the boy, "It is all a dodge about my calling myself your uncle. I am not
your uncle a bit; only I want a strong daring sort of boy to do something
for me which I am too old to do myself. I am a wizard, and if you do what
I tell you I will reward you well; but if you attempt to resist or escape you
may be sure you will suffer for it."

"Tell me what I have to do before we talk about resisting and escaping,"
replied the boy; "maybe I shan't mind doing it."

They were walking on as they talked, and the boy observed that they
got over much more ground than by ordinary walking, and they were now
in a wild desolate country. The wizard said nothing till they reached a
spot where there was a flat stone in the ground. Here he stopped, and as
he lifted up the stone, he said, "This is what you have to do. I will let you
down with this rope, and you must go all along through the dark till you
come to a place where is a beautiful garden. At the gate of the garden sits

a fierce dog, which will fly out at you, and bark fearfully. I will give you some bread and cheese to throw to him, and, while he is devouring the bread and cheese, you must pass on. Then all manner of terrible noises will cry after you, calling you back; but take no heed of them, and, above all, do not look back; if you look back you are lost. As soon as you are out of sound of the voices you will see on a stone an old lantern, take that and bring it back to me."

The boy showed no unwillingness to try his fortune, and the magician gave him the bread and cheese he had promised, and let him down by a rope. He gave him also a ring, saying, "If anything else should happen, after you have got the lantern, to prevent your bringing it away, rub this ring and wish at the same time for deliverance, and you will be delivered."

The boy did all the wizard had told him, and something more besides; for when he got into the garden he found the trees all covered with beautiful fruits, which were all so many precious stones; with these he filled his pockets till he could hardly move for the weight of them; then he came back to the opening of the cave, and called to the wizard to pull him up.

"Send up the lantern first," said the magician, "and I'll see about pulling you up afterwards."

But the boy was afraid lest he should be left behind; so he refused to send up the lantern unless the wizard hauled him up with it. This the wizard would by no means do.

"Ah! the youngster will be frightened if I shut him up in the dark cave a bit," said he, and closed the stone, meaning to call to him by and by to see if he had come round to a more submissive mind. The boy, however, finding himself shut up alone in the cave, bethought him of the ring, and rubbed it, wishing the while to be at home. Instantly he found himself there, lantern in hand. His parents were very much astonished at all he told them of his adventures, and, poor as they were, were very glad to have him safe back.

"I wonder what the magician wanted this ugly old lantern for," said the boy to himself one day. "It must be good for something or he would not have been so anxious to have it; let me try rubbing it, and see if that answers as well as rubbing the ring." He no sooner did so than One appeared, and asked his pleasure. "A table well laid for dinner!" said the boy; and immediately a table appeared covered with all sorts of good things, with real silver spoons and forks. Then he called on his mother and father, and they made a good meal; after that they lived for a month on the price of the silver which the mother took out and pawned. One day she found the town all illuminated. What is going on?" she asked of the neighbours. "The daughter of the Sultan is going to marry the son of the Grand Vizier, and there is a distribution of alms to the people on the occasion; that is why they rejoice." Such was the answer.

When she came home she told her son what she had heard. He said, "That will not be, because the daughter of the Sultan will have to marry me!" but she only laughed at him. The next day he brought her three neat little baskets filled with the precious stones which he had gathered in the underground garden, and he said, "These you must take to the Sultan, and say I want to marry his daughter." But she was afraid and would not go; and when at last he made her go, she stood in a corner apart behind all the people, for there was a public audience, and came back and said she could not get at the Sultan; but he made her go again the next two days following, and she always did the same. The last day, however, the Sultan sent for her, saying, "Who is that old woman standing in the corner quite apart? Bring her to me." So they brought her to him all trembling.

"Don't be afraid, old woman," said the Sultan. "What have you to say?"

"My son, who must have lost his senses, sent me to say he wanted to marry the daughter of the Sultan," said the old woman, crying for very fear; "and he sends these baskets as a present."

When the Sultan took the baskets and saw of what great value were the contents, he said, "Don't be afraid, old woman; go back and tell your son I will give him an answer in a month."

She went back and told her son; but at the end of a week the princess was married, nevertheless, to the son of the Grand Vizier.

"There!" said the mother, when she heard it; "I thought the Grand Sultan was only making game of you. Was it likely that the daughter of the Sultan should marry a beggar like you?"

"Don't be in too great a hurry, Mother," replied the lad; "leave it to me, leave it to me."

With that he went and took out the old lantern, and rubbed it till One appeared asking his pleasure.

"Go tonight, at three hours of night," was his reply, "and take the daughter of the Sultan and lay her on a poor wallet in the out-house here."

At three hours of night he went into the out-house and found the princess on the poor wallet as he had commanded. Then he laid his sabre on the bed between them, and sat down and talked to her; but she was too frightened to answer him. This he did three nights running. The princess, however, went crying to her mother, and told her all that had happened. The Sultana could not imagine how it was. "But," she said, "something wrong there must be;" and she went and told the Sultan, and he, too, said it was all wrong, and that the marriage must be annulled. Also the son of the Grand Vizier went to his father and complained, saying, "Every night my wife disappears just at bed-time, and, though the door is locked, I see nothing of her till the next morning."

His father, too, said, "There must be something wrong," and when the Sultan said the marriage must be annulled, the Grand Vizier was quite willing. So the marriage was annulled.

At the end of the month, the lad made his mother go back to the Sultan for his answer, and he gave her three other baskets of precious stones to take with her. The Sultan, when he saw the man had so many precious stones to give away, thought he must be in truth a prince in disguise, and he answered, "He may come and see us." He also said, "What is his name that I may know him?"

And his mother said, "His name is Cajusse."

So she went home and told her son what the Sultan had said. Then he rubbed the lantern and asked for a suit to wear, all dazzling with gold and silver, and a richly caparisoned horse, and six pages in velvet dresses, four to ride behind, and one to go before with a purse scattering alms to the people, and one to cry, "Make place for the Signor Cajusse!" Thus he came to the Sultan, and the Sultan received him well, and gave him his daughter to be his wife; but Cajusse had brought the lantern with him, and he rubbed it, and ordered that there should stand by the side of the Sultan's palace a palace a great deal handsomer, furnished with every luxury, and that all the windows should be encrusted round with precious stones, all but one.

This was all done as he had said, and he took the princess home with him to live there. Then he showed her all over the beautiful palace, and showed her the windows all encrusted with gems, "and in this vacant one," said he, "we will put those in the six baskets I sent you before the Sultan consented to our marriage." And they did so; but they did not suffice.

But the magician meantime had learnt by his incantations what had happened, and in order to get possession of the lantern he watched till Cajusse was gone out hunting; then he came by dressed as a peddler of metal work, and offered to exchange old lanterns for new ones. The princess thought to make a capital bargain by exchanging Cajusse's shabby old lantern for a brand new one, and thus fell into his snare. The magician no sooner had possession of it than he rubbed it, and ordered that the palace and all that was in it should be transported on to the high seas.

The Sultan happened to look out of window just as the palace of Cajusse had disappeared. "What is this?" he cried. And when he found the palace was really gone, he uttered so many furious threats that the people, who loved Cajusse well, ran out to meet him as he came home from hunting, and told him of all that had happened, and warned him of the Sultan's wrath. Instead of going back to be put in prison by the Sultan therefore, he rubbed his ring and desired to be taken to the place wherever the princess was. Instantly he found himself on a floating rock in mid ocean, at the foot of the palace. Then he went to the gate and sounded the horn. The princess knew her husband's note of sounding and ran to the window. Great was her delight when she saw that it was really he, and she told him that there was a horrid old man who had possession of the palace, and persecuted her every day to marry him, saying her husband was dead. And she, to keep him at a distance, yet without offending him lest he should kill her, had said: "No, I have always resolved never to marry an old man, because then if he dies I should be left alone, and that would be too sad." "But when I say that," she continued, "he always says, 'You need not be afraid of that, for I shall never die!' so I don't know what to say next."

Then the prince said, "Make a great feast tonight, and say you will marry him if he tells you one thing: say it is impossible that he should never die, for all people die some day or other; it is impossible but that there should be some one thing or other that is fatal to him; ask him what that one fatal thing is, and he, thinking you want to know it that you may guard him against it, will tell; then come and tell me what he says."

The princess did all her husband had told her, and then came back and repeated what the magician had said: "One must go into the wood," she repeated, "where is the beast called hydra, and cut off all his seven heads. In the head which is in the middle of the other six, if it is split open, will be found a leveret; if this leveret is caught and his head split open there is a bird; if this bird is caught and his head split open, there is in it a precious stone. If that stone is put under my pillow I must die."

The prince did not wait for anything more: he rubbed the ring, and desired to be carried to the wood where the hydra lived. Instantly he found himself face to face with the hydra, who came forward spewing fire. But Cajusse had also asked for a coat of mail and a mighty sword, and with one blow he cut off the seven heads. Then he called to his servant to take notice which was the head which was in the middle of the other six, and the servant pointed it out. Then he said, "Watch when I split it open, for a leveret will jump out. Beware lest it escapes." The servant stood to catch it, but it was so swift it ran past the servant. The prince, however, was swifter than it, and overtook it and killed it. Then he said, "Beware when I split open the head of the leveret. A little bird will fly out; mind that it escapes not, for we are undone if it escapes." So the servant stood ready to catch the bird, but the bird was so swift it flew past the servant. The prince, however, was swifter than the bird, and he overtook it and killed it, and split open its head and took out the precious stone. Then he rubbed the ring and bade it take him back to the princess. The princess was waiting for him at the window.

"Here is the stone," said the prince; and he gave it to her, and with it a bottle of opium. "Tonight," he said, "you must say you are ready to marry the wizard; make a great feast again, and have ready some of this opium in his wine. He will sleep heavily, and not see what you are doing; then you can put the stone under his pillow and when he is dead call me."

All this the princess did. She told the wizard that she was now ready to do as he wished. The magician was so delighted that he ordered a great banquet.

"Here," said the princess at the banquet, "is a little of my father's choicest wine, which I had with me in the palace when it was brought hither," and she poured out to him to drink of the wine mixed with opium.

After this, when the wizard went to bed, he was heavy and took no notice what she did, and thus she put the stone under his pillow. No sooner did he, therefore, lay his head on the pillow than he gave three terrible yells, turned himself round and round three times, and was dead.

There was no need to call the prince, for he had heard the death yells, and immediately came up. They found the lantern, after they had hunted everywhere in vain, tied on to the magician's body under all his clothes, for he had hid it there that he might never part with it. By its power Cajusse ordered the palace to be removed back to its place, and there they lived happily for ever afterwards.

The Marriage of Signor Cajusse

THERE WAS A RICH FARMER who had one only daughter, and she was to be his heiress. She fell in love with a count who had no money – at least only ten scudi a month. When he went to the farmer to ask her in marriage he would not hear of the alliance, and sent him away.

But the girl and he were bent on the marriage, and this is how they brought it about. The girl had a thousand scudi of her own; half of this she gave to him, and said: "Go over a certain tract of the Campagna and visit all the peasants about, and give five piastres to one and ten to another according to their degree, that they may say when they are asked that they all belong to Signor Cajusse. Then take Papa round to hear what they say, and he will think you are a great proprietor, and will let us marry."

Signor Cajusse, for such was his name, took the money and did as she told him, and then hired a carriage and came to her father, and said: "You are quite mistaken in thinking I'm too poor to marry your daughter; come and take a drive with me, and I will show you what a great man I am."

So the farmer got into his carriage, and he drove him round to all the peasants he had bribed. First they stopped at a farm.

"Good morning, Signor Cajusse," said the tenant, who had been duly primed, bowing down to the ground; and then he began to tell him about his crops, as if he had been really proprietor.

After this he proposed to walk a little way, and all the labourers left their work and flocked after him, crying, "Good day, Signor Cajusse; health to you and long life, and may God prosper you!" and they tried to kiss his hand.

Further along they came to a villa where Cajusse had ascertained that the real proprietor would not come that day. Here he went straight up to the casino, where the servant in charge, who had been also duly bribed, received him with all the honours due to a master.

"Welcome, Signor Cajusse," he said, and opened the doors and shutters and set the chairs.

"Bring a little of that fine eight-year-old wine," ordered Cajusse; "we have brought a packet of biscuits, and will have some luncheon."

"Very good, Signor Cajusse," replied the servant respectfully, and shortly after brought in a bottle of wine handed to him for the purpose by Cajusse the day before. When they had drunk they took a stroll round the place, and wherever they turned the labourers all had a greeting and a blessing for Signor Cajusse.

When the merchant saw all this he hardly knew how to forgive himself for having run the risk of losing such a son-in-law. He was all smiles and civility as they drove home, and the next day was as anxious to hurry on the match as he had been before to put it off. As all were equally in a hurry to have it, of course it was not long before it was celebrated. With the girl's remaining five hundred scudi a handsome apartment was hired to satisfy appearances before the parents, and for a few days they lived on what was left over.

They sat counting their last two or three scudi. "What is to be done now?" said Cajusse; "that will soon be spent, and then how are we to live?"

"I'll set it right," answered the bride. "Now we're married that's all that signifies. Now it's done they can't help it."

So she went to her mother and told her all, and the good woman, knowing the thing could not be altered, talked over the father; and he gave them something to live upon and found a place for Cajusse, and they were very happy.

The Daughter of Count Lattanzio

COUNT LATTANZIO had a daughter who was in love with a lawyer, but the Count was not at all inclined to let her marry beneath her station, and he took all the pains imaginable to prevent them from meeting; so much so that he scarcely let her out of his sight. One day he was obliged to go to his vineyard outside the gates, and before he left he gave strict injunctions to his servant to let no one in till he came back at 21 o'clock.

It was an hour before 21 o'clock, and there was a knock at the door.

"Is the Count Lattanzio in?"

"No, he won't be in just yet."

"Ah, I know, he won't be in till 21 o'clock; he said I was to wait. I'm come to measure him for a pair of new boots.

"If he told you to wait I suppose you must," said the servant; "otherwise he had told me not to let anyone in." And as he showed him in he thought he was a rather gentlemanly shoemaker.

Soon after there was another knock.

"Is the Count Lattanzio in?"

"No, he won't be in for some time yet."

"Ah, never mind; he said I was to wait if he hadn't come in. I'm the tailor, come to measure him for a new suit."

"If he said you were to wait I suppose you must," answered the servant; "but it's very odd he should have told you so, as he particularly told me to let no one in." However, he showed him in also. Directly after there came another knock.

"Is the Count Lattanzio at home?"

"No, he won't be in for some time yet."

"Never mind; I'm the lawyer engaged in his cause before the courts. He said I was to wait if he wasn't in."

But the servant began to get alarmed at having to disobey orders so many times, and he thought he would make a stand.

"I'm very sorry," he said, "but master said I wasn't to show anyone in."

"What! when I've come here with my two clerks, on particular business of the greatest importance to your master, do you suppose I'm going away again like that, fellow?"

The servant was so amazed by his imperative manner that he let him in, too.

Twenty-one o'clock came at last, and with it Count Lattanzio. Having given orders that no one should be let in, of course he expected to find no one. What was his astonishment, therefore, when, as he opened the drawing-room door, a loud cry of "Long live Count Lattanzio!" uttered by several voices met his ear.

The shoemaker was the bridegroom, the tailor the best man, the lawyer and his two clerks were the notary and his witnesses. The marriage articles had been duly drawn up and signed, and as the parties were of age there was no rescinding the contract.

Count Lattanzio sent away the servant for not attending to orders; but that made no difference – the deed was done.

The Simple Wife

THERE WERE A MAN and his wife who had a young daughter to marry; and there was a man who was seeking a wife. So the man who was seeking a wife came to the man who had a daughter to marry, and said, "Give me your daughter for a wife."

"Yes," said the man who had a daughter to marry; "you'll do very well; you're just about the sort of son-in-law I want." And then he added: "If our daughter is to be betrothed today, it is the occasion for a feast." So to the wife he said, "Prepare the table;" and to the daughter he said, "Draw the wine."

The daughter went down into the cellar to draw the wine. But as she drew the wine she began to cry, saying: "If I am to be married I shall have a child, and the child will be a son, and the son will be a priest, and the priest will be a bishop, and the bishop will be a cardinal, and the cardinal will be a Pope." And she cried and cried, and the wine was running all the time, so that the bottle she was filling ran over, and went on running over.

Then said the father and mother: "What can the girl be doing down in the cellar so long?" But the mother said: "I must go and see."

So the mother went down to see why she was so long, but the moment she came into the cellar she, too, began to cry; so that the wine still went on running over.

Then the father said: "What can the girl and her mother both be doing so long down in the cellar? I must go and see."

So the father went down into the cellar; but the moment he got into the cellar he, too, began to cry, and could do nothing for crying; so the wine still went on running over.

Then he who had come to seek a wife said: "What can these people all be doing so long down in the cellar?" So he, too, went down to see, and found them all crying in the cellar and the wine running over. Only when the wine was all run out they left off crying and came upstairs again.

Then the betrothal and the marriage were happily celebrated.

One day after they were married the husband went into the market to buy meat, and he bought a large provision because he had invited a friend to dinner. When the wife saw him buy such a quantity of meat she began to cry, saying: "What can we do with such a lot of meat?"

"Oh, never mind, don't make a misery of it," said the husband; "put it behind you."

The simple wife took the meat and went home, saying to her parents, and crying the while: "My husband says I am to put all this meat behind me! Do tell me what *can* I do?"

"You can't put the whole lot of it behind you, that's certain," replied the equally simple mother; "but we can manage it between us."

Then she took the meat and put all the hard, bony part on one chair, where she made the father sit down on it; all the fat, skinny part she put on another chair, and made the wife sit down on it; and the fleshy, meaty part she put on another chair, and sat down on that herself.

Presently the husband came with his friend, ready for dinner, knocking at the door. None of the three dared to move, however, that they might not cease to be fulfilling his injunctions. Then he looked through the keyhole, and, seeing them all sitting down without moving when he knocked, he thought they must all be dead; so he ran and fetched a locksmith, who opened the door for him.

"What on earth are you all doing there," exclaimed the hungry husband, "instead of getting dinner ready?"

"You told me to put the meat behind me, and I have done so," answered the simple wife.

Then he saw they were sitting on the meat. Out of all patience with such idiocy, he exclaimed: "This is the last you'll ever see of me. At least I promise you not to come back till I have met three other people as idiotic as you, and that's hardly likely to occur."

With that he took his friend to a tavern to dine, and then put on a pilgrim's dress and went wandering over the country.

In the first city he came to there was great public rejoicing going on. The princess had just been married, and the court was keeping high festival. As he came up to the palace the bride and bridegroom were just come back from church. The bride wore one of those very high round headdresses that they used to wear in olden times, with a long veil hanging from it. It was so very high that she could not by any means get in at the door, and there she stuck, not knowing what to do. Then she began to cry, saying: "What shall I do? What shall I do?"

"Shall I tell you what to do?" said the pilgrim-husband, drawing near.

"Oh, pray do, if you can; I will give you a hundred scudi if you will only show me how to get in."

So he went and made her go a few steps backwards, and then bow her head very low, and so she could pass under the door.

"Really, I have found one woman as simple as my people at home," said the pilgrim-husband, as he sat down to the banquet at the special invitation of the princess, in reward for his services. Afterwards she counted out a hundred scudi to him, and he went further.

Further along the road he came to a farm, with barns and cattle and plenty of stock about, and a large well at which a woman was drawing water. Instead of dipping in the pail, she had got the well-rope knotted into a huge knot, which she kept dipping into the water and squeezing out into the pail, and she kept crying as she did so: "Oh, how long shall I be filling the pail! The pail will never be full!"

"Shall I show you how to fill it?" asked the pilgrim-husband, drawing near.

"Oh, yes, do show me if you can. I will give you a hundred scudi if you will only show me."

Then he took all the knots out of the rope and let down the pail by it, and filled it in a minute.

"Here's a second woman as stupid as my people at home," said the pilgrim-husband, as the farmer's wife asked him in to dinner in reward for his great services; "if I go on at this rate I shall have to return to her at last, in spite of my protestations."

After that the farmer's wife counted out the hundred scudi of the promised reward, and he went on further, having first packed six eggs into his hollow staff as provision for the journey.

Towards nightfall he arrived at a lone cottage. Here he knocked and asked a bed for his night's lodging.

"I can't give you that," said a voice from the inside; "for I am a lone widow. I can't take a man in to sleep here."

"But I am a pilgrim," replied he; "let me in at least to cook a bit of supper."

"*That* I don't mind doing," said the good wife, and she opened the door.

"Thanks, good friend!" said the pilgrim-husband as he sat down by the stove; "now add to your charity a couple of eggs in a pan."

So she gave him a pan and two eggs, and a bit of butter to cook them in; but he took the six eggs out of his staff and broke them into the pan, too.

Presently, when the good wife turned her head his way again, and saw eight eggs swimming in the pan instead of two, she said: "Lack-a-day! you must surely be some strange being from the other world. Do you know so-and-so there?" She asked, naming her dead husband.

"Oh, yes," said the pilgrim-husband, enjoying the joke; "I know him very well; he lives just next to me."

"Only to think of that!" replied the poor woman. "And do tell me, how do you get on in the other world? What sort of a life is it?"

"Oh, not so very bad; it depends what sort of a place you get. The part where we are is not very bad, except that we get very little to eat. Your husband, for instance, is nearly starved."

"No, really!" cried the good wife, clasping her hands. "Only fancy! My good husband starving out there; so fond as he was of a good dinner, too!" Then she added, coaxingly: "As you know him so well, perhaps you wouldn't mind doing him the charity of taking him a little something to give him a treat. There are such lots of things I could easily send him."

"O, dear no, not at all; I'll do it with great pleasure," answered he; "but I'm not going back till tomorrow; and if I don't sleep here I must go on further, and then I shan't come by this way."

"That's true," replied the widow. "Ah, well, I mustn't mind what the folks say, for such an opportunity as this may never occur again. You must sleep in my bed, and I must sleep on the hearth; and in the morning I'll load a donkey with provisions for my poor dear husband."

"Oh, no," replied the pilgrim; "you shan't be disturbed in your bed; only let me sleep on the hearth, that will do for me; and as I'm an early riser I can be gone before anyone's astir, so folks won't have anything to say."

So it was done, and an hour before sunrise the woman was up loading the donkey with the best of her stores. There were ham, and maccaroni, and flour, and cheese, and wine. All this she committed to the pilgrim, saying: "You'll send the donkey back, won't you?"

"Of course I would send him back; he'd be no use to us out there: but I shan't get out again myself for another hundred years or so, and I fear he won't find his way back alone, for it's no easy way to find."

"To be sure not; I ought to have thought of that," replied the widow. "Ah, well, so as my poor husband gets a good meal never mind the donkey."

So the pretended pilgrim from the other world went his way. He hadn't gone a hundred yards before the widow called him back.

"Ah, she's beginning to think better of it!" said he to himself; and he continued his way, pretending not to hear.

"Good pilgrim!" shouted the widow; "I forgot one thing. Would any money be of use to my poor dear husband?"

"Oh dear yes, all the use in the world," replied the pilgrim; "you can always get anything for money everywhere."

"Oh, do come back then, and I'll trouble you with a hundred scudi for him."

The pretended pilgrim came back willingly for the hundred scudi, and the widow counted them out to him.

"There is no help for it," soliloquized he as he went his way; "I must go back to those at home. I have actually found three women each more stupid than they."

So he went home to live, and complained no more of the simplicity of his wife.

The Foolish Woman

THERE WAS ONCE a couple well-to-do in the world, who had one only daughter.

The son of a neighbour came to ask her in marriage, and as the father thought he would do, the father asked him to dinner, and sent the daughter down into the cellar to draw the wine.

"If I am married," said the girl to herself, and began to cry as she drew the wine, "I shall have a child, and the child will be a boy, and the boy will be called Petrillo, and by and by he will die, and I shall be left to lament him, and to cry all day long 'Petrillo! Petrillo! where are you!'" and she went on crying, and the wine went on running over.

Then the mother went down to see what kept her so long, and she repeated the story all over to her, and the mother answered, "Right you are, my girl!" and she, too, began to cry, and the wine was all the time running over.

Then the father went down, and they repeated the story to him, and he, too, said, "Right you are!" and he, too, began to cry, and the wine all the time went on running all over the floor.

Then the young man also goes down to see what is the matter, and stops the wine running, and makes them all come up.

"But," he says, "I'll not marry the girl till I have wandered over the world and found other three as simple as you." He dines with them, and sets out on his search.

The first night he goes to bed in an inn, and in the morning he hears in the room next him such lamenting and complaining that he goes in to see what is the matter. A man is sitting by the side of the bed lamenting because he cannot get his stockings on.

The young man says, "Take hold of one side this way, and the other side that way, and pull them up."

"Ah, to be sure!" cries the man, and gives him a hundred scudi for the benefit he has done him.

"There's one of my three simpletons, at all events," says the young man, and journeys on.

The next day, at the inn where he spends the night, he hears a noise *bru, bru!* goes in to see, and finds a man fruitlessly trying to put walnuts into a sack by sticking a fork into them.

"You'll never do it that way," says the young man; and he shows him how to scoop them up with both his hands and so pour them in.

"Ah, to be sure!" answers the man, and gives him a hundred scudi for the favour he has done him.

"There is my second simpleton," says the young man, and goes further.

The third day – Ah! I can't remember what he meets the third day; but it is something equally stupid, and he gets another hundred scudi, and goes back and marries the girl as he had promised.

When they had been married some time, he goes out for two or three days to shoot.

"I'll come with you," says the wife.

"Well, it's not quite the thing," answered he; "but perhaps it's better than leaving you at home; but mind you pull the door after you."

"Oh yes, of course," answers the simple wife, and pulls it so effectually that she lifts it off its hinges and carries it along with her.

When they have gone some way he looks back and sees her carrying the door.

"What on earth are you bringing the door along for?" he cries.

"You told me to pull it after me," answers she.

"Of course, I only meant you to pull it to, to make the house secure," he says.

"If merely pulling it to, made the house secure, how much securer it must be when I pull it all this way!" answers she.

He finds it useless to reason with her, and they go on. At night they climb up into a tree to sleep, the woman still carrying the door with her. A band of robbers come and count their gains under the tree; the woman from sheer weariness, and though she believes it will rouse the robbers to come and kill them, drops the door upon them. They take it for an earthquake and run away. The man and his wife then gather up the money, and are rich for the rest of their lives.

The Booby

THEY SAY THERE WAS once a widow woman who had a very simple son. Whatever she set him to do he muddled in some way or other.

"What am I to do?" said the poor mother to a neighbour one day. "The boy eats and drinks, and has to be clothed; what am I to do if I am to make no profit of him?"

"You have kept him at home long enough;" answered the neighbour. "Try sending him out, now; maybe that will answer better."

The mother took the advice, and the next time she had got a piece of linen spun she called her boy, and said to him:

"If I send you out to sell this piece of linen, do you think you can manage to do it without committing any folly?"

"Yes, Mama," answered the booby.

"You always say, "Yes, Mama," but you do contrive to muddle everything all the same," replied the mother. "Now, listen attentively to all I say. Walk straight along the road without turning to right or left; don't take less than such and such a price for it. Don't have anything to say to women who chatter; whether you sell it to anyone you meet by the way, or carry it into the market, offer it only to some quiet sort of body whom you may see standing apart, and not gossiping and prating, for such as they will persuade you to take some sort of a price that won't suit me at all."

The booby promised to follow these directions very exactly, and started on his way.

On he walked, turning neither to the right hand nor to the left, thus passing the turnings which led to the villages, to one or other of which he ought to have gone. But his mother had only meant that he was not to turn off the pathway and lose himself.

Presently he met the wife of the syndic of the next town, who was driving out with her maids, but had got out to walk a little stretch of the way, as the day was fine. The syndic's wife was talking cheerfully with her maids, and when one of them caught sight of the simpleton, she said to her mistress:

"Here is the simple son of the poor widow by the brook."

"What are you going to do, my good lad?" said the syndic's wife kindly.

"Not going to tell you, because you were chattering and gossiping," replied the booby boorishly, and tried to pass on.

The syndic's wife forgave his boorishness, and added:

"I see your mother has sent you to sell this piece of linen. I will buy it of you, and that will save you walking further; put it in the carriage, and I'll give you so much for it."

Though she had offered him twice as much as his mother had told him to get for it, he would only answer:

"Can't sell it to you, because you were chattering and gossiping."

Nor could they prevail on him to stop a moment longer.

Further along he came to a statue by the roadside.

"Here's one who stands apart and doesn't chatter," said the booby to himself. "This is the one to sell the linen to." Then aloud to the statue, "Will you buy my linen, good friend?" Then to himself. "She doesn't speak, so it's all right." Then to the statue, "The price is so-and-so; have the money ready against I come back, as I have to go on and buy some yarn for Mother."

On he went and bought the yarn, and then came back to the statue. Someone passing by meanwhile, and seeing the linen lie there had picked it up and walked off with it.

Finding it gone, the booby said to himself, "It's all right, she's taken it." Then to the statue, "Where's the money I told you to have ready against I came back?" As the statue remained silent, the booby began to get uneasy. "My mother will be finely angry if I go back without the linen or the money," he said to himself. Then to the statue, "If you don't give me the money directly I'll hit you on the head."

The booby was as good as his word; lifting his thick, rough walking-stick, he gave the statue such a blow that he knocked the head off.

But the statue was hollow, and filled with gold coin.

"That's where you keep your money, is it?" said the booby, "all right, I can pay myself." So he filled his pockets with money and went back to his mother.

"Look, Mama! Here's the price of the piece of linen."

"All right!" said the mother out loud; but to herself she said, "Where can I ever hide all this lot of money? I have got no place to hide it but in this earthen jar, and if he knows how much it is worth, he will be letting out the secret to other people, and I shall be robbed."

So she put the money in the earthen jar, and said to the boy:

"They've cheated you in making you think that was coin; it's nothing but a lot of rusty nails; but never mind, you'll know better next time." And she went out to her work.

While she was gone out to her work there came by an old rag-merchant.

"Ho! here, rag-merchant!" said the booby, who had acquired a taste for trading. "What will you give me for this lot of rusty nails?" and he showed him the jar full of gold coin.

The rag-merchant saw that he had to do with an idiot, so he said:

"Well, old nails are not worth very much; but as I'm a good-natured old chap, I'll give you twelve pauls for them," because he knew he must offer enough to seem a prize to the idiot.

"You may have them at that," said the booby. And the rag-merchant poured the coin out into his sack, and gave the fool the twelve pauls.

"Look Mama, look! I've sold that lot of old rusty worthless nails for twelve pauls. Isn't that a good bargain?"

"Sold them for twelve pauls!" cried the widow, tearing her hair, "Why, it was a fortune all in gold coin."

"Can't help it, Mama," replied the booby; "you told me they were rusty nails."

Another day she told him to shut the door of the cottage; but as he went to do it he lifted the door off its hinges. His mother called after him in an angry voice, which so frightened him that he ran away, carrying the door on his back.

As he went along, someone, to tease him, said, "Where did you steal that door?" which frightened him still more, and he climbed up in a tree with it to hide it.

At night there came a band of robbers under the tree, and counted out all their gains in large bags of money. The booby was so frightened at the sight of so many fierce-looking robbers that he began to tremble and let go of the door.

The door fell with a bang in the midst of the robbers, who thinking it must be that the police were upon them, decamped, leaving all their money behind.

The booby came down from the tree and carried the money home to his mother, and they became so rich that she was able to appoint a servant to attend to him, and keep him from doing any more mischief.

The Preface of a Franciscan

A FRANCISCAN FRIAR was travelling on business of his order when he was overtaken by three brigands, who stole from him his ass, his saddle and his doubloons. Moreover, they told him that if he informed any man of what they had done they would certainly come after him again and take his life; for they could only sell the ass and the saddle that were known to be his by representing that he had sold them to them, otherwise no one would have bought them.

The friar told no man what had happened to him, for fear of losing his life; yet he knew that if he could only let his parishioners know what had occurred, they would soon retake for him all that he had lost.

So he hit on the following expedient: next Sunday, as he was saying Mass, when he came to the place in the Preface where special additions commemorative of the particular festivals are inserted, after the enumeration of the praises of God, he added the words, "Nevertheless, me, Thy poor servant, evil men have robbed of my ass and her saddle, and all my doubloons; but to no man have I declared the thing, save unto Thee only, Omnipotent Father, who knowest all things, and helpest the poor;" and then he went on, "et ideò cum angelis et archangelis," &c.

The parishioners were no sooner thus informed of what had occurred than they went after the brigands and made them give up all they had taken. The next time, therefore, the father was out in the Campagna, the brigands came after him and said:

"Now, we take your life; last time we let you off, saying we would spare you if you told no man what we had done; but you cannot keep your own counsel, so you must die like the rest."

But the good monk showed them that he had not spoken to man of the thing, but had only lamented his loss before God, which every man was free to do. And the brigands, when they heard that, could say nothing, and they let him go by uninjured, him and his beast.

Animal Tales

ANIMALS IN FAIRY TALES are often humans in disguise. The protagonist of the first tale in this section turns into a dove when her evil stepmother kills her, while the monstrous beast in 'The Enchanted Rose Tree' is, of course, a handsome prince who has been cursed. More unusual is the female donkey who, when she is turned back into the woman she once was, still bears the signs of the beatings she received for her nastiness.

Magical animals can make for powerful helpers, such as the bird acting like the better-known fairy godmother in 'Cenorientola' and the cow who saves Maria from her murderous stepmother in 'Vaccarella'. Not all enchanted animals are desirable, however: Bellacuccia is a monkey who behaves like a perfect housekeeper, but is revealed to be a man possessed by the devil. Nor are all animals enchanted. Some of them are, quite simply, animals: the white serpent in the eponymous tale indicates the site of a buried treasure; Nina the donkey shares the miller's daughter's name, allowing the trickster miller to deceive his greedy and more powerful landlord. And although in 'Signor Lattanzio' the cats are in fact fairies, punished for their malice, the cats in the last three tales of this section are quite plainly themselves – tricksters, always: from the one who killed his owner because she left him with servants who ate the chicken destined to him, to the explanation of why cats and dogs do not get along, to the cats who made their owner rich by saving America from the mice that overran it.

Palombelletta

THEY SAY THERE WAS a peasant whose wife had died and left him one little girl, who was the most beautiful creature that ever was seen; no one on earth could compare with her for beauty. After a while the peasant married again: this time he married a peasant-woman who had a daughter who was the most deformed object that ever was seen; no cripple on earth could compare with her for deformity; and, moreover, her skin was quite black and shrivelled, and altogether no one could bear to look at her, she was so hideous.

One day when everyone was out, and only the fair daughter at home, the king came by from hunting thirsty, and he stopped at the cottage and asked the fair maid for a glass of water. When he saw how fair she was and with what grace she waited on him, he said, "Fair maiden, if you will, I will come back in eight days and make you my wife." The maiden answered, "Indeed I will it, Your Majesty!" and the king rode away.

When the stepmother came home the simple maiden told her all that had happened, and she answered her deceitfully, congratulating her on her good fortune. Before the day came round, however, she shut the fair maiden in the cellar. When the king came she went out to meet him with a smiling face, saying, "Good day, Sire! What is your royal pleasure?" And the king answered, "To marry your daughter am I come." Then the stepmother brought out her own daughter to him, all wrapped up in a wide mantle, and her face covered with a thick veil, and a hood over that.

"Rest assured, good woman, that your daughter will be my tenderest care," said the king; "but you must take those wrappers off."

"By no means, Sire!" exclaimed the stepmother. "And beware you do it not. You have seen how fair she is above all the children of earth. But this exceeding beauty she has on one condition. If one breath of air strike her she loses it all. Therefore, oh, king! let not the veil be removed."

When the king heard that he called for another veil, and another hood, and wrapping her still more carefully round, handed her into the carriage he had brought for her, shut the door close, and rode away on horseback by her side.

When they arrived at the palace the hideous daughter of the stepmother was married to the king all wrapped up in her veils.

The stepmother, however, went into her room, full of triumph at what she had done. "But what am I to do with the other girl?" she said to herself; "somehow or other someday she will get out of the cellar, and the king will see her, and it will be worse for my daughter than before." And as she knew not what to do she went to a witch to help her. "This is what you must do," said the witch; "take this pin" (and she gave her a long pin with a gold head), "and put it into the head of the maiden, and she will become a dove. Then have ready a cage, and keep her in it, and no one will ever see her for a maiden more."

The stepmother went therefore, and bought a cage, and taking the large pin down into the cellar, she drove the pin into the fair maiden's head, holding open the cage as she did so.

As soon as the pin entered the maiden's head she became a dove, but instead of flying into the cage she flew over the stepmother's head far away out of sight.

On she flew till she came to the king's palace, right against the window of the kitchen where the cook was ready preparing a great dinner for the king. The cook looked round as he heard the poor little dove beating its frightened breast against the window, and, fearful lest it should hurt itself, he opened the window.

In flew the dove as soon as he opened the window, and flew three times round his head, singing each time as she did so: "O cook! O cook! of the royal kitchen, what shall we do with the Queen? All of you put yourselves to sleep, and may the dinner be burnt up!"

As soon as she had sung this the third time the cook sank into a deep sleep; the dinner from want of attention was all burnt up; and when the king sat down to table, there was nothing to set before him.

"Where is the dinner?" exclaimed the king, as he looked over the empty table to which he had brought his bride, still wrapped up in her thick veils.

"Please Your Majesty, the dinner is all burnt up as black as charcoal," said the chamberlain; "and the cook sits in the kitchen so fast asleep that no one can wake him."

"Go and fetch me a dinner from the inn," said the king; "and the cook, when he comes to himself, let him be brought before me."

After a time the cook came to himself, and the chamberlain brought him before the king.

"Tell me how this happened," said the king to the cook. "All these years you have served me well and faithfully; how is it that today, when the dinner should have been of the best in honour of my bride, everything is burnt up, and the king's table is left empty?"

"Indeed, the dinner had been of the best, Sire," answered the cook. "So had I prepared it. Only, when all was nearly ready, there came a dove flying in at the window, and flew three times round my head, singing each time,

> *Cook of the royal kitchen,*
> *What shall we do with the Queen?*
> *Sleep ye all soundly, and burnt be the meal*
> *Which on the King's board should have been.*

After that a deep sleep fell on me and I know nothing more of what happened."

"That must have been a singular dove," said the king; "bring her to me and you shall be forgiven."

The cook went down to look for the dove, and found her midway, flying to meet him.

"There is the dove, Sire," said the cook, handing the dove to the king.

"So you spoilt my dinner, did you, palombelletta?" said the king. "But never mind; you are a dear little dove, and I forgive you," and he put her in his breast and stroked her. Thus, as he went on stroking and fondling her, calling her "palombelletta bella!" he felt the gold head of the stepmother's big pin through the feathers. "What have you got in your head, palombelletta dear?" he said, and pulled the pin out.

Instantly the fair maiden stood before him in all her surpassing beauty as he had seen her at the first. "Are you not my fair maiden who promised to marry me?" exclaimed the king.

"The very same, and no other," replied the maiden.

"Then who is this one?" said the king, and he turned to the stepmother's daughter beside him, and tore off her veil. Then he understood the deceit that had been played on him, and he sent for the stepmother, and ordered that she and her daughter should be punished with death.

La Cenorientola

THEY SAY THERE WAS a merchant who had three daughters. When he went out into foreign countries to buy wares he told them he would bring them rare presents, whatever they might ask for. The eldest asked for precious jewels, the second for rich shawls, but the youngest who was always kept out of sight in the kitchen by the others, and made to do the dirty work of the house, asked only for a little bird.

"So you want a little bird, do you? What is the use of a little bird to you?" said the sisters mocking her, and, "Papa will have something else to think of than minding little birds on a long journey."

"But you will bring me a little bird, won't you, Papa?" pleaded the little girl; "and I can tell you that if you don't the boat you are on will stand still, and will neither move backwards nor forwards."

The merchant went away into a far country and bought precious wares, but he forgot all about the little bird. It was only when he had got on board a boat to go down a mighty river on his homeward way, and the captain found the boat would not move by any means, that he remembered what his daughter had said to him. Then while the captain was wondering how it was the boat would not move, he went to him and told him what he had done. But the captain said, "That is easily set right. Here close by is a garden full of thousands of birds; you can easily creep in and carry off one. *One* will never be missed among so many thousands."

The merchant followed his directions and went into the garden where there were so many thousand birds that he easily caught one. The captain gave him a cage, and he brought it safely home and gave it to his daughter.

That night the elder sisters said as usual, "We are going to the ball; you will stay at home and sweep up the place and mind the fire."

Now all the birds in the garden which the captain had pointed out to the merchant were fairies; so when the others were gone to the ball and the youngest daughter went into her room to her bird, she said to it:

> *Give me splendid raiment,*
> *And I will give you my rags.*

Immediately, the bird gave her the most beautiful suit of clothes, with jewels and golden slippers, and a splendid carriage and prancing horses. With these the maiden went to the ball which was at the king's palace. The moment the king saw her he fell in love with her, and would dance with no one else. The sisters were furious with the stranger because the king danced all night with her and not with them, but they had no idea it was their sister.

The second night she did the same, only the bird gave her a yet more beautiful dress, and the king did all he could to find out who she was, but she would not tell him. Then he asked her name and she said,

"They call me *Cenorientola*."

"*Cenorientola*," said the king; "what a pretty name! I never heard it before."

He had also told the servants that they must run after her carriage and see where it went; but though they ran as fast as the wind they could not come near the pace of her horses.

The third night the sisters went to the ball and left her at home, and she stayed at home with her little bird and said to it,

> *Give me splendid raiment,*
> *And I will give you my rags.*

Then the bird gave her a more splendid suit still, and the king paid her as much attention as ever. But to the servants he had said, "If you don't follow fast enough tonight to see where she lives I will have all your heads cut off." So they used such extra diligence that she in her hurry to get away dropped one of her golden slippers; this the servants picked up and brought to the king.

The next day the king sent a servant into every house in the city till he should find her whom the golden slipper fitted, but there was not one; last of all he came to the merchant's house, and he tried it on the two elder daughters and it would fit neither. Then he said,

"There must be some other maiden in this house;" but they only shrugged their shoulders. "It is impossible; another maiden there must be, for every maiden in the city we have seen and the slipper fits none, therefore one there must be here."

Then they said,

"In truth we have a little sister who sits in the kitchen and does the work. She is called *Cenorientola*, because she is always smutty. We are sure she never went to a ball, and it would only soil the beautiful gold slipper to let her put her smutty feet into it."

"It may be so," replied the king's servant, "but we must try, nevertheless."

So they fetched her, and the king's servant found that the shoe fitted her; and they went and told the king all.

The moment the king heard them say *Cenorientola* he said, "That is she! It is the name she gave me."

So he sent a carriage to fetch her in all haste. The bird meantime had given her a more beautiful dress than any she had had before, and priceless jewels, so that when they came to fetch her she looked quite fit to be a queen. Then the king married her; and though her sisters had behaved so ill to her she gave them two fine estates, so that all were content.

Vaccarella

THEY SAY THERE WAS once a husband and a wife; but I don't mean that they were husband and wife of each other. The husband had lost his wife, and the wife had lost her husband, and each had one little daughter. The husband sent

his daughter to the wife to be brought up along with her own daughter, and as the girl came every morning to be trained and instructed, the wife used to send a message back by her every evening, saying, "Why doesn't your father marry me? Then we should all live together, and you would no longer have this weary walk to take."

The father, however, did not see it in the same light; but the teacher continued sending the same message. In short, at last she carried her point, having previously given a solemn promise to him that Maria, his little girl, should be always as tenderly treated as her own.

Not many months elapsed, however, before she began to show herself a true stepmother. After treating Maria with every kind of harshness, she at last sent her out into the Campagna to tend the cow, so as to keep her out of sight of her father, and estrange him from her. Maria had to keep the cow's stall clean with fresh litter every day; sometimes she had to take the cow out to grass, and watch that it only grazed over the right piece of land; at other times she had to go out and cut grass for the cow to eat. All this was work enough for one so young; but Maria was a kind-hearted girl, and grew fond of her cow, so that it became a pleasure to her to attend to it.

When the cruel stepmother saw this she was annoyed to find her so light-hearted over her work, and to vex her more gave her a great heap of hemp to spin. It was in vain that Maria reminded her she had never been taught to spin; the only answer she got was, "If you don't bring it home with you tonight all properly spun you will be finely punished;" and Maria knew to her cost what that meant.

When Maria went out into the Campagna that day she was no longer light-hearted; and as she littered down the stall she stroked the cow fondly, and said to her, as she had no one else to complain to, "Vaccarella! Vaccarella! what shall I do? I have got all this hemp to spin, and I never learnt spinning. Yet if I don't get through it somehow I shall get sadly beaten tonight. Dear little cow, tell me what to do!"

But the cow was an enchanted cow, and when she heard Maria cry she turned round and said quickly and positively:

> *Throw it on to the horns of me,*
> *And go along, cut grass for me!*

Maria did as she was told, went out and cut a good basketful of grass, and imagine her delight on coming back with it to find all the whole lot of hemp beautifully spun.

The surprise of the stepmother was still greater than hers, at finding that she had got through her task so easily, for she had given her enough to have occupied an ordinary person for a week. Next day, therefore, she determined to vex her with a more difficult task, and gave her a quantity of spun hemp to weave into a piece of fine cloth. Maria's pleadings were as fruitless as before, and once more she went to tell her tale of woe to her "dear little cow."

Vaccarella readily gave the same answer as before:

> *Throw it on to the horns of me,*
> *And go along, cut grass for me!*

Once more, when Maria came back with her basket of grass, she found all her work done, to her great surprise and delight. But her stepmother's surprise was quite of another order. That Maria should have woven the cloth, not only without instruction, but even without a loom, proved clearly enough she must have had someone to help her – a matter which roused the stepmother's jealousy in the highest degree, and wherein this help consisted she determined to find out. Accordingly, next day she gave her a shirt to make up, and then posted herself out of sight in a corner of the cow-house to see what happened. Thus she overheard Maria's complaint to her dear little cow, and Vaccarella's reply:

> *Throw it on to the horns of me,*
> *And go along, cut grass for me!*

She thus also saw what Maria did not see, that as soon as she had gone out the cow assumed the form of a woman, and sat down and stitched and stitched away till the shirt was made, and that in a surprisingly short space of time. As soon as it was finished, and before Maria came in, the woman became a cow again.

The cruel stepmother determined that Maria should be deprived of a friend who enabled her to set all her hard treatment at defiance, and next morning told her that she was going to kill the cow. Maria was broken-hearted at the announcement, but she knew it was useless to remonstrate; so she only used her greatest speed to reach her "dear little cow," and warn her of what was going to happen in time to make her escape.

"There is no need for me to escape," replied Vaccarella; "killing will not hurt me. So dry your tears, and don't be distressed. Only, after they have killed me, put your hand under my heart, and there you will find a golden ball. This ball is yours, so take it out, and whenever you are tired of your present kind of life, you have only to say to it on some fitting occasion – "Golden ball, golden ball, dress me in gold and give me a lover," and you shall see what shall happen."

Vaccarella had no time to say more, for the stepmother arrived just then with a man who slaughtered the cow at her order.

Under Vaccarella's heart Maria found the promised golden ball, which she hid away carefully against some fitting occasion for using it arose.

Not long after there was a *novena,* or a great festival, during which Maria's stepmother, with all her disposition to overwork her, durst not keep her from church, lest the neighbours should cry "Shame!" on her.

Maria accordingly went to church with all the rest of the people, and when she had made her way through the crowd to a little distance from her stepmother, she took her golden ball out of her pocket and whispered to it: "Golden ball, golden ball, dress me in gold and give me a lover."

Instantly the golden ball burst gently open and enveloped her, and she came out of it all radiant with beautiful clothing, like a princess. Everybody made way for her in her astonishing brightness.

The eyes of the king's son were turned upon her, no less than the eyes of all the people; and the prayers were no sooner over than he sent some of his attendants to call her and bring her to him. Before they could reach her, however, Maria had restored her beautiful raiment to the golden ball, and, in the sordid attire in which her stepmother dressed her, she could easily pass through the crowd unperceived.

At home, her stepmother could not forbear talking, like everyone else in the town, about the maiden in glittering raiment who had appeared in the midst of the church; but, of course, without the remotest suspicion that it was Maria herself. But Maria sat still and said nothing.

So it happened each day of the Novena; for, though Maria was not at all displeased with the appearance and fame of the husband whom her "dear little cow" seemed to have appointed for her, she did not wish to be too easy a prize, and thought it but right to make him take a little trouble to win her. Thus she every day restored all her bright clothing to the golden ball before the prince's men could overtake her. Only on the last day of the Novena, when the prince, fearful lest it might also be the last on which he would have an opportunity of seeing her, had told them to use extra diligence, they were so near overtaking her that, in the hurry of the moment, she dropped a slipper. This the prince's men eagerly seized, feeling no compunction in wresting it from the mean-looking wench (so Maria now looked) who disputed possession of it with them, not in the least imagining that she could be the radiant being of whom they were in search.

The Novena over, Maria once more returned to her ceaseless toil; but the stepmother's hatred had grown so great that she determined to rid herself of her altogether and in the most cruel way.

Down in the cellar there stood a large barrel, which had grown dirty and mouldy from neglect, and wanted scalding out. "Get into the barrel, Maria girl," she bade her next morning for her task, "and scrape it and rub it well before we scald it."

Maria did as she was bidden, and the stepmother went away to boil the water.

Meantime, the prince's men had taken Maria's slipper to him, and he, delighted to have any token of his fair one, appointed an officer to go into every house, and proclaim that the maiden whom the slipper might fit should be his bride. The officer went round from house to house, trying the slipper on everybody's foot. But it fitted no one, for it was under a spell.

But the stepmother's own daughter had gone down to the cellar to help Maria, unbeknown to her mother; and it so happened that, just as she was inside the barrel and Maria outside, the king's officer happened to come by that way. He opened the door, and, seeing a damsel standing within, tried on the sandal without waiting to ask leave. As the sandal fitted Maria to perfection, the officer was all impatience to carry her off to the prince, and placed her in the carriage which was waiting outside, and drove off with her before anyone had even observed his entrance.

Scarcely had all this passed than the stepmother came back with her servants, each carrying a can of boiling water. They placed themselves in a ring round the barrel, and each emptied her charge into it. As it was the stepmother's daughter who was inside at the time, instead of Maria, it was she who got scalded to death in her place.

By and by, when the house was quiet, the bad stepmother went to the barrel, intending to take out the body of Maria and hide it. What was her dismay when she found, instead of Maria's body, that of her own daughter! As soon as her distress and grief subsided sufficiently to enable her to consider what she had to do, the idea suggested itself to conceal the murder by putting the blame of it on someone else. For this purpose she took the body of her daughter, and, dressing it in dry clothes, seated it on the top of the stairs against her husband's return.

Presently, home he came with his ass-load of wood, and called to her daughter to come and help him unload it, as usual. But the daughter continued sitting on the top of the stairs, and moved not. Again and again he called, louder and louder, but still she moved not; till at last, irritated beyond all endurance, he hurled one of his logs of wood at her, which brought the badly balanced corpse rolling and tumbling all the way down the stairs, just as the stepmother had designed.

The husband, however, was far from being deceived by the device. He could see the body presented no appearance of dying from a recent fall.

"Where's Maria?" he asked, as soon as he got up into the room.

"Nobody knows; she has disappeared!" replied the stepmother; nor was he slow to convince himself she was nowhere in the house.

"This is no place for me to stay in," said the husband to himself. "One child driven away, and one murdered; who can say what may happen next?"

Next morning, therefore, he called to him the little daughter born to him since his marriage with Maria's stepmother, and went away with her for good and all. So that bad woman was deprived, as she deserved, of her husband and all her children in one day.

Just as the father and his daughter were starting to go away, Maria drove by in a gilded coach with the prince her husband; so he had the satisfaction, and her stepmother the vexation, of seeing her triumph.

The Enchanted Rose Tree

THEY SAY THERE WAS once a merchant who, when he was going out to buy rare merchandise, asked his daughter what rich present he should bring home to her. She, however, would hear of nothing but only a simple rose tree.

"That," said her father, "is too easy. However, as you are bent on having a rose tree, you shall have the most beautiful rose tree I can find in all my travels."

In all his travels, however, he met with no rose tree that he deemed choice enough. But one day, when he was walking outside the walls of his own city, he came to a garden which he had never observed before, filled with all manner of beautiful flowers.

"This is a wonderful garden indeed," said the merchant to himself; "I never saw it before, and yet these luxuriant plants seem to have many years' growth in them. There must be something wonderful about them, so this is just the place to look for my daughter's rose tree." In he went therefore to look for the rose tree.

In the midst of the garden was a casino, the door of which stood open; when he went in he found a banquet spread with the choicest dishes; and though he saw no one, a kind voice invited him to sit down and enjoy himself. So he sat down to the banquet, and very much he did enjoy himself, for there was everything he could desire.

When he had well eaten and drunk, he bethought him to go out again into the garden and seek a choice rose tree.

"As the banquet was free," he thought to himself, "I suppose the flowers are free too."

So he selected what seemed to him the choicest rose of all; while it had petals of the richest red in the world, within it was all shining gold, and the leaves too were overlaid with shining gold. This rose tree, therefore, he proceeded to root up.

A peal of thunder attended the attempt, and with a noise of rushing winds and waters a hideous monster suddenly appeared before him.

"How dare you root up my rose trees?" said the monster; "was it not enough that I gave you my best hospitality freely? Must you also rob me of my flowers, which are as my life to me? Now you must die!"

The merchant excused himself as best he could, saying it was the very freedom of the hospitality which had emboldened him to take the rose, and that he had only ventured to take it because he had promised the prettiest rose tree he could find to his daughter.

"Your daughter, say you?" replied the monster. "If there is a daughter in the case perhaps I may forgive you; but only on condition that you bring her hither to me within three days' time."

The father went home sad at heart, but within three days he kept his promise of taking his daughter to the garden. The monster received them very kindly, and gave them the casino to live in, where they were well fed and lodged. At the end of eight days, however, a voice came to the father and told him he must depart; and when he hesitated to leave his daughter alone he was taken by invisible agency and turned out of the garden.

The monster now often came and talked to the daughter, and he was so gentle and so kind that she began quite to like him. One day she asked him to let her go home and see her friends, and he, who refused her nothing, let her go; but begged her to promise solemnly she would come back at the end of eight days, "for if you are away longer than that," he added, "I know I shall die of despair." Then he gave her a mirror into which she could look and see how he was.

Thus she went home, and the time passed quickly away, and eight days were gone and she had not thought of returning. Then by accident the mirror came under her hand, and, looking into it, she saw the monster stretched on the ground as if at the point of death. The sight filled her with compunction, and she hurried back with her best speed.

Arrived at the garden, she found the monster just as she had seen him in the mirror. At sight of her he revived, and soon became so much better that she was much touched when she saw how deeply he cared for her.

"And were you really so bad *only* because I went away?" she asked.

"No, not only because you went away, for it was right you should go and see your parents; but because I began to fear you would never come back, and if you had never come back I should quite have died."

"And now you are all right again?"

"Yes, now you are here I am quite happy; that is, I should be quite happy if you would promise always to remain and never go away anymore."

Then when she saw how earnest and sincere he was in wishing her to stay, she gave her consent never to leave him more.

No sooner had she spoken the promise than in the twinkling of an eye all was changed. The monster became a handsome prince, the casino a palace, the garden a flourishing country, and each rose tree a city. For the prince had been enchanted by an enemy, and had to remain transformed as a monster till he should be redeemed by the love of a maiden.

The Transformation-Donkey

THERE WAS ONCE a poor chicory-seller: all chicory-sellers are poor, but this was a very poor one, and he had a large family of daughters and two sons. The daughters he left at home with their mother, but the two sons he took with him to gather chicory. While they were out gathering chicory one day, a great bird flew down before them and dropped an egg and then flew away again. The boys picked up the egg and brought it to their father, because there were some figures like strange writing on it which they could not read; but neither could the father read the strange writing, so he took the egg to a farmer. The farmer read the writing, and it said:

"Whoso eats my head, he shall be an emperor."

"Whoso eats my heart, he shall never want for money."

"Ho, ho!" said the farmer to himself, "it won't do to tell the fellow this; I must manage to eat both the head and the heart myself." So he said, "The meaning of it is that whoever eats the bird will make a very good dinner; so tomorrow when the bird comes back, as she doubtless will to lay another egg, have a good stick ready and knock her down; then you can make a fire, and bake it between the stones, and I will come and eat it with you if you like."

The poor chicory-seller thought his fortune was made when a farmer offered to dine with him, and the hours seemed long enough till next morning came.

With next morning, however, came the bird again. The chicory-seller was ready with his stick and knocked her down, and the boys made a fire and cooked the bird. But as they were not very apt at the trussing and cooking, the head dropped into the fire, and the youngest boy said: "This will never do to serve up, all burnt as it is;" so he ate it. The heart also fell into the fire and got burnt, and the eldest boy said: "This will never do to serve up, all burnt as it is;" so he ate that.

By and by the farmer came, and they all sat down on a bank – the farmer quite jovial at the idea of the immense advantage he was going to gain, and the chicory-seller quite elated at the idea of entertaining a farmer.

"Bring forward the roast, boys," said the father; and the boys brought the bird.

"What have you done with the head?" exclaimed the farmer, the moment he saw the bird.

"Oh, it got burnt, and I ate it," said the younger boy.

The merchant ground his teeth and stamped his foot, but he dared not say why he was so angry; so he sat silent while the chicory-seller took out his knife and cut the bird up in portions.

"Give me the piece with the heart, if I may choose," said the merchant; "I'm very fond of birds' hearts."

"Certainly, any part you like," replied the chicory-seller, nervously turning all the pieces over and over again; "but I can't find any heart. Boys, had the bird no heart?"

"Yes, Papa," answered the elder brother, "it had a heart, sure enough; but it tumbled into the fire and got burnt, and so I ate it."

There was no object in disguising his fury any longer, so the farmer exclaimed testily, "Thank you, I'll not have any then; the head and the heart are just the only parts of a bird I care to eat." And so saying he turned on his heel and went away.

"Look, boys, what you've done! You've thrown away the best chance we ever had in our lives!" cried the father in despair. "After the farmer had taken dinner with us he must have asked us to dine with him, and, as one civility always brings another, there is no saying what it might not have led to. However, as you have chosen to throw the chance away, you may go and look out for yourselves. I've done with you." And with a sound cudgelling he drove them away.

The two boys, left to themselves, wandered on till they came to a stable, when they entered the yard and asked to be allowed to do some work or other as a means of subsistence.

"I've nothing for you to do," said the landlord; "but, as it's late, you may sleep on the straw there, on the condition that you go about your business tomorrow first thing."

The boys, glad to get a night's lodging on any condition, went to sleep in the straw. When the elder brother woke in the morning he found a box of sequins under his head.

"How could this have come here," soliloquized the boy, "unless the host had put it there to see if we were honest? Well, thank God, if we're poor there's no danger of either of us taking what doesn't belong to us." So he took the box to the host, and said: "There's your box of sequins quite safe. You needn't have taken the trouble to test our honesty in that way."

The host was very much surprised, but he thought the best way was to take the money and say nothing but "I'm glad to see you're such good boys." So he gave them breakfast and some provisions for the way.

Next night they found themselves still in the open country and no inn near, and they were obliged to be content to sleep on the bare ground. Next morning when they woke the younger boy again found a box of sequins under his head.

"Only think of that host not being satisfied with trying us once, but to come all this way after us to test our honesty again. However, I suppose we must take it back to him."

So they walked all the way back to the host and said: "Here's your box of sequins back; as we didn't steal it the first time it was not likely we should take it the second time."

The host was more and more astonished; but he took the money without saying anything, only he praised the boys for being so good and gave them a hearty meal. And they went their way, taking a new direction.

The next night the younger brother said: "Do you know I've my doubts about the host having put that box of sequins under your head. How could he have done it out in the open country without our seeing him? Tonight I will watch, and if he doesn't come, and in the morning there is another box of sequins, it will be a sign that it is your own."

He did so, and next morning there was another box of sequins. So they decided it was honestly their own, and they carried it by turns and journeyed on. About noon they came to a great city where the emperor was lately dead, and all the people were in great excitement about choosing another emperor. The population was all divided in factions, each of which had a candidate, and none would let the candidate of the others reign. There was so much fighting and quarrelling in the streets that the brothers got separated, and saw each other no more.

At this time it happened that it was the turn of the younger brother to be carrying the box of sequins. When the sentinels at the gate saw a stranger coming in carrying a box they said, "We must see what this is," and they took him to the minister. When the minister saw his box was full of sequins he said, "This must be our emperor." And all the people said, "Yes, this is our emperor. Long live our emperor!" And thus the boy became an emperor.

But the elder brother had entered unperceived into the town, and went to ask hospitality in a house where was a woman with a beautiful daughter; so they let him stay. That night also there came a box of sequins under his head; so he went out and bought meat and fuel and all manner of provisions, and gave them to the mother, and said, "Because you took me in when I was poor last night, I have brought you all these provisions out of gratitude," and for the beautiful daughter he bought silks and damasks, and ornaments of gold. But the daughter said, "How comes it, tell me, that you, who were a poor footsore wayfarer last night, have now such boundless riches at command?" And because she was beautiful and spoke kindly to him, he suspected no evil, but told her, saying, "Every morning when I wake now, I find a box of sequins under my head."

"And how comes it," said she, "that you find a box of sequins under your head now, and not formerly?" "I do not know," he answered, "unless it be because one day when I was out with Father gathering chicory, a great bird came and dropped an egg with some strange writing on it, which we could not read. But a farmer read it for us; only he would not tell us what it said, but that we should cook the bird and eat it. While we were cooking it the heart fell into the fire and got burnt, and I ate it: and when the farmer heard this he grew very angry. I think, therefore, the writing on the egg said that he who ate the heart of the bird should have many sequins."

After this they spent the day pleasantly together; but the daughter put an emetic in his wine at supper, and so made him bring up the bird's heart, which she kept for herself, and the next morning when he woke there was no box of sequins under his head. When he rose in the morning also the beautiful girl and her mother turned him out of the house, and he wandered forth again.

At last, being weary and full of sorrow, he sat down on the ground by the side of a stream crying. Immediately three fairies appeared to him and asked him why he wept. And when he told them, they said to him: "Weep no more, for instead of the bird's heart we give you this sheepskin jacket, the pockets of which will always be full of sequins. How many soever you may take out they will always remain full." Then they disappeared; but he immediately went back to the house of the beautiful girl, taking her rich and fine presents; but she said to him, "How comes it that you, who had no money left when you went away, have now the means to buy all these fine presents?" Then he told her of the gift of the three fairies, and they let him sleep in the house again, but the daughter called her maid to her and said: "Make a sheepskin jacket exactly like that in the stranger's room." So she made one, and they put it in his room, and took away the one the fairies

74

had given him, and in the morning they drove him from the house again. Then he went and sat down by the stream and wept again; but the fairies came and asked him why he wept; and he told them, saying, "Because they have driven me away from the house where I stayed, and I have no home to go to, and this jacket has no more sequins in the pockets." Then the fairies looked at the jacket, and they said, "This is not the jacket we gave you; it has been changed by fraud:" so they gave him in place of it a wand, and they said, "With this wand strike the table, and whatever you may desire, be it meat or drink or clothes, or whatsoever you may want, it shall come upon the table." The next day he went back to the house of the woman and her daughter, and sat down without saying anything, but he struck the table with his wand, wishing for a great banquet, and immediately it was covered with the choicest dishes. There was no need to ask him questions this time, for they saw in what his gift consisted, and in the night, when he was asleep, they took his wand away. In the morning they drove him forth out of the house, and he went back to the stream and sat down to cry. Again the fairies appeared to him and comforted him; but they said, "This is the last time we may appear to you. Here is a ring; keep it on your hand; for if you lose this gift there is nothing more we may do for you;" and they went away. But he immediately returned to the house of the woman and her beautiful daughter. They let him in, "Because," they said, "doubtless the fairies have given him some other gift of which we may take profit." And as he sat there he said, "All the other gifts of the fairies have I lost, but this one they have given me now I cannot lose, because it is a ring which fits my finger, and no one can take it from my hand."

"And of what use is your ring?" asked the beautiful daughter.

"Its use is that whatever I wish for while I have it on I obtain directly, whatever it may be."

"Then wish," said she, "that we may be both together on the top of that high mountain, and a sumptuous *merenda* spread out for us."

"To be sure!" he replied, and he repeated her wish. Instantly they found themselves on the top of the high mountain with a plentiful *merenda* before them; but she had a vial of opium with her, and while his head was turned away she poured the opium into his wine. Presently after this he fell into a sound sleep, so sound that there was no fear of waking him. Immediately she took the ring from his finger and put it on her own; then she wished that she might be replaced at home and that he might be left on the top of the mountain. And so it was done.

In the morning when he woke and found himself all alone on the top of the high mountain and his ring gone, he wept bitter tears, and felt too weary to attempt the descent of the steep mountain side. For three days he remained there weary and weeping, and then, becoming faint from hunger, he took some of the herbs that grew on the mountain top for food. As soon as he had eaten these he was turned into a donkey, but as he retained his human intelligence, he said to himself, this herb has its uses, and he filled one of the panniers on his back with it. Then he came down from the mountain, and when he was at the foot of it, being hungry with the long journey, he ate of the grass that grew there, and, behold! he was transformed back into his natural shape; so he filled the other basket with this kind of grass and went his way.

Having dressed himself like a street seller, he took the basket of the herb which had the property of changing the eater into a donkey, and stood under the window of the house where he had been so evil entreated, and cried, "Fine salad! fine salad! Who will buy my fine salad?"

"What is there so specially good about your salad?" asked the maid, looking out. "My young mistress is particularly fond of salad, so if yours is so very superfine, you had better come up."

He did not wait to be twice told. As soon as he saw the beautiful daughter, he said, "This is fine salad, indeed, the finest of the fine, all fresh gathered, and the first of its kind that ever was sold."

"Very likely it's the first of its kind that ever was sold," said she; "but I don't like to buy things I haven't tried; it may turn out not to be nice."

"Oh, try it, try it freely; don't buy without trying;" and he picked one of the freshest and crispest bunches.

She took one in her hand and bit a few blades, and no sooner had she done so than she too became a donkey. Then he put the panniers on her back and drove her all over the town, constantly cudgelling her till she sank under the blows. Then one who saw him belabour her thus said, "This must not be; you must come and answer before the emperor for thus belabouring the poor brute;" but he refused to go unless he took the donkey with him;

so they went to the emperor and said, "Here is one who is belabouring his donkey till she has sunk under his blows, and he refuses to come before the emperor to answer his cruelty unless he bring his donkey with him." And the emperor made answer, "Let him bring the beast with him."

So they brought him and his donkey before the emperor. When he found himself before the emperor he said, "All these must go away; to the emperor alone can I tell why I belabour my donkey." So the emperor commanded all the people to go to a distance while he took him and his donkey apart. As soon as he found himself alone with the emperor he said, "See, it is I, thy brother!" and he embraced him. Then he told him all that had befallen him since they parted. Then said the emperor to the donkey, "Go now with him home, and show him where thou hast laid all the things – the bird's heart, the sheepskin jacket, the wand, and the ring, that he may bring them hither; and if thou deliver them up faithfully I will command that he give thee of that grass to eat which shall give thee back thy natural form."

So they went back to the house and fetched all the things, and the emperor said, "Come thou now and live with me, and give me of thy sequins, and I will share the empire with thee." Thus they reigned together.

But to the donkey they gave of the grass to eat, which restored her natural form, only that her beauty was marred by the cudgelling she had received. And she said, "Had I not been so wilful and malicious I had now been empress."

Signor Lattanzio

THEY SAY THERE WAS a duke who wandered over the world seeking a beautiful maiden to make his wife.

After many years he came to an inn where was a lady, who asked him what he sought.

"I have journeyed half the earth over," answered the duke, "to find a wife to my fancy, and have not found one; and now I go back to my native city as I came."

"How sad!" answered the lady. "I have a daughter who is the most beautiful maiden that ever was made; but three fairies have taken possession of her, and locked her up in a casino in the Campagna, and no one can get to see her."

"Only tell me where she is," replied the duke, "and I promise you I'll get to see her, in spite of all the fairies in the world."

"It is useless!" replied the lady. "So many have tried and failed. So will you."

"Not I!" answered the duke. "Tell me how they failed, and I will do otherwise."

"I have told so many, and all say the same as you, and all go to seek her, but none ever come back."

"Never mind! Tell it once again, and I promise you it shall be the last time, for I will surely come back."

"If you are bent on sacrificing yourself uselessly," proceeded the lady, "this is the story. You must go to the mountain of Russia, and at the foot of it there will meet you three most beautiful maidens, who will come round you, and praise you, and flatter you, and pour out all manner of blandishments, and will ask you to go into their palace with them, and will entreat you so much that you will not be able to resist; then you will go into their palace with them, and they will turn you into a cat, for they are three fairies. But, on the other hand, if you can resist only for the space of one hour to all they will say to you, then you will have conquered, and they will be turned into cats, and you will have free access to my daughter to release her."

"I will go," said the duke firmly; and he rose up and went his way to the mountain of Russia.

"Now, if all these other men have failed in this same attempt," he mused within himself as he went along, "it behooves me to be prudent. I know what I will do; I will put a bandage over my eyes, and then I shan't see the fairies, and their blandishments will have no power over me." And so he did.

Then the fairies came out to him and said, "Signor Lattanzio! welcome, welcome! How fair you are; do take the bandage off and let us see you; how noble you look. Do let us see your face. We are dying to have you with us!"

But the duke remained firm, and seemed to take no heed, though their voices were so soft and persuasive that he longed to look at them, or even to lift up one corner of the bandage and take a peep. But he remained firm.

"Signor Lattanzio! Signor Lattanzio! Don't be so ungallant," pursued the fairies. "Here are we at your feet, as it were, begging you to give us your company, and you will not so much as speak to us, or even look at us!"

But the duke remained firm, and seemed to take no heed, though his head was turned by their accents, and he felt that if he could only go with them as they wished he should want no more. But he remained firm.

"Signor Lattanzio! Signor Lattanzio! Signor Lattanzio!" cried the three fairies disdainfully, for now they began to suspect in right good earnest that at last one had come who was too strong for them. "The fact is you are afraid of us. If you are a man, show you have no fear, and come and talk with us."

But the duke remained firm, though a vanity, which had nearly lost him, whispered that it would be a grander triumph to look them in the face and yet resist them, than to conquer without having ventured to look at them, yet prudence prevailed, and he remained firm.

So they went on, and the duke felt that the hour was drawing to a close. He took out his repeater and struck it, and the hour of trial was over.

"Traitor!" cried the three fairies, and in the same instant they were turned into cats. Then the duke went into their palace, and took their wand, and with it he could open the gates of the casino where the lady's daughter was imprisoned.

When he saw her, he found her indeed fairer than the fairest; fairer even than his conception.

When, therefore, with the wand he had restored all the cats that were upon the mountain to their natural shapes as those that had failed in their enterprise, he took her home with him to be his wife.

The White Serpent

MY STORY IS ALSO of a husband and wife, but they were peasants, and lived outside the gates.

"It is so cold tonight," said the husband to the wife, as they went to bed, "we shall freeze if we have another night like it. We must contrive to wake before it is light, and go and get some wood somewhere before we go to work, to make a fire tomorrow night."

So they woke very early, before it was light, and went out to get wood. The husband stood up in the tree, and the wife down below in a ditch, or hole. As she stood there she saw a great white serpent glide past her. "Look, look!" she cried to her husband; "see that great white serpent; surely there is something unnatural about it!"

"A white serpent!" answered her husband; "what nonsense! Who ever heard of such a thing as a white serpent!"

"There it goes, then," said the wife; "you can see it for yourself."

"I see nothing of the kind," said the husband. "There are no serpents about Rome this many a long year; and as for a white one, such a thing doesn't exist."

While he spoke the serpent went through a hole in the ground. As the husband was so positive, the wife said no more, but they gathered up the wood and went home.

In the night, however, the wife had a dream. She saw an Augustinian friar, long since dead, standing before her, who said, "Angela! (that was indeed her name) if you would do me a favour listen to me. Did you see a white serpent this morning?"

"Yes," she answered; "that I did, though my husband said there was no such thing as a white serpent in existence."

"Well, if you would do me a pleasure, go back to the place where you saw the white serpent go in – not where he came out, but where you saw him go into the earth. Dig about that place, and, when you have dug a pretty good hole, a dead man will start up; but don't be afraid, he can't hurt you, and won't want to hurt you. Take no notice of him, and go on digging, and no harm will come to you; you have nothing to be afraid of. If you dig on you will come to a heap of money. Take some of the biggest pieces of gold and carry them to St. Peter's, and take some of the smaller pieces and carry them to S. Agostino, and let masses be said for that dead man. But you must tell no one alive anything about it."

The woman was much too frightened to do what the friar had said, but she managed to keep the story to herself, though it made her look so anxious her husband could not help noticing something.

The next night the friar came again, and said the same words, only he added: "If you are so frightened, Angela, you may take with you for company a little boy, but he must not be over seven, nor under six; and what you do you must tell no one. But you have nothing to fear, for if you do as I have said no one can harm you."

For all his assurances, however, she could not make up her mind to go, nor this day could she even keep the story from her husband, for it weighed upon her mind. When he heard the story he said, "I'll go with you."

"Ah! if you'll go, then I don't mind," she said. "But how will it be? The friar was so particular that I should tell no one, evil may happen if I take another with me."

"If there is nothing in the story, there's nothing to fear," said the husband; "and, if the story is true, there is a heap of money to reward one for a little fear; so let's go. Besides, if you think any harm will happen to you for taking me, I can stand on the top of the bank while you go down to the hole, and it can't be said properly that I'm there, while I shall yet be by to give you courage and help you if anything happens."

"That way, I don't mind it," answered the wife; and they went out together to the place, the husband, as he had said, standing by on a bank, and the wife creeping down into a hole. They took also two donkeys with them to bring away the treasure.

At the first stroke of the woman's spade there came such lugubrious cries that she was frightened into running away.

"Don't be afraid," said the husband; "cries don't hurt!" So the woman began digging again, and then there came out cries again worse than before, and the noise of rattling of chains, dreadful to hear. So terrified was the woman that she swooned away.

The husband then went down into the hole with what water he could find to bring her to herself, but the moment he got into the hole the spirits set upon him and beat him so that he had great livid marks all over.

After that neither of them had the heart to go back to try it again.

But the woman was in the habit of going to confession to one of the Augustinian fathers, and she told him all. The fathers sent and had the place dug up all about, and thought they had proved there was nothing there; but for all that, it generally happens that when a thing like that has to be done, it must be done by the person who is sent, and anybody else but that person trying it proves nothing at all.

One thing is certain, that when those horrid assassins hide a heap of money they put a dead man's body at the entrance of the hole where they hide it, and say to it, "Thou be on guard till one of such a name, be it Teresa, be it Angela, be it Pietro, comes;" and no one else going can be of any use, for it may be a hundred years before the coincidence can happen of a person just of the right name lighting on the spot – perhaps never.

"Yes, yes! that's a fact; that is not old wives' nonsense," was the chorus which greeted this enunciation.

Bellacuccia

T**HERE WAS ONCE a pleader who sat writing in his room all day whenever he was not in court.**

One day as he so sat there came in at the window a large monkey, and began whisking about the room. The lawyer, pleased with the antics of the monkey, called it *scimmia bellacuccia*, and caressed and fed it. By and by he had to go out on his business, and though he was in some fear of the pranks the monkey might be up to in his absence, he had taken such a fancy to it that he did not like to send it away, and at last left it alone in his apartment.

When he came home, instead of the monkey having been at any mischievous pranks, the whole suite of rooms was put in beautiful order, and out of very scanty materials in the cupboard an excellent dinner was cooked and laid ready.

"*Scimmia bellacuccia!* is this your doing?" said the lawyer, and the monkey nodded assent.

"Then you are a precious monkey, indeed," he replied, and he called it to him and fed it, and gave it part of the dinner.

The next day the monkey did the work of the house, and the lawyer sent away his servant because he had no further need for one, the monkey did all much better and in a more intelligent way.

All went well for a time, when one day the lawyer had occasion to visit a friar he knew at St. Nicolò da Tolentino, for in those days there were friars there instead of nuns as now.

He did not fail to tell him of the treasure he had found in his *bellacuccia*, as he called his monkey.

"Don't let yourself be deceived, friend!" exclaimed the friar. "This is no monkey; it is not in the nature of a monkey to do thus."

"Come and see it yourself," said the lawyer. "You will find I have over-stated nothing of what it can do and does every day."

Some days after this the friar came, having taken care to provide himself with his stole and a stoup of holy water. Directly he came into the lawyer's apartment he put on his stole and sprinkled the holy water.

The monkey no sooner saw the shadow of his habit than it took to flight, and, after scrambling all round the room to get away from the sight of him, finally hid itself under the bed.

"You see!" said the friar to the lawyer.

But the lawyer cried, "Here *bellacuccia*; come here!" and as the monkey was by habit very docile and obedient, when he had said, "*bellacuccia*" a great many times, it at last forced itself to come to him, but stealthily and warily, showing great fear of the monk.

When it had got quite close to the lawyer, and he was holding it, the friar once more put on his stole, sprinkled it with holy water and exorcised it.

Instantly *bellacuccia* burst away from the lawyer, and, clambering up to the window, broke away through the upper panes and disappeared, leaving smoke and a smell of brimstone behind.

But it was really a man who had been put under a spell by evil arts, and when thus released by the monk's exorcism he went and became a monk, I forget in what order, but I know it.

Ass or Pig

🪕

A COUNTRYMAN WAS GOING along driving a pig before him. "Let's have a bit of fun with that fellow," said the brother porter of a monastery to the father guardian, as they saw him coming along the road. "I'll call his pig an ass, and of course he'll say it's a pig; then I shall laugh at him for not knowing better, and he will grow angry. Then I'll say, "Well, will you have the father guardian to settle the dispute? And if he decides I'm right I shall keep the beast for myself." Then you come and say it is an ass, and we'll keep it."

The father guardian agreed, with a hearty laugh; and as soon as the countryman came up the brother porter did all as he had arranged.

The countryman was so sure of his case that he willingly submitted to the arbitration of the father guardian; but great was his dismay when the father guardian decided against him, and he had to go home without his pig.

But what did the countryman do? He dressed himself up as a poor girl, and about nightfall, and a storm coming on, he rang at the bell of the monastery and entreated the charity of shelter for the night.

"Impossible!" said the brother porter; "we can't have any womenkind in here."

"But the dark, and the storm!" clamoured the pretended girl; "think of that. You can't leave me out here all alone."

"I'm very sorry," said the porter, "but the thing's impossible. I can't do it."

The good father guardian, hearing the dispute at that unusual hour, put his head out of the window and asked what it was all about.

"It is a difficult case, brother porter," he said when he had heard the girl's request. "If we take her in we infringe our rule in one way; if we leave her exposed to every kind of peril we sin against its spirit in another direction. I only see one way out of it. I can't send her into any of your cells; but I will let her pass the night in mine, provided she is content not to undress, and will consent to sit up in a chair."

This was exactly what the countryman wanted, therefore he gave a ready assent, and the father guardian took him up into his cell. The pretended girl sat up in a chair quietly enough through the dark of the night, but when morning began to dawn, out came a stick that had been hidden under the petticoats, and whack, whack – a fine drubbing the poor father guardian got, to the tune of – "So you think I don't know a pig from an ass, do you?"

When he had well bruised him all over, the countryman made the best of his way downstairs, and off and away he was before anyone could catch him.

The next day what did he do? He dressed up like a doctor, and came round asking if anyone had any ailments to cure.

"That's just the thing for us," said the brother porter to himself as he saw him come by. "The father guardian was afraid to let the doctor of the neighbourhood attend him, for fear of the scandal of all the story coming out; the strange doctor will just do, as there is no need to tell him anything."

The countryman in his new disguise, therefore, was taken up to the father guardian's cell.

"There's nothing very much the matter," he said when he had examined the wounds and bruises; "it might all be set right in a day by a certain herb," which he named.

The herb was a difficult one to find, but as it was so important to get the father guardian cured immediately, before any enquiry should be raised as to the cause of his sufferings, the whole community set out to wander over the Campagna in search of it.

As soon as they were a good way off, the pretended doctor took out a thick stick which he held concealed under his long robe, and whack, whack – belaboured the poor father guardian more terribly even than before, to the tune of "So you think I don't know an ass from a pig, do you?"

How far soever the brothers were gone, his cries were so piteous that they recalled them, but not till the countryman had made good his escape.

"We have sinned, my brethren," said the father guardian when they were all gathered round him; "and I have suffered justly for it. We had no right to take the man's pig, even for a joke. Let it now, therefore, be restored to him, and in amends let there be given him along with it an ass also."

So the countryman got his pig back, and a donkey into the bargain.

The Greedy Daughter

THERE WAS A MOTHER who had a daughter so greedy that she did not know what to do with her. Everything in the house she would eat up. When the poor mother came home from work there was nothing left.

But the girl had a godfather-wolf. The wolf had a frying-pan, and the girl's mother was too poor to possess such an article; whenever she wanted to fry anything she sent her daughter to the wolf to borrow his frying-pan, and he always sent a nice omelette in it by way of not sending it empty. But the girl was so greedy and so selfish that she not only always ate the omelette by the way, but when she took the frying-pan back she filled it with all manner of nasty things.

At last the wolf got hurt at this way of going on, and he came to the house to enquire into the matter.

Godfather-wolf met the mother on the step of the door, returning from work.

"How do you like my omelettes?" asked the wolf.

"I am sure they would be good if made by our godfather-wolf," replied the poor woman; "but I never had the honour of tasting them."

"Never tasted them! Why, how many times have you sent to borrow my frying-pan?"

"I am ashamed to say how many times; a great many, certainly."

"And every time I sent you an omelette in it."

"Never one reached me."

"Then that hussy of a girl must have eaten them by the way."

The poor mother, anxious to screen her daughter, burst into all manner of excuses, but the wolf now saw how it all was. To make sure, however, he added: "The omelettes would have been better had the frying-pan not always been full of such nasty things. I did my best always to clean it, but it was not easy."

"Oh, godfather-wolf, you are joking! I always cleaned it, inside and out, as bright as silver, every time before I sent it back!"

The wolf now knew all, and he said no more to the mother; but the next day, when she was out, he came back.

When the girl saw him coming she was so frightened and self-convicted that she ran under the bed to hide herself.

But to the wolf it was as easy to go under a bed as anywhere else; so under he went, and he dragged her out and devoured her. And that was the end of the Greedy Daughter.

Nina

THERE WAS A MILLER who got into difficulties, and could not pay his rent. The landlord sent to him a great many times to say that if he could not pay his rent he must go out; but as he paid no attention to the notice, the landlord went himself at last, and told him he must go. The miller pleaded that his difficulties were only temporary, and that if he would give him but a little time he would make it all straight. The landlord, however, was pitiless, and said he had waited long enough, and now he had come to put an end to it; adding, "Mind, this is my last word: If you do not go out tonight peaceably, I shall send someone tomorrow to turn you out by force."

As he turned to leave, after pronouncing this sentence, he met the miller's daughter coming back from the stream where she had been washing. "Who is this buxom lass?" enquired the landlord.

"That is my daughter Nina," answered the miller.

"A fine girl she is too," replied the landlord. "And I tell you what, miller, listen to me; give Nina to me, and I will not only forgive you the debt, but will make over the mill and the homestead to you, to be your own property for ever."

"Give me a proper document to that effect, duly signed by your own hand," replied the miller, with a twinkle in his eye, "and I will give you 'Nina.'"

The landlord went back into the house, and taking two sheets of paper drew up first a formal quittance of the back rent, and then a conveyance of the mill and homestead absolutely to the miller and to his heirs for ever. These he handed to the miller; and then he said, "Tonight, an hour before sundown, I will send for 'Nina.'"

"All right," said the miller; "you shall have 'Nina,'" and so they parted.

An hour before sundown a servant came with a carriage to fetch "Nina".

"Where's 'Nina'?" said the servant. "Master has sent me to fetch 'Nina.'"

"In the stable – take her!" answered the miller.

In the stable was nothing to be seen but a very lean old donkey.

"There's nothing here but an old donkey," exclaimed the servant.

"All right, that's 'Nina,' so take her," replied the miller.

"But this can't be what master meant me to fetch!" expostulated the servant.

"What have you got to say to it?" replied the miller. "Your master told you to fetch 'Nina'; we always call our donkey 'Nina'; so take her, and be off."

The servant saw there was nothing to be gained by disputing, so he took the donkey and went home. When he got back, his master had got company with him, so he did not know what to say about the donkey. But his master seeing he was come back, took it for granted the business was done; and calling him to him privately said, "Take 'Nina' upstairs into the best bedroom and light a fire, and give her some supper."

"Take her upstairs into the best bedroom!" exclaimed the man.

"Yes! do what you're told, and don't repeat my words."

The servant could not venture to say any more; so he took the donkey up into the best bedroom, and lit a fire, and put some supper there. As soon as his company was gone, the master called the servant:

"Is 'Nina' upstairs?" asked he.

"Si, Signore; she's lying before the fire," answered the servant.

"Did you take some supper up? I'll have my supper up there with 'Nina.'"

"Si, Signore," replied the servant, and he turned away to laugh, for he thought his master had gone mad.

The landlord went upstairs; but it had now grown dark, so he groped his way to the fireplace, and there sure enough was "Nina," the donkey, lying down, and as he stroked her he said, "What fine soft hair you've got, Nina!"

Presently the servant brought the lights; and when he saw the dirty old worn-out donkey, and understood what a trick the miller had played off on him, it may be imagined how furious he was.

The next day, as soon as the courts were opened, he went before the judge, and told all the tale. Then the miller came too, and told his; but the judge examined the documents, and pronounced that the miller was in the right; for his part of the contract was that he was to deliver over "Nina," and he had delivered over "Nina." There was no evidence that any other "Nina" was intended but "Nina" the donkey, and so the miller remained in undisputed possession of the mill.

And that is the truth, for it actually happened as I have told you.

The Countessa's Cat

THERE WAS A very rich Countessa who was a widow and lived all alone, with no companion but only a cat, after her husband died. The greatest care was taken of this cat, and every day a chicken was boiled on purpose for him.

One day the Countessa went out to spend the day at a friend's villa in the Campagna, and she said to the waiting woman:

"Mind the cat has his chicken just the same as if I were at home."

"Yes! Signora Countessa, leave that to me," answered the woman; but the Countessa was no sooner gone out than she said to the man-servant:

"The cat has the chicken every day; suppose we have it today?"

The man said, "To be sure!" and they ate the chicken themselves, giving the cat only the inside; but they threw the bones down in the usual corner, to make it appear as if he had eaten the whole chicken.

The cat said nothing, but looked on with great eyes, full of meaning.

When the Countessa came back that evening the cat, instead of going out to meet her as he always did, remained still in his place and said nothing.

"What's the matter with the cat? Hasn't he had his chicken?" asked the Countessa, immediately.

"Yes! Signora Countessa," answered the cameriera. "See, there are the bones on the floor, where he always leaves them."

The Countessa could not deny the testimony of her eyes, so she said nothing more but went up to bed.

The cat followed her as he always did, for he slept on her bed; but he followed at a distance, without purring or rubbing himself against her. The Countessa saw something was wrong, but she didn't know what to make of it, and went to bed as usual.

That night the cat throttled the Countessa, and killed her.

The cat is very intelligent in his own interest, but he is a traitor.

"It would have been more intelligent," I observed, "if he had throttled the waiting woman in this instance."

Not at all; the cat's reasoning was this: If thou hadst not gone out and left me to the mercy of menials, this had not happened; therefore it was thou who hadst to die.

This is quite true, for cats are always traitors. Dogs are faithful, cats are traitors.

Why Cats and Dogs Always Quarrel

"WHY DO DOGS and cats always fight, Papa?" we used to say. And he used to answer, "I'll tell you why;" and we all stood round listening.

"Once on a time dogs and cats were very good friends, and when the dogs went out of town they left their cards on the cats, and when the cats went out of town they left their cards on the dogs."

And we all sat round and listened and laughed.

"Once the dogs all went out of town and left their cards as usual on the cats; but they were a long time gone, for they were gone on a rat-hunt, and killed all the rats. When the cats heard that the dogs had taken to killing rats, they were furious against the dogs, and lay in wait for them and set upon them.

"'Set upon the dogs! At them! Give it them!'" shouted the cats, as they flew at them; and from that time to this, dogs and cats never meet without fighting.

And we all stood round and laughed fit to split our sides.

The Cats Who Made Their Master Rich

"**A**H! AS TO CATS and mice, listen and *I'll* tell you something worth hearing!

"In America, once upon a time, there were no cats. Mice there were in plenty; mice everywhere; not peeping out of holes now and then, but infesting everything, swarming over every room; and when a family sat down to meals, the mice rushed upon the table and disputed the victuals with them.

"Then one thought of a plan; he freighted three ships; full, full of cats, and off to America with them. There he sold them for their weight in gold and more, and *whiff!* the mice were swept away, and he made a great fortune. A great fortune, all out of cats!"

Food Stories

THERE ARE chicory gatherers and tripe sellers in Busk's book, people who purvey the least expensive of foods for the same social class to which her narrators belong. Chicory grows wild and costs nothing other than the effort to find and pick it. Tripe is what remains of the animal after the choice cuts have been sold, and Roman cuisine is famous for its inventive uses of the *'quinto quarto'*, or offal – abundant in this city due to the large number of slaughterhouses.

But Busk's book also features precious fruits such as oranges, and variations of the three stories that open this section appear in many Italian folk and fairy tales, as far back as Basile's, who wrote the oldest known version of it in his *Tale of Tales*. In addition to maiden-enclosing citrus fruit, the protagonist of 'The Three Love-Oranges' claims the prince's attention by tricking the cook into burning his food every day. Food is not something to take for granted among the urban poor who were Busk's informants. In the Roman adaptation of 'Hansel and Gretel', titled 'The King Who Goes Out to Dinner', every episode centres on eating and drinking. The stepmother twice distracts the children with cake and wine when she abandons them; the girl cooks such a good dinner for the prince and his mother that she becomes queen; the stepmother makes a whale swallow the girl and asks to drink the boy's own blood. Busk also includes a tale similar to 'Love Like Salt', made famous in King Lear, where the youngest and most beloved daughter loses favour with her father because she refuses to flatter him. In both Shakespeare and Busk, it is through the critical addition of salt to food that the daughter explains her love.

The Three Love-Oranges

THEY SAY THERE WAS a king's son who went out to hunt. It was a winter's day, and the ground was covered with snow, so that when he brought down the birds with his arquebus the red blood made beautiful bright marks on the dazzling white snow.

"How beautiful!" exclaimed the prince. "Never will I marry till I find one with a complexion fair as this snow, and tinted like this rosy blood."

When his day's sport was at an end, he went home and told his parents that he was going to wander over the world till he found one fair as snow, tinted like rosy blood. The parents approved his design and sent him forth.

On, on, on he went, till one day he met a little old woman, who stopped him, saying: "Whither so fast, fair prince?"

He replied, "I walk the earth till I find one who is fair as snow, tinted like rosy blood, to make her my wife."

"That can I help you to, and I alone," said the little old woman, who was a fairy; and then she gave him the three love-oranges, telling him that when he opened one such a maiden as he was in search of would appear, but he must immediately look for water and sprinkle her, or she would disappear again.

The prince took the oranges, and wandered on. On, on, on he went, till at last the fancy took him to break open one of the oranges. Immediately a beautiful maiden appeared, whose complexion was indeed fair as snow, and tinted like rosy blood, but it was only when she had already disappeared that he recollected about the water. It was too late, so on he wandered again till the fancy took him to open another orange. Instantly another maiden appeared, fairer than the other, and he lost no time in looking for water to sprinkle her, but there was none, and before he came back from the search she was gone.

On he wandered again till he was nearly home, when one day he noticed a handsome fountain standing by the road, and over against it a fine palace. The sight of the fountain made him think of his third orange, and he took it out and broke it open.

Instantly a third maiden appeared, far fairer than either of the others; with the water of the fountain he sprinkled her the moment she appeared, and she vanished not, but stayed with him and loved him.

Then he said, "You must stay here in this bower while I go on home and fetch a retinue worthy to escort you."

In a palace opposite the fountain lived a Saracen woman, and just then she went down to the fountain to draw water, and as she looked into the water she said, "My mistress says that I am so ugly, but I am so fair, therefore I break the pitcher and the little pitcher."

Then she looked up in the bower, and seeing the beautiful maiden, she called her down, and caressed her, and stroked her hair, and praised her beauty; but as she stroked her hair she took out a magic pin, and stuck it into her head, and instantly the maiden became a dove and perched on the side of the fountain.

Then she broke the pitcher and the little pitcher, and the prince came back.

When the prince saw the woman standing in the bower where he had left his beautiful maiden, he was quite bewildered, and looked all about for her.

"I am she whom you seek, prince," said the woman. "It is the sun has changed me thus while standing here waiting for you; but all will come right when I get away from the sun."

The prince did not know what to make of it, but there was no help for it but to take her and trust to her coming right when she got away from the sun. He took her home, therefore, and right grand preparations were made for the royal marriage. Tapestries were hung on the walls, and flowers strewed the floor, while in the kitchen was the cook as busy as a bee, preparing I know not how many dishes for the royal banquet.

Then, lo, there came and perched on the kitchen window a little dove, which sang, "Cook, cook, for whom are you cooking; for the son of the king, or the Saracen Moor? May the cook fall asleep, and may all the viands be burnt!"

After this nothing would go right in the kitchen; every day all the dishes got burnt, and it was impossible to give the wedding banquet, because there was nothing fit to send up to the table. Then the king's son came into the kitchen to learn what had happened, and they showed him the dove which had done all. "Sweet little dove!" said the prince, and, catching it in his hand, began to caress it; thus he felt the pin in its head, and pulled it out. Instantly his own fair maiden stood before him, white as snow, rosy as blood. Then the mystery was cleared up, and there was great rejoicing, and the old witch was burnt.

The King Who Goes Out to Dinner

THEY SAY THERE WAS a well-to-do peasant whose wife died leaving him two children – a boy and a girl. Both were beautiful children, but the girl was of the most inconceivable beauty.

As both were still young, and the father did not know how to supply a mother's place to them, he sent them to a woman, who was to teach them and train them, and do all that a mother would have done for them. So to her they went every day. The woman, however, was bent on marrying their father, and used to send a message every day to ask why he did not marry her. The father sent in answer that he did not want to marry; but the woman continued to repeat the same message so frequently that, wearied by her importunity, he sent an answer to the effect that when a pair of strong woollen stockings, which he also gave the children to take to her, were rotted away he would marry her, and not before. The woman took the pair of stockings and hung them up in a loft and damped them with water twice a day till they were soon quite rotted; then she showed them to the children, and told them to tell their father what they had seen. When the children went home they said, "Papa! we saw your pair of stockings today; they are all rotted away." But the father said, "Nonsense! Those thick stockings could not have rotted in this time; there must be some unfair play."

The next morning he gave them a large pitcher of water, and told them to take it to their teacher, saying that when all the water had dried up he would marry her, and not before. The teacher took the children up every day to see how rapidly the water diminished in the jug; but the fact was she used to go first and pour out a little every day. At last she showed them the pitcher empty, and bade them tell their father that they had seen it so. "Impossible!" said their father; but when they assured him they had seen the water in it gradually diminish day by day, he saw there was no way of disputing the fact, and that he was bound by the condition he himself had fixed.

Accordingly he married the teacher. No sooner, however, was she in possession of the house than she told the father she would not have the children about the place; they were not her children, and she could not bear the sight of them. The father expostulated, saying he had no place to send them to, but the stepmother continued so persistently in her representations that, for the sake of peace, he ceased to oppose her, and she took upon herself the task of disposing of them.

One day, therefore, she made them a large cake, and putting it in a basket with a bottle of wine, she took them for a walk outside the gates. When they had gone a long, long way, she proposed that they should sit down and lunch off their cake and wine. The children were nothing loth; but, while they were eating, the stepmother slipped away unperceived, and left them alone, thinking that they would be lost. But the fact was the boy had overheard their father and stepmother talking about getting rid of them, and he had provided himself with a paper parcel of ashes, and had strewn them all along the road they had come, unperceived by his stepmother, and so now by this track they found their way home again.

The stepmother was furious at seeing them come back, but she said nothing in order not to rouse their suspicions. A few days after, however, she made another cake and proposed to take them on another walk. The children accompanied her willingly; but the little boy provided himself with a parcel of millet, and strewed the grain on the ground as they walked along. They were in no haste, therefore, to finish their refection. But, alas! when they came to trace the track by which they were to return, there was no means of finding it, for the birds had come meanwhile and eaten up all the grain. The little girl was appalled when she saw they were lost, and sat down to cry; but the little boy said, "Never mind; our stepmother was very cross and unkind to us; perhaps we shall meet with someone who will behave better to us. Come, let us look for shelter before night comes on." The little girl took courage at her brother's words, and, joining hands, they walked on together.

Before night they came to a little cottage, the only one in sight; so they knocked at the door. "Who's there?" said a voice within, and when they answered "Friends," an old man opened the door. "Will you please take us in and give us shelter for the night, for our stepmother has turned us out of our home?" said the little boy. "Come in, and welcome," answered the old man, "and you shall be my children." So they went in and lived with him as his children.

When they had been living there some time, it happened that one day when the old man and her brother were both out, the king came by hunting, and he came to the hut and asked for some water to drink. The extraordinary beauty of the maiden astonished the king, and he asked her whence she was, and so learnt all her story. When he went home he told his mother, saying, "When I was out today I saw the most beautiful maiden that ever was created. You must come and see her." The queen-mother did not like going to the poor hut, but the prince urged her so much that at last she consented to accompany him. The king drove out beforehand to the cottage and gave notice that he would like to dine there, and, giving the maiden plenty of money, told her to prepare the best dinner that ever she could for him and the queen-mother. The maiden tidied up the cottage so neatly, and prepared the dinner so well, and did the honours of it so gracefully, that the queen-mother was won to admire her as much as her son had been, and when the king told her of his intention to make the girl his wife she was well pleased. So Albina (such was her name) was married to the king, and her brother was made viceroy.

In the meantime, the stepmother had begun to wonder what had become of the children. But she was a witch, and had a divining rod; this rod she struck, and asked it where the children were. The answer came, "The girl is married to the king, and the lad is made viceroy."

When she heard this she went to her husband and said, "Do you know a sort of remorse has taken me that we let those poor children go we know not whither. I am resolved to put on a pilgrim's dress and go and seek them that I may bring them home to us again." The father was very glad to hear her speak thus, and gave his consent to her taking the journey. The next day, therefore, she put on a pilgrim's dress and went forth.

On, on, on she went till she came to the city where Albina was married to the king. Here she took up her stand opposite the palace windows, and with her divining rod she called up a golden hen with golden chickens, and made them strut about under the palace window. When Queen Albina looked out and saw the wonderful brood, she sent down at once to call the pilgrim-woman to her and offered to buy them of her. "My hen and chickens I neither sell nor pledge," answered the pretended pilgrim; "I only part with them at one price."

"And what is the price, good pilgrim, say?" answered the queen.

"My price is that the queen herself take me down to the palace garden and show me the whale which I know there is in the fishpond."

"That is a condition easily accepted," answered Albina. "I will take you there at once, good woman."

The queen and the pretended pilgrim then went down together to the pond. The pretended pilgrim no sooner came in sight of the whale than she touched the water with her rod and bade the whale swallow the queen. The whale obeyed the stroke of the wand imparted through the water, and the stepmother went up and threw herself on the queen's bed. When she had well wrapped herself in the coverlets so as to be hidden, she called the maids to her and bade them tell the king that the queen was sick. The king immediately came in all haste to assure himself of the state of the queen. "I am ill indeed, very ill!" cried the pretended queen, groaning between whiles; "and there is no hope for me, for there is only one remedy for my malady, and that I cannot take."

"Tell me the one remedy at least," said the king.

"The one only remedy for me is the blood of the viceroy, and that I could not take."

"It is a dreadful remedy indeed," said the king; "but if it is the only thing to save your life, I must make you take it."

"Oh, no! I could not take it!" exclaimed the pretended queen, for the sake of appearing genuine.

But the king, bent on saving her life at any price, sent and had the viceroy taken possession of and secured, ready to be slain, in one of the lower chambers of the palace. The windows of this chamber looked out upon the fishpond.

The viceroy looked out of the window on to the fishpond, and immediately there came a voice up to him, speaking out of the whale, and saying, "Save me, my brother, for here am I imprisoned in the whale, and behold two children are born to me."

But her brother could only answer, "I can give help to none, for I also am in peril of death, being bound and shut up ready to be slain!"

Then a voice of lamentation came up from within the whale saying, "Woe is me that my brother is to be slain, and I and my children are shut up in this horrible place! Woe is me!"

Presently, the gardener hearing these lamentations, went to the king, saying, "O, king! come down thyself and hear the voice of one that waileth, and the voice cometh as from within the whale."

The king went down, and at once recognized the voice of the queen; then he commanded that the whale should be ripped open; no sooner was this done than the queen and her two children were brought to light. The king embraced them all, and said, "Who then is she that is in the queen's bed?" and he commanded that she should be brought before him. When the queen had seen her she said, "This is my stepmother;" and when the pilgrim's weeds, which she had taken off, were also found, and it was shown that it was she who had worked all this mischief, the king pronounced that she was a witch, and she was put to death, and the viceroy was set at liberty.

A Yard of Nose

THERE WAS ONCE a poor orphan youth left all alone, with no home, and no means of gaining a living, and no place of shelter.

Not knowing what to do he wandered away over the Campagna, straight on; when he had wandered all day and was ready to die of hunger and weariness, he at last saw a fig tree covered with ripe figs.

"There's a godsend!" said the poor orphan; and he set to upon the figs without ceremony. But, lo! he had scarcely eaten half a dozen when his nose began to feel very odd; he put his hand up to it and it felt much bigger than usual; however, he was too hungry to trouble himself about it, and he ate on. As he ate on his nose felt queerer and queerer; he put his hand up and found it was quite a foot long! But he was so hungry he went on eating still, and before he had done he had fully a yard of nose.

"A pretty thing I have done for myself now! As well might I have died of starvation as make myself such an object as this! Never can I appear among civilised beings again." And he laid himself down to sleep, hiding himself in the foliage of the fig tree lest anybody passing by should see his nose.

In the morning the first thing he thought of when he awoke was his nose; he had no need to put up his hand to feel it for it reached down to his hand, a full yard of it waggling about.

"There's no help for it," he said. "I must keep away from all habitable places, and live as best I may."

So he wandered on and on over the Campagna away from all habitations, straight on; and when he had wandered all day and was ready to die of hunger and weariness he saw another fig tree covered with ripe figs.

Right glad he was to see anything in the shape of food. "If it had only been anything else in the world but figs!" he said. "If I go on at this rate I shan't be able to carry my nose along at all! Yet starving is hard, too, and I'm such a figure now, nothing can make me much worse, so here goes!" and he began eating at the figs without more ado.

As he ate this time, however, his nose, instead of feeling queerer and queerer as it had before, began to feel lighter and lighter.

Less, less, and still less it grew, till at last he had to put his hand up to feel where it was, and by the time he had done eating, it was just its natural size again.

"*Now* I know how to make my fortune!" he cried, and he danced for delight.

With a basketful of the figs of the first tree he trudged to the nearest town, still clad in his peasant's dress, and cried, "Fine figs! fine figs! Who'll buy my beautiful ripe figs!"

All the people ran out to see the new fruit-seller, and his figs looked so tempting that plenty of people bought of him. Among the foremost was the host of the inn, with his wife and his buxom daughter, and every one of them, as they ate the figs, their noses began to grow and grow till every one of them had a nose fully a yard long.

Then there was a hue and cry through the whole town, everyone with his yard of nose dangling and waggling, came running out, calling, "Ho! Here! Wretch of a fruit-seller!"

But our fruit-seller had had the good sense to foresee the coming storm, and had taken care to get far out of the way of pursuit.

But the next day he dressed himself like a doctor, all in black, with a long false beard, and came to the same town, where he entered the druggist's shop, and gave himself out for a great doctor.

"You come in good season!" said the druggist. "A doctor is wanted here just now, if ever one was, for to everyone almost in the town is grown a nose so big! So big! In fact, a full yard of nose! Anyone who could reduce these noses might make a fortune indeed!"

"Why, that's just what I excel at of all things. Let me see some of these people," answered our pretended doctor.

The druggist looked incredulous at a real remedy turning up so very opportunely; but at the same moment a pretty peasant girl came into the shop to buy some medicine for her mother; that is, she would have been pretty if it had not been for the terrible nose, which made a fright of her. The false doctor was seized with compunction when he saw what a fright his figs had made of this pretty girl, and he took out some figs of the other tree and gave her to eat, and immediately her tremendous nose grew less, and less, and less, and she was a pretty girl again. Of course it need not be said that he did not give her the figs in their natural state and form; he had peeled and pounded, and made them up with other things to disguise them.

The druggist no sooner saw this wonderful cure than he was prompt to publish it, and there was quite a strife who should have the new doctor the first.

It was the innkeeper who succeeded in being the first to possess himself of him. "What will you give me for the cure?" said the strange doctor.

"Whatever you have the conscience to ask," replied the host, panting to be rid of the monstrosity.

"Four thousand scudi apiece," replied the false doctor; and the host, his wife, and his buxom daughter stood in a row waiting to be cured. With the same remedy that had cured the peasant girl he cured the host first, and next his daughter. After he had cured her he said, "Instead of the second premium of four thousand scudi, I will take the hand of your daughter, if you like?"

"Yes, if you wish; it's a very good idea," replied the host.

"Never, while I live!" said the wife.

"Why not? He's a very good husband!" said the host.

"An ugly old travelling doctor, who comes no one knows whence, to marry my daughter indeed!" said the wife.

"I'm sure we're under great obligations to his cleverness," said the husband.

"Then let him be paid his price, and go about his business, and not talk impudence!" said the wife.

"But I choose that he *shall* marry her!" said the husband.

"And *I* choose that he shan't," said the wife; "and you'll find that much stronger."

Just then a customer came in, and the host had to go and attend upon him, and while he was gone the wife called the servants, and bade them turn the doctor out, and give him a good drubbing into the bargain, saying, "I'll have some other doctor to cure me!"

So he left them, and went on curing people's noses all day, till he had made a lot of money. Then he went away, but limping all the time from the beating he had received. The next day he came back dressed like a Turk, so that no one would have known him for the same man, and he came back to the same inn, saying he, too, could cure noses.

The mistress of the inn gave him a hearty welcome, as she was very anxious to find another doctor who could cure her nose.

"My treatment is effectual, but it is rude," said the pretended Turk. "I don't know if you'll like to submit to it."

"Oh yes! Anything, whatever it may be, only to be rid of this monstrous nose," said the hostess.

"Then you must come into a room by yourself with me," said the pretended Turk; "and I have a stick here made out of the root of a particular tree. I must thump you on the back with it, and in proportion as I thump you the nose will draw in. Of course it will hurt very much, and make you cry out, so you must tell your servants and people outside that however much you may call they are not to come in. For if they should come in and interrupt the cure, it would all have to be begun over again, and all you had suffered would go for nothing."

So the hostess gave strict orders, saying, "I am going into this room with the Turk to be cured by him, and however much I may call out, or whatever I may say, mind none of you, on pain of losing your places, open the door, or come near the room."

Then she took the Turk into a room apart, and shut the door. The Turk no sooner got her alone than he made her lie with her face downwards on a sofa, and then – *whack, whack, whack!* – he gave her such a beating that she felt the effects of it to the end of her days.

Of course it was in vain she screamed and roared for help; the servants had had their orders, and none of them durst approach the room. It was only when she had fainted that the Turk left her alone and went his way.

But she never got her nose cured, and he married the pretty peasant girl who was the subject of his first cure.

The Fishpond of St. Francis

ST. FRANCIS HAD a little fishpond, where he kept some gold and silver fish as a pastime.

Some bad people wanted to vex him, and they went and caught these poor little fish and fried them, and sent them up to him for dinner. But St. Francis when he saw them knew that they were his goldfish, and made the sign of the cross over them, and blessed them, and soon they became alive again, and he took them and put them back into the fishpond, and no one durst touch them again after that.

Padre Vincenzo

THERE WAS PADRE VINCENZO TOO, who wasn't much less than "good Philip" himself. He was a miracle of obedience. One day when he was ill the Father-General sent him a codfish. Padre Vincenzo sent back word to thank him, but said he couldn't eat it. "Nonsense!" answered the Father-General, who thought he spoke out of regard to his love of abstinence. "Nonsense! tell him he is to eat it all." The message was given to Padre Vincenzo, who was really too ill to eat anything; but in his simplicity thinking he ought to obey, he ate the whole fish, head, tail, bones and all.

By and by the Father-General came to see him. He seemed almost at the last gasp, suffocated by the effort he had made, and his throat all lacerated with swallowing the fishbones. The Father-General praised the simplicity of his obedience, but told the brother who took the message that he ought to have explained it better.

But Padre Vincenzo did not lose anything by his obedience, for that same evening he was cured of his illness altogether, and was quite well again....

One morning Padre Vincenzo had to pass through the Rotonda on business of his community. A temptation of the throat took him as he saw a pair of fine plump pigeons such as you, perhaps, cannot see anywhere out of the Rotonda hanging up for sale. Padre Vincenzo bought the pigeons, and took them home secretly under his cloak. In his cell he plucked the pigeons, and cooked them over a little fire. The unwonted smell of roast pigeon soon perfumed the corridor, and two or three brothers, having peeped through the keyhole and seen what was going on in Padre Vincenzo's cell, ran off to say to the Father-General,

"What do you think Padre Vincenzo, whom we all reckon such a saint, is doing now? He is cooking pigeons privately in his cell."

"It's a calumny! I can't believe it of him," answered the Father-General indignantly.

The spying brothers bade him come and see.

"I am certain if I do, it will be to cover you with confusion in some way or other for telling tales!" replied the Father-General as he went with them.

As they passed along the corridor there was the smell of roast pigeon most undeniably; but when the Father-General opened the cell door what did they see?

Padre Vincenzo was on his knees, praying for forgiveness in a tone of earnest contrition; round his throat were tied the two pigeons, burning hot, as he had taken them from the fire. A spirit of compunction had seized him as he was about to accomplish the unmortified act of eating in his cell in contravention of his rule, and he had adopted this penance for yielding in intention to the temptation.

Smaller Ghost and Treasure Stories and Family and Local Traditions

"HERE'S ANOTHER THING I have heard that will do for you. There were two who took a peasant and carried him into the Campagna."

"What! two ghosts?"

"No, no! Two fellows who had more money than they knew what to do with. They took him into the Campagna and made an omelette very good, with plenty of sweet-scented herbs in it, and made him eat it.

"Then they took a barrel and measured him against it, and then another, till they found one to fit, and killed him and filled it up with money, and made a hole in the earth and buried it.

"And they said over it, 'No one may disturb you till one comes who makes an omelette with just the same sweet-scented herbs as we have used, and makes it just on the top of this hole. Then, come out and say, "This gold is yours."'

"And, of course, in the ordinary course of things, no one would have thought of making an omelette with just those same herbs, just on the top of that hole. But there was one who knew the other two, and suspected something of what they were going to do, and he went up and hid himself in a tree, and watched all that was done, and heard the words.

"As soon as they were gone he came down and took some nice fresh eggs, and just the same sweet-scented herbs the others had used, and made an omelette just over the hole where he had seen them bury the barrel with the money and the man in it.

"He had no sooner done so than the man came out all whole and well, and said: "Oh, how many years have I been shut up in that dark place" (though he hadn't been there half an hour) "till you came to deliver me? Therefore all the gold is yours."

"Such things can't be true, so I don't believe them; but that's what they tell."

The Wooing of Cassandro

"**DID YOU EVER HEAR of Sor Cassandro?**"
"**No, never.**"
"**Do you know where Panìco is?**"

"I know the Via di Panìco which leads down to Ponte S. Angelo."

"Very well; at the end of Panìco there is a frying-shop, which, many years ago, was kept by an old man with a comely daughter. Both were well known all over the Rione.

"One day there came an old gentleman, with a wig and tights, and a comical old-fashioned dress altogether, and said to the shopkeeper:

"'I've observed that daughter of yours many days as I have passed by, and should like to make her my wife."

"'It's a great honour for me, Sor Cassandro, that you should talk of such a thing,' answered the old man; and he said 'Sor Cassandro' like that because everybody knew old Sor Cassandro with his wig, and his gold-knobbed stick, and his tights, and his old-fashioned gait. 'But,' he added, as a knowing way of getting out of it, 'you see it wouldn't do for a *friggitora* to marry a gentleman; a *friggitora* must marry a *friggitore.*'

"'I don't know that that need be a bar,' replied Sor Cassandro.

"'You don't understand me, Sor Cassandro,' pursued the man.

"'Yes, I understand perfectly,' answered the other. 'You mean that if she must marry a *friggitore*, I must become a *friggitore.*'

"'You a *friggitore*, Sor Cassandro! That would never do. How could you so demean yourself?'

"'Love makes all sweet,' responded Sor Cassandro. 'You've only to show me what to do and I'll do it as well as anyone.'

"The *friggitore* was something of a wag, and the idea of the prim little Sor Cassandro turned into a journeyman *friggitore* tickled his fancy, and he let him follow his bent.

"The next morning Sor Cassandro was at Panìco as soon as the shop was open. They gave him a white jacket and a large white apron, and put a white cap on his head, with a carnation stuck in it. And the whole neighbourhood gathered round the shop to see Sor Cassandro turned into a *friggitore*. The work of the shop was increased tenfold, and it was well there was an extra hand to help at it.

"Sor Cassandro was very patient, and adapted himself to his work surprisingly well, and though the master fryer took a pleasure in ordering him about, he submitted to all with good grace, and not only did he make him do the frying and serving out to perfection, but he even taught him to clip his words and leave off using any expression that seemed inappropriate to his new station.

"There was no denying that Sor Cassandro had become a perfect *friggitore*, and no exception could be taken to him on that score. As soon as he felt himself perfect he did not fail to renew his suit.

"The father was puzzled what objection to make next. He knew, however, that Sor Cassandro was very miserly, so he said, "You've made yourself a *friggitore* to please me, now you must do something to please the girl. Suppose you bring her some trinkets, if you can spare the price of them."

"'Oh, anything for love!' answered Sor Cassandro; and the next day he brought a pair of earrings.

"'How did she like my earrings?' he whispered next night to her father.

"'Oh, pretty well!' replied the father. 'You might try something more in that style.'

"The next day he brought her a necklace, the next day a shawl, and after that he brought fifty scudi to buy clothes such as a girl should have when she's going to be married.

"After all this he asked for the girl herself.

"'You must take her,' said the father, and Sor Cassandro went to take her. But she was a sprightly, impulsive girl, and the moment he came near her she screamed out:

"'Get away, horrid old man!' and wouldn't let him approach her.

"'Leave her alone tonight, and try tomorrow. I'll try to bring her round in the meantime.'

"Sor Cassandro came next day; but the girl was more violent than ever, and would say nothing but, 'Get away, horrid old man!'

"Finding this went on day after day without amendment, Sor Cassandro indignantly asked for his presents back.

"'You shall have them!' cried the girl, and the clothes she tore up to rags, and the trinkets she broke to atoms and threw them all at him.

"But for the rest of his life, wherever he went, the boys cried after him, '*Sor Cassandro, la friggitora! Sor Cassandro, la friggitora!*'"

The Two Friars

TWO FRIARS ONCE WENT out on a journey, that is to say, a friar and a lay brother. One day of their journey, when they were far from their convent, the friar said to the lay brother:

"We fare poorly enough all the days of our life in our convent, let us, for one day of our lives, taste the good things of this world which others enjoy every day."

"You know better than I, who am only a poor simple lay brother," answered the other, "whether such a thing may be done. I don't mean to say I should not like to have a jolly good dinner for once; but there is the uneasiness of conscience to spoil the feast, and the penance afterwards. I think we had better leave it alone."

They journeyed on, therefore, and said no more about it that day, but the next, when they were very hungry after a long walk through the cold mountain air, the scent of the viands preparing in the inn as they drew near brought the subject of yesterday's conversation to their minds again, and the friar said to the lay brother: "You know even our rule says that when we are journeying we cannot live as we do in our convent; we must eat and drink whatever we find in the places to which we are sent; moreover, some relaxation is allowed for the restoration of the body under the fatigues of the journey. Now, if we come, as it has often happened to us, to a poor little mountain village, where scarcely a wholesome crust of bread is to be found, to be washed down with a glass of sour wine, we have to take it for all our dinner, and eat it with thanksgiving. Therefore why, now, when we come to a place where the fare is less scanty, even as by the odours we perceive is the case here, should we not also take what is found ready, and eat it with thanksgiving?"

"What you say seems right and just enough," said the lay brother, not at all sorry to have his scruples so speciously explained away. "But there is one thing you have not thought of. It is all very well to say we will eat and drink this and that, but how are we poor friars, who possess nothing, to command the delicacies which are smoking round the fire, and which have to be paid for by well-stored purses?"

"Oh! that is not the difficulty," replied the friar; "leave that to me."

By this time they had reached the threshold of the inn, and, taking his companion's last feeble resistance for consent, the friar strutted into the eating-room with so bold an air that the lay brother hardly knew him for the humble religious he had been accompanying anon.

"Ho! here! John, Peter, Francis, whatever you are called!"

"Francesco, to your service," replied the host humbly, thinking by his commanding tone he must be some son of a great family.

"Francesco *guercino*, then," continued the friar in the same high-sounding voice, "take away this foul tablecloth, and bring the cleanest and finest in your house; remove these cloudy glasses and bring out the bright ones you have there locked up in the glass case, and replace these bone spoons and forks with the silver ones out of your strong box."

"Your Excellency is served!" said the host, who, as well as his wife and son, had bustled so fast to do what he was so peremptorily ordered that all was done as soon as spoken.

"Now then Francesco *guercino*, what have you got to put before a hungry gentleman in this poor little place of yours?"

"Eccellenza! when you have tasted the cooking of my poor little house," said the host, "you will not, I am sure, be displeased; all unworthy as it is of your Excellency's palate. For what we have ready, we have beef for our boiled meat, good brains for our fried, the plumpest poultry for our grilled, and the freshest eggs for our omelette; or, if your Excellency prefers it, we have hashed turkey, with crisp watercresses; and as for our soup, there is not an inn in the whole province can beat us, I know. And for dessert we have cheese and fruits, and—"

"Well done, Francesco *guercino*," said the friar, interrupting him. "You know how to cry your own wares, at all events. Bring us the best of what you have; it is not for poor friars to complain of what is set before us."

The last sentence gave the host a high idea of the piety of his guest just as the hectoring tone he had assumed had convinced him he must be high-born, and in a trice the best of everything in the house was made ready for the table of the friar. All other guests had to wait, or go away unserved; the host was intent only on serving the friar.

Every dish he took to the table himself, and as he did so each time the friar, fixing on him a look of sanctity, exclaimed,

"Blessed Francesco! Blessed Francesco!"

At the close of the meal, as he was hovering about the table, nervously wiping away a crumb, or polishing a plate, he said, with trembling:

"Eccellenza! Permit a poor man to put one question. What is there you see about me that makes you look at me as though you saw happiness in store, and exclaim with so much unction as quite to fill me with joy, 'Blessed Francesco!'?"

"True, something I see wherefore I call thee blessed," replied the friar; "but I cannot tell it thee now. Tomorrow, perhaps, I may find it easier. Impossible now, friend. Now, pray thee, show us our rooms."

It needed not to add any injunctions concerning the rooms; of course, the cleanest and the best were appointed by Francesco spontaneously for such honoured guests.

"How do you think we are getting on?" said the friar to the lay brother when they were alone.

"Excellently well so far," replied the other; "things have passed my lips this night which never have they tasted before, nor ever may again. But the reckoning, the reckoning; that is what puzzles me: when it comes to paying the bill, what'll you do then?"

"Leave it all to me," returned the friar; "I'm quite satisfied with the man we have to deal with. It will all come right, never fear."

The next morning the two brothers were astir betimes, but Francesco was on the look-out to serve them.

"Eccellenza! you will not leave without breakfast, Eccellenza!"

"Yes, Francesco; poor friars must not mind going without breakfast."

"Never, from my house, Eccellenza!" responded Francesco. "I have the table ready with a bottle of wine freshly drawn from the cellar, eggs that were born since daylight, only waiting your appearance to be boiled, rolls this moment drawn from the oven, and my wife is at the stove preparing a fried dish fit for a king."

"Too much, too much, Francesco! You spoil us; we are not used to such things," said the lay brother as they sat down; but Francesco had flown into the kitchen, and returned with the dish.

"Blessed Francesco!" said the friar as he set it on the table.

"I will not disturb your Excellency now," said Francesco; "but, after you have breakfasted, I crave your remembrance of your promise of last night, that you would reveal to me this morning wherefore you say with such enthusiasm 'Blessed Francesco!'"

"It is not time to speak of it now," said the friar; "first we have our reckoning to make."

The lay brother hid his face in his table-napkin in terror, and seemed to be seized with a distressing fit of coughing.

"Oh, don't speak of the reckoning, Eccellenza; that is as nothing."

"Nay," said the friar; "that must not be;" and he made a gesture as if he would have drawn out a purse, while under the table he had to press his feet against those of the lay brother to silence his rising remonstrance for his persistence.

"I couldn't think of taking anything from your Eccellenza," persisted the host, putting his hands behind him that no money might be forced upon him. The more steadfastly he refused the more perseveringly the friar continued to press the payment, till, with his companion, he had gained the threshold of the door.

As they were passing out, however, the host once more exclaimed, "But the explanation your Excellency was to give me of why you said 'Blessed Francesco!'"

"Impossible, friend; I cannot tell it here. Wait till I have gained the height of yonder mound, while you stand at its foot, and I will tell it you from thence." With this they parted.

When the friar and his companion had reached the height he had pointed out, and were at a sufficient distance to be saved the fear of pursuit, he turned to the host, who stood gaping at the bottom, and said:

"Lucky for you, Francesco, that when you come to die you will only have the trouble of shutting one eye, instead of two, like other men."

The Seven Clodhoppers

S EVEN CLODHOPPERS went to confession.
"Father, I stole something," said the first.
"What was it you stole?" asked the priest.

"Some *mistuanza*, because I was starving," replied the country bumpkin.

That the poor fellow, who really looked as if he might have been starving, should have stolen some herbs did not seem such a very grave offence; so with due advice to keep his hands from picking and stealing, and a psalm to say for his penance, the priest sent him to communion.

Then came the second, and there was the same dialogue. Then the third and the fourth, till all the seven had been up.

At last the priest began to think it was a very odd circumstance that such a number of full-grown men should all of a sudden have taken into their heads to go stealing salad herbs; and when the seventh had had his say he rejoined,

"But what do you mean by *mistuanza*?"

"Oh, any mixture of things," replied the countryman.

"Nay; that's not the way we use the word," responded the priest; "so tell me *what* 'things' you mean."

"Oh, some cow, some pig, and some fowl."

"You men of the *mistuanza*!" shouted the priest in righteous indignation, starting out of the confessional; "Come back! Come back! You can't go to communion like that."

The seven clodhoppers, finding themselves discovered, began to fear the rigour of justice, and decamped as fast as they could.

The Little Bird

THERE WAS AN OLD COUPLE who earned a poor living by working hard all day in the fields.

"See how hard we work all day," said the wife; "and it all comes of the foolish curiosity of Adam and Eve. If it had not been for that we should have been living now in a beautiful garden, with nothing to do all day long."

"Yes," said the husband; "if you and I had been there, instead of Adam and Eve, all the human race had been in Paradise still."

The Count, their master, overheard them talking in this way, and he came to them and said: "How would you like it if I took you up into my palazzo there to live, and gave you servants to wait on you, and plenty to eat and drink?"

"Oh, that would be delightful indeed! That would be as good as Paradise itself!" answered husband and wife together.

"Well, you may come up there if you think so. Only remember, in Paradise there was one tree that was not to be touched; so at my table there will be one dish not to be touched. You mustn't mind that," said the Count.

"Oh, of course not," replied the old peasant; "that's just what I say: when Eve had all the fruits in the garden, what did she want with just that one that was forbidden? And if we, who are used to the scantiest victuals, are supplied with enough to live well, what does it matter to us whether there is an extra dish or not on the table?"

"Very well reasoned," said the Count. "We quite understand each other, then?"

"Perfectly," replied both husband and wife.

"You come to live at my palace, and have everything you can want there, so long as you don't open one dish which there will be in the middle of the table. If you open that you go back to your former way of life."

"We quite understand," answered the peasants.

The Count went in and called his servant, and told him to give the peasants an apartment to themselves, with everything they could want, and a sumptuous dinner, only in the middle of the table was to be an earthen dish, into which he was to put a little bird alive, so that if one lifted the cover the bird would fly out. He was to stay in the room and wait on them, and report to him what happened.

The old people sat down to dinner, and praised everything they saw, so delightful it all seemed.

"Look! that's the dish we're not to touch," said the wife.

"No; better *not* look at it," said the husband.

"Pshaw! there's no danger of wanting to open it, when we have such a lot of dishes to eat our fill out of," returned the wife.

So they set to, and made such a repast as they had never dreamed of before. By degrees, however, as the novelty of the thing wore off, they grew more and more desirous for something newer and newer still. Though when they at first sat down it had seemed that two dishes would be ample to satisfy them, they had now had seven or eight and they were wishing there might be others coming. There is an end to all things human, and no other came; there only remained the earthen dish in the middle of the table.

"We might just lift the lid up a little wee bit," said the wife.

"No; don't talk about it," said the husband.

The wife sat still for five minutes, and then she said: "If one just lifted up one corner of the lid it could scarcely be called opening it, you know."

"Better leave it alone altogether, and not think about it at all," said the husband.

The wife sat still another five minutes, and then she said: "If one peeped in just the least in the world it would not be any harm, surely; and I *should* so like to know what there can possibly be. Now, what *can* the Count have put in that dish?"

"I'm sure I can't guess in the least," said the husband; "and I must say I can't see what it can signify to him if we did look at it."

"No; that's what I think. And besides, how would he know if we peeped? it wouldn't hurt him," said the wife.

"No; as you say, one could just take a look," said the husband.

The wife didn't want more encouragement than that. But when she lifted one side of the lid the least mite she could see nothing. She opened it the least mite more, and the bird flew out. The servant ran and told his master, and the Count came down and drove them out, bidding them never complain of Adam and Eve anymore.

The Gluttonous Girl

THERE WAS A POOR WOMAN who went out to work by the day. She had one idle, good-for-nothing daughter, who would never do any work, and cared for nothing but eating, always taking the best of everything for herself, and not caring how her mother fared.

One day the mother, when she went out to her work, left the girl some beans to cook for dinner, and some pieces of bacon-rind to stew along with them. When the pieces of bacon-rind were nicely done, she took them out and ate them herself, and then found a pair of dirty old shoe-soles, which she pared in slices, and put them into the stew for her mother.

When the poor mother came home, not only were there no pieces of bacon which she could eat, but the beans themselves were rendered so nasty by the shoe-soles that she could not eat them either. Determined to give her daughter a good lesson, once and for all, on this occasion, she took her outside her cottage door, and beat her well with a stick.

Just as she was administering this chastisement, a farmer came by.

"What are you beating this pretty lass for?" asked the man.

"Because she *will* work so hard at her household duties that she works on Sundays and holidays the same as common days," answered the mother, who, bad as her daughter was, yet had not the heart to give her a bad character.

"That is the first time I ever heard of a mother beating her child for doing too much work; the general complaint is that they do too little. Will you let me have her for a wife? I should like such a wife as that."

"Impossible!" replied the mother, in order to enhance her daughter's value; "she does all the work of the house, I can't spare her; what shall I do without her?"

"I must give you something to make up for the loss," replied the merchant; "but such a notable wife as this I have long been in search of, and I must not miss the chance."

"But I cannot spare such a notable daughter, either," persisted the mother.

"What do you say if I give you five hundred scudi?"

"If I let her go, it is not because of the five hundred scudi," said the mother; "it is because you seem a husband, who will really appreciate her; though I don't say five hundred scudi will not be a help to a poor lone widow."

"Let it be agreed then. I am going now to the fair; when I come back let the girl be ready, and I'll take her back with me."

Accordingly, when the farmer returned from the fair, he fetched the girl away.

When he got home his mother came out to ask how his affairs had prospered at the fair.

"Middling well, at the fair," replied the man; "but, by the way, I found a treasure, and I have brought her home to make her my wife. She is so hardworking that she can't be kept from working, even on Sundays."

"She doesn't look as if there was much work in her," observed the mother dryly; "but if you're satisfied that's enough."

All went well enough the first week, because she was not expected to do much just at first, but at the end of that time the husband had to go to a distant fair which would keep him absent three weeks. Before he went he took his new wife up into the store-room, and said, "Here are provisions of all sorts, and you will have all you like to eat and drink; and here is a quantity of hemp, which you can amuse yourself with spinning and weaving if you want more employment than merely keeping the place in order."

Then he gave her a set of rooms to herself, next the store-chamber, that there might be no cause of quarrel with the mother-in-law, who, he knew, was inclined to be jealous of her, and said goodbye.

Left to herself, she did no more work than she could help; all the nice things she found she cooked and ate, and that was all the work she did. As to the hemp, she never touched it; nor did she even clean up the place, or attempt to put it tidy.

When the husband had been gone a fortnight, the mother-in-law came up to see how she was going on, and when she saw the hemp untouched, and the place in disorder, she said, "So this is how you go on when your husband is away!"

"You mind your affairs, and I'll mind mine," answered the wife, and the mother-in-law went away offended.

Nevertheless, it was true that in eight days the husband would be back, and might expect to see something done, so she took up a lot of hemp and began trying to spin it; but, as she had no idea of how to do it, she went on in the most absurd way imaginable with it.

As she stood on the top of the outside staircase, twisting it this way and that, there passed three deformed fairies. One was lame, and one squinted, and one had her head all on one side, because she had a fishbone stuck in her throat.

The three fairies called out to ask what she was doing, and when she said, "spinning," the one who squinted laughed so much that her eyes came quite right, and the one who had a bone stuck in her throat laughed so much that the bone came out, and her head became straight again like other people's, and when the lame one saw the others laughing so much, she ran so fast to see what it was that her lameness was cured.

Then the three fairies said:

"Since she has cured us of our ailments, we must go in and do her a good turn."

So they went in and took the hemp and span it, and wove it, and did as much in the six remaining days as any human being could have done in twenty years; moreover, they cleaned up everything, and made everything look spick-and-span new.

Then they gave her a bag of walnuts, saying, "In half an hour your husband will be home; go to bed and put this bag of walnuts under your back. When he comes in say you have worked so hard that all your bones are out of joint; then move the bag of walnuts and they will make a noise, *c-r-r-r-r*, and he will think it is your bones which are loosened, and will say you must never work again."

When the husband came home his mother went out to meet him, saying,

"I told you I did not think there was much work in your "treasure." When you go up you'll see what a fine mess the place is all in; and as to the hemp, you had better have left it locked up, for a fine mess she has made of that."

But the husband went up and found the place all in shining order, and so much hemp spun and woven as could scarcely be got through in twenty years. But the wife was laid up in bed.

When the husband came near the bed she moved the bag of walnuts and they went *c-r-r-r-r*.

"You have done a lot of work indeed!" said the husband.

"Yes," replied the wife; "but I have put all my bones out of joint; only hear how they rumble!" and she moved the walnuts again, and they went c-r-r-r-r. "It will be some time before I am about again."

"Oh, dear! oh, dear!" said the husband; "only think of such a treasure of a wife being laid up by such marvellous diligence."

And to his mother he said: "A mother-in-law has never a good word for her daughter-in-law; what you told me was all pure invention."

But to the wife he said: "Mind I will never have you do any work again as long as you live."

So from that day forth she had no work to do, but ate and drank and amused herself from morning till night.

The Old Miser

T HEY SAY THERE WAS ONCE an old man who had so much money he didn't know what to do with it. He had cellars and cellars, where all the floors were strewn with gold; but the house was all tumbling down, because he would not spend a penny in repairing it; and for all food he took nothing all day but a crust of bread and a glass of water.

He was always afraid lest someone should come to rob him of his wealth, so he seldom so much as spoke to anyone.

One day, however, a busy, talkative neighbour would have her say out with him, and among other things she said: "How can you go on living in that ugly old house all alone now? Why don't you take a wife?"

"A wife!" replied the old miser. "How can I take a wife? How am I to afford to keep a wife, I should like to know?"

"Nonsense!" persisted the loquacious neighbour; "you've got plenty of money, you know. And how much better you'd be if you had a wife. Do you mean to tell me, now, you wouldn't be much better off with one? Now answer me fairly."

"Well, if I must speak the truth, as you are so urgent for an answer," replied the old miser, "I don't mean to say I haven't often thought I should like a wife; but I am waiting till I find one who can live upon air."

"Well, maybe there might be such a one even as you say," returned the busy neighbour; "though she might not be easy to find." And she said no more for that day.

She went, however, to a young woman who lived opposite, and said: "If you want a rich husband I will find you one."

"To be sure I should like a rich husband," replied the young woman. "Who would not?"

"Very well, then," continued the neighbour; "I will tell you what to do. You have only, every day at dinnertime, to stand at the window and suck in the air, and move your lips as if you were eating. But eat nothing; take nothing into your mouth but air. The old miser who lives opposite wants a wife who can live on air; and if he thinks you can do this he will marry you. And when you are once installed it'll be odd if you don't find means, in the midst of so much money, to lay hold of enough to get a dinner every day without working for it."

The young woman thanked her friend for the advice, and next day, when the bells rang at noon, she threw open the window and stood sucking in the air, and then moving her lips as if she was eating. This she did several days.

At last the old miser came across under the window, and said to her: "What are you doing at the window there?"

"Don't you see it's dinnertime, and I'm taking my dinner? Don't interrupt me!" replied the young neighbour.

"But, excuse me, I don't see you are eating anything, though your lips move."

"O! I live upon air; I take nothing but air," replied the young woman; and she went on with her mock munching.

"You live upon air, do you? Then you're just the wife I'm looking for. Will you come down and marry me?"

As this was just what she wanted she did not keep him waiting, and soon they were married and she was installed in the miser's house.

But it was not so easy to get at the money as she had thought. At first the miser would not let her go near his cellars; but as he spent so much time down there she said she could not be deprived of his company for so long, she must come down too.

All the time she was down with him the miser held both her hands in his, as if he was full of affection for her; but in reality it was to make sure she did not touch any of his money.

She, however, bought some pitch, and put it on the soles of her shoes, and as she walked about in the gold plenty of it stuck to her shoes; and when she came up again she took the gold off her shoes, and sent her maid to the *trattoria* for the most delicious dinners. Shut up in a room apart they fared sumptuously – she and her maid. But every day at midday she let the miser see her taking her fancied dinner of air.

This went on for long, because the miser had so much gold that he never missed the few pieces that stuck to her shoes every day.

But at last there came a Carnival Thursday, when the maid had brought home an extra fine dinner; and as they were an extra length of time over this extra number of dishes and glasses, the old miser, always suspicious, began to guess there must be something wrong; and to find it out he instituted a scrutiny into every room in the crazy house. Thus he came at last to the room where his wife and her maid were dining sumptuously.

"This is how you live on air, is it?" he roared, red with fury.

"Oh, but on Carnival Thursday," replied the wife, "one may have a little extra indulgence!"

"Will you tell me you have not had a private dinner every day?" shouted the excited miser.

"If I have," replied the wife, not liking to tell a direct falsehood, "how do you know it is not with my own money? Tell me, have you missed any of yours?"

The miser was only the more angry at her way of putting the question, because he could not say he had actually missed the money; yet he was convinced it was his money she had been spending.

"How do I know it is not your money, do you ask?" he thundered; "because if you had had any money of your own you would never have come to live here, you would not have married me."

But weak as he was with his bread and water diet, the excitement was too much for him. As he said these words a convulsion seized him, and he fell down dead.

Thus all his riches came into possession of the wife.

The Beggar and the Chick-Pea

THERE WAS ONCE a poor man who went about from door to door begging his bread. He came to the cottage of a poor peasant and said: "Give me something, for the love of God."

The peasant's wife said, "Good man, go away; I have nothing."

But the poor man said, "Leave me out something against I come again."

The peasant's wife answered, "The most I can give you is a single chick-pea."

"Very well; that will do," replied the poor man; "only mind the hen doesn't eat it."

The peasant's wife was as good as her word, and put out a chick-pea on the dresser against the beggar came by next time. While her back was turned, however, the hen came in and gobbled it up. Presently after the beggar came by.

"Where's the chick-pea you promised me?" he asked.

"Ah! I put it out for you, but the hen gobbled it up!"

At this he assumed an air of terrible authority, and said: "Did I not tell you to beware lest the hen should eat it? Now, you must give me either the pea or the hen!"

As it was impossible for the peasant's wife now to give him the pea, she was obliged to give him the hen. The beggar, therefore, took the hen, and went to another cottage.

"Good woman," he said to the peasant's wife; "can you be so good as to take care of this hen for me?"

"Willingly enough!" said the peasant's wife.

"Here it is then," said the beggar; "but mind the pig doesn't get it."

"Never fear!" said the peasant's wife; and the poor man went his way.

Next day the beggar came back and claimed his hen.

"Oh, dear me!" said the peasant's wife, "while my back was turned, the pig gobbled it up!"

Assuming an air of terrible authority, the man said: "Didn't I warn you to beware lest the pig gobbled it up? Now, you must give me either the hen or the pig."

As the peasant's wife couldn't give him the hen, she was obliged to give him the pig. So the poor man took the pig and went his way.

He came now to another cottage, and said to the peasant's wife: "Good woman, can you take care of this pig a little space for me?"

"Willingly!" said the peasant's wife; "put him in the yard."

"Mind the calf doesn't get at him," said the man.

"Never fear," said the peasant's wife, and the beggar went his way.

The next day he came back and claimed his pig.

"Oh, dear!" answered the peasant's wife; "while I wasn't looking, the calf got at the pig, and seized it by the throat, and killed it, and trampled it all to pieces."

Assuming an air of terrible authority, the beggar said: "Did I not warn you to beware lest the calf got at it? Now you must give me the pig or the calf."

As the poor woman could not give him the pig, she was forced to give him the calf. The beggar took the calf and went away.

He went on to another cottage, and said to the peasant's wife: "Good woman, can you take care of this calf for me?"

"Willingly!" said the peasant's wife; "put it in the yard."

The poor man put the calf in the yard; but he said: "I see you have a sick daughter there in bed; mind she doesn't desire the calf."

"Never fear!" said the peasant's wife; and the man went his way.

He was no sooner gone, however, than the sick daughter arose, and saying, "Little heart! little heart! I must have you," she went down into the yard and killed the calf, and took out its heart and ate it.

The next day the beggar man came back and claimed the calf.

"Oh, dear!" said the peasant's wife, "while I wasn't looking, my sick daughter got up and killed the calf, and ate its heart."

Assuming an air of terrible authority, the beggar said: "Did not I warn you not to let the sick daughter get at the calf? Now, either calf or maiden I must have; make haste with your choice; calf or maiden, one or the other!"

But the poor woman could not get back the calf, seeing it was dead, and she was resolved not to give up her daughter. So she said: "I can't give you the calf, because it is dead. So I must give you my daughter, only if I went to take her now while she's awake, she would make such a fuss you would never get her along; so leave me your sack, that while she's asleep I may put her in it, and then when you come back you can have her."

So the beggar left his sack and went away. As soon as he was gone the peasant's wife took the sack and put some stones at the bottom, to make it heavy, and thrust in a ferocious mad dog; then having made fast the mouth of the sack, she stood it up against the wall.

Next day the beggar came back and asked for his sack.

"There it is against the wall," said the peasant's wife.

So the beggar put it on his shoulder and went away.

As soon as he got home, he opened the sack to take out the maiden; but the ferocious mad dog rushed out upon him and killed him.

The Value of Salt

T HEY SAY THERE WAS a king who had three daughters. He was very anxious to know which of them loved him most; he tried them in various ways, and it always seemed as if the youngest daughter came out best by the test. Yet he was never satisfied, because he was prepossessed with the idea that the elder ones loved him most.

One day he thought he would settle the matter once and for all, by asking each separately how much she loved him. So he called the eldest by herself, and asked her how much she loved him.

"As much as the bread we eat," ran her reply; and he said within himself, "She must, as I thought, love me the most of all; for bread is the first necessary of our existence, without which we cannot live. She means, therefore, that she loves me so much she could not live without me."

Then he called the second daughter by herself, and said to her, "How much do you love me?"

And she answered, "As much as wine!"

"That is a good answer too," said the king to himself. "It is true she does not seem to love me quite so much as the eldest; but still, scarcely can one live without wine, so that there is not much difference."

Then he called the youngest by herself, and said to her, "And you, how much do you love me?"

And she answered, "As much as salt!"

Then the king said, "What a contemptible comparison! She only loves me as much as the cheapest and commonest thing that comes to table. This is as much as to say, she doesn't love me at all. I always thought it was so. I will never see her again."

Then he ordered that a wing of the palace should be shut up from the rest, where she should be served with everything belonging to her condition in life, but where she should live by herself apart, and never come near him.

Here she lived, then, all alone. But though her father fancied she did not care for him, she pined so much at being kept away from him, that at last she was worn out, and could bear it no longer.

The room that had been given her had no windows on to the street, that she might not have the amusement of seeing what was going on in the town, but they looked upon an inner court-yard. Here she sometimes saw the cook come out and wash vegetables at the fountain.

"Cook! cook!" she called one day, as she saw him pass thus under the window.

The cook looked up with a good-natured face, which gave her encouragement.

"Don't you think, cook, I must be very lonely and miserable up here all alone?"

"Yes, Signorina!" he replied; "I often think I should like to help you to get out; but I dare not think of it, the king would be so angry."

"No, I don't want you to do anything to disobey the king," answered the princess; "but would you really do me a favour, which would make me very grateful indeed?"

"O! yes, Signorina, anything which I can do without disobeying the king," replied the faithful servant.

"Then this is it," said the princess. "Will you just oblige me so far as to cook Papa's dinner today without any salt in anything? Not the least grain in anything at all. Let it be as good a dinner as you like, but no salt in anything. Will you do that?"

"I see!" replied the cook, with a knowing nod. "Yes, depend on me, I will do it."

That day at dinner the king had no salt in the soup, no salt in the boiled meat, no salt in the roast, no salt in the fried.

"What is the meaning of this?" said the king, as he pushed dish after dish away from him. "There is not a single thing I can eat today. I don't know what they have done to everything, but there is not a single thing that has got the least taste. Let the cook be called."

So the cook came before him.

"What have you done to the victuals today?" said the king, sternly. "You have sent up a lot of dishes, and no one alive can tell one from another. They are all of them exactly alike, and there is not one of them can be eaten. Speak!"

The cook answered:

"Hearing Your Majesty say that salt was the commonest thing that comes to table, and altogether so worthless and contemptible, I considered in my mind whether it was a thing that at all deserved to be served up to the table of the king; and judging that it was not worthy, I abolished it from the king's kitchen, and dressed all the meats without it. Barring this, the dishes are the same that are sent every day to the table of the king."

Then the king understood the value of salt, and he comprehended how great was the love of his youngest child for him; so he sent and had her apartment opened, and called her to him, never to go away anymore.

The King of Portugal

T HEY SAY THAT ONCE there was a king of Portugal who had a beautiful daughter, and there came a prince to marry her. When the prince saw how old and feeble the king was, he seized him, and shut him up in prison, and ordered him to be fed

on only bread and water, that he might die without killing him. "And then," he said, "I shall take the government."

Then he would send and ask, "How does he look today? Does he grow lean and pale? Does he look like to die?"

But the answer ever was, "Nay, prince, he looks hale and stout. Every day his face is fresher and fatter. Every day he seems stronger and firmer."

Then the prince grew in despair of ever accomplishing his design, and he said, "It cannot be as you say, unless there is treachery," and he changed the guards, and set a watch upon them; but the same thing happened, and the old king continued to grow stouter and stronger. He made them search the princess, too, when she went to see her father, and they assured themselves that she took nothing to him. Then he bade them watch her, and they saw that she placed her breast against the prison bars, and fed him with her own milk.

For it had been thus, that when she learnt what was the design of the prince, she was filled with earnest desire to save her father's life, and prayed so hard that she might have wherewith to support him, that, young girl as she was, the means was afforded her, and thus by her devotion she preserved him in life and health.

When the prince heard what she did, he was seized with compunction, and sent and released the king, and restored him to his throne, and went his way in shame. But the king sent for him back, and forgave him: he gave him his daughter also, and when he died he left him the succession to the kingdom.

Love & Marriage

THE JOYS OF young love and the excitement of a forbidden courtship, along with the equally common woes of an unhappy marriage, are some of the most common themes in Busk's collection. They appear in every category of tales, both in Busk's original division and in the present edition.

The first three stories in this section are Roman versions of well-known, international fairy tales; they feature persecuted heroines, monstrous husbands and happy endings. Other stories, though not fairy tales proper, rely on familiar motifs that were probably not uncommon occurrences in the lives of Busk's narrators and their family and friends: the yearning for children that do not appear, no matter how much one tries; a fatal outcome for star-crossed lovers; abusive arranged marriages; a wife beaten almost to death because she had a crush on another man – a priest, no less – and another thrashed for her extravagant spending habits. Despite so many marriages leading to unhappiness and even to death, the last tale in this section provides some hope, when open communication prevents a loving couple from falling victim to a joke gone wrong. The message is clear: jealousy is no joking matter.

Maria Wood

THEY SAY THERE WAS A KING, whose wife, when she came to die, said to him,

"When I am dead, you will want to marry again; but take my advice: marry no woman but her whose foot my shoe fits."

But this she said because the shoe was under a spell, and would fit no one whom he could marry.

The king, however, caused the shoe to be tried on all manner of women; and when the answer always was that it would fit none of them, he grew quite bewildered and strange in his mind.

After some years had passed, his young daughter, having grown up to girl's estate, came to him one day, saying,

"Oh, Papa; only think! Mama's shoe just fits me!"

"Does it!" replied the simple king. "Then I must marry you."

"Oh, that cannot be, Papa," said the girl, and ran away.

But the simple king was so possessed with the idea that he must marry the woman whom his wife's shoe fitted, that he sent for her every day and said the same thing. But the queen had not said that he should marry the woman whom her shoe fitted, but that he should not marry any whom it did not fit.

When the princess found that he persevered in his silly caprice, she said at last,

"Papa, if I am to do what you say, you must do something for me first."

"Agreed, my child," replied the king; "you have only to speak."

"Then, before I marry," said the girl, "I want a lot of things, but I will begin with one at a time. First, I want a dress of the colour of a beautiful noontide sky, but all covered with stars, like the sky at midnight, and furnished with a parure to suit it."

Such a dress the king had made and brought to her.

"Next," said the princess, "I want a dress of the colour of the sea, all covered with golden fishes, with a fitting parure."

Such a dress the king had made, and brought to her.

"Next," said the princess, "I want a dress of a dark blue, all covered with gold embroidery and spangled with silver bells, and with a parure to match."

Such a dress the king had made and brought to her.

"These are all very good," said the princess; "but now you must send for the most cunning artificer in your whole kingdom, and let him make me a figure of an old woman just like life, fitted with all sorts of springs to make it move and walk when one gets inside it, just like a real woman."

Such a figure the king had made, and brought it to the princess.

"That is just the sort of figure I wanted," said she; "and now I don't want anything more."

And the simple king went away quite happy.

As soon as she was alone, however, the princess packed all the three dresses and many of her other dresses, and all her jewellery and a large sum of money, inside the figure of the old woman, and then she got into it and walked away. No one seeing an old woman walking out of the palace thought she had anything to do with the princess, and thus she got far away without anyone thinking of stopping her.

On, on, on, she wandered till she came to the palace of a great king, and just at the time that the king's son was coming in from hunting.

"Have you a place in all this fine palace to take in a poor old body?" whined the princess inside the figure of the old woman.

"No, no! get out of the way! How dare you come in the way of the prince!" said the servants, and drove her away.

But the prince took compassion on her, and called her to him.

"What's your name, good woman?" said the prince.

"Maria Wood is my name, Your Highness," replied the princess.

"And what can you do, since you ask for a place?"

"Oh, I can do many things. First, I understand all about poultry, and then—"

"That'll do," replied the prince; "take her, and let her be the henwife, and let her have food and lodging, and all she wants."

So they gave her a little hut on the borders of the forest, and set her to tend the poultry.

But the prince as he went out hunting often passed by her hut, and when she saw him pass she never failed to come out and salute him, and now and then he would stop his horse and spend a few moments in gossip with her.

Before long it was Carnival time; and as the prince came by Maria Wood came out and wished him a "good Carnival." The prince stopped his horse and said, his young head full of the pleasure he expected,

"Tomorrow, you know, we have the first day of the feast."

"To be sure I know it; and how I should like to be there: won't you take me?" answered Maria Wood.

"You shameless old woman," replied the prince, "to think of your wanting to go to a *festino* at your time of life!" and he gave her a cut with his whip.

The next day Maria put on her dress of the colour of the noontide sky, covered with stars like the sky at midnight, with the parure made to wear with it, and came to the feast. Every lady made place before her dazzling appearance, and the prince alone dared to ask her to dance. With her he danced all the evening, and fairly fell in love with her, nor could he leave her side; and as they sat together, he took the ring off his own finger and put it on to her hand. She appeared equally satisfied with his attentions, and seemed to desire no other partner. Only when he tried to gather from her whence she was, she would only say she came from the country of Whipblow, which set the prince wondering very much, as he had never heard of such a country. At the end of the ball, the prince sent his attendants to watch her that he might learn where she lived, but she disappeared so swiftly it was impossible for them to tell what had become of her.

When the prince came by Maria Wood's hut next day, she did not fail to wish him again a "good Carnival."

"Tomorrow we have the second *festino*, you know," said the prince.

"Well I know it," replied Maria Wood; "shouldn't I like to go! Won't you take me?"

"You contemptible old woman to talk in that way!" exclaimed the prince. "You ought to know better!" And he struck her with his boot.

Next night Maria put on her dress of the colour of the sea, covered all over with gold fishes, and the parure made to wear with it, and went to the feast. The prince recognized her at once, and claimed her for his partner all the evening, nor did she seem to wish for any other, only when he tried to learn from her whence she was, she would only say she came from the country of Bootkick. The prince could not remember ever to have heard of the Bootkick country, and thought she meant to laugh at him; however, he ordered his attendants to make more haste this night in following her; but what diligence soever they used she was too swift for them.

The next time the prince came by Maria Wood's hut, she did not fail to wish him again a "good Carnival."

"Tomorrow we have the last *festino*!" exclaimed he, with a touch of sadness, for he remembered it was the last of the happy evenings that he could feel sure of seeing his fair unknown.

"Ah! you must take me. But, what'll you say if I come to it in spite of you?" answered Maria Wood.

"You incorrigible old woman!" exclaimed the prince; "you provoke me so with your nonsense, I really cannot keep my hand off you;" and he gave her a slap.

The next night Maria Wood put on her dress of a dark blue, all covered with gold embroidery and spangled with silver bells, and the parure made to wear with it. The prince constituted her his partner for the evening as before, nor did she seem to wish for any other, only when he wanted to learn from her whence she was, all she would say was that she came from Slapland. This night the prince told his servants to make more haste in following her, or he would discharge them all. But they answered, "It is useless to attempt the thing, as no mortal can equal her in swiftness."

After this, the prince fell ill of his disappointment, because he saw no hope of hearing any more of the fair domino with whom he had spent three happy evenings, nor could any doctor find any remedy for his sickness.

Then Maria Wood sent him word, saying, "Though the prince's physicians cannot help him, yet let him but take a cup of broth of my making, and he will immediately be healed."

"Nonsense! How can a cup of broth, or how can any medicament, help me?" exclaimed the prince. "There is no cure for my ailment."

Again Maria Wood sent the same message; but the prince said angrily, "Tell the silly old thing to hold her tongue; she doesn't know what she's talking about."

But again, the third time, Maria Wood sent to him, saying, "Let the prince but take a cup of broth of my making, and he will immediately be healed."

By this time the prince was so weary that he did not take the trouble to refuse. The servants finding him so depressed began to fear that he was sinking, and they called to Maria Wood to make her broth, because, though they had little faith in her promise, they knew not what else to try. So Maria Wood made ready the cup of broth she had promised, and they put it down beside the prince.

Presently the whole palace was roused; the prince had started up in bed, and was shouting,

"Bring hither Maria Wood! Quick! Bring hither Maria Wood!"

So they ran and fetched Maria Wood, wondering what could have happened to bring about so great a change in the prince. But the truth was that Maria had put into the cup of broth the ring the prince had put on her finger the first night of the feast, and when he began to take the broth he found the ring with the spoon. When he saw the ring, he knew at once that Maria Wood could tell where to find his fair partner.

"Wait a bit! There's plenty of time!" said Maria, when the servant came to fetch her in all haste; and she waited to put on her dress of the colour of the noontide sky.

The prince was beside himself for joy when he saw her, and would have the betrothal celebrated that very day.

The Dark King

🎵

THEY SAY THERE WAS ONCE a poor chicory-gatherer who went out every day with his wife and his three daughters to gather chicory to sell for salad. Once, at Carnival time, he said,

"We must gather a fine good lot today," and they all dispersed themselves about trying to do their best. The youngest daughter thus came to a place apart where the chicory was of a much finer growth than any she had ever seen before. "This will be grand!" she said to herself, as she prepared to pull up the finest plant of it. But what was her surprise when with the plant, up came all the earth round it and a great hole only remained!

When she peeped down into it timidly she was further surprised to find it was no dark cave below as she had apprehended, but a bright apartment handsomely furnished, and a most appetizing meal spread out on the table. There was, moreover, a commodious staircase reaching to the soil on which she stood, to descend by.

All fear was quickly overcome by the pleasant sight, and the girl at once prepared to descend, and, as no one appeared to raise any objection, she sat down quite boldly and partook of the good food. As soon as she had finished eating, the tables were cleared away by invisible hands, and, as she had nothing else to do she wandered about the place looking at everything. After she had passed through several brilliant rooms she came to a passage, out of which led several store-chambers, where was laid up a good supply of everything that could serve in a house. In some there were provisions of all sorts, in some stuffs both for clothes and furniture.

"There seems to be no one to own all these fine things," said the girl. "What a boon they would be at home!" and she put together all that would be most useful to her mother. But what was her dismay when she went back to the dining-hall to find that the staircase by which she had descended was no longer there!

At this sight she sat down and had a good cry, but by and by, suppertime came, and with it an excellent supper, served in as mysterious a way as the dinner; and as a good supper was a rare enjoyment for her, she almost forgot her grief while eating it. After that, invisible hands led her into a bedroom, where she was gently undressed and put to bed without seeing anyone. In the morning she was put in a bath and dressed by invisible hands, but dressed like a princess all in beautiful clothes.

So it all went on for at least three months; every luxury she could wish was provided without stint, but as she never saw anyone she began to get weary, and at last so weary that she could do nothing but cry. At the sound of her crying there came into the room a great black King. Though he was so dark and so big that she was frightened at the sight of him, he spoke very kindly, and asked her why she cried so bitterly, and whether she was not provided with everything she could desire. As she hardly knew herself why she cried, she did not know what to answer him, but only went on whimpering. Then he said, "You have not seen half the extent of this palace yet or you would not be so weary; here are the keys of all the locked rooms which you have not been into yet. Amuse yourself as much as you like in going through them; they are all just like your own. Only into the room of which the key is not among these do not try to enter. In all the rest do what you like."

The next morning she took the keys and went into one of the locked rooms, and there she found so many things to surprise and amuse her that she spent the whole day there, and the next day she examined another, and so on for quite three months together, and the locked room of which she had not the key she never thought of trying to enter. But all amusements tire at last, and at the end of this time she was so melancholy that she could do nothing but cry. Then the Dark King came again and asked her tenderly what she wanted.

"I want nothing you can give me," she replied this time. "I am tired of being so long away from home. I want to go back home."

"But remember how badly you were clothed, and how poorly you fared," replied the Dark King.

"Ah, I know it is much pleasanter here," said the girl, "for all those matters, but one cannot do without seeing one's relations, now and then at least."

"If you make such a point of it," answered the Dark King, "you shall go home and see Papa and Mama, but you will come back here. I only let you go on that condition."

The arrangement was accepted, and next day she was driven home in a fine coach with prancing horses and bright harness. Her appearance at home caused so much astonishment that there was hardly room for pleasure, and even her own mother would hardly acknowledge her; as for her sisters, they were so changed by her altered circumstances and so filled with jealousy they would scarcely speak to her. But when she gave her mother a large pot of gold which the Dark King had given her for the purpose, their hearts were somewhat won back to her, and they began to ask all manner of questions concerning what had befallen her during her absence. So much time had been lost at first, however, that none was left for answering them, and, promising to try and come back to them soon, she drove away in her splendid coach.

Another three months passed away after this, and at the end of it she was once more so weary, her tears and cries again called the Dark King to her side.

Again she confided to him that her great grief was the wish to see her friends at home. She could not bear being so long without them. To content her once more he promised to let her drive home the next day; and the next day accordingly she went home.

This time she met with a better reception, and having brought out her pot of gold at her first arrival, everyone was full of anxiety to know how it came she had such riches at her disposal.

"What, that pot of money?" replied the girl, in a tone of disparagement. "That's nothing. You should see the beautiful things that are scattered about in my new home, just like nothing at all;" and then she went on to describe the magnificence of the place, till nothing would satisfy them but that they should go there too.

"That's impossible," she replied. "I promised him not even to mention it."

"But if he were got rid of, *then* we might come," replied the elder sisters.

"What do you mean by 'got rid of'?" asked the youngest.

"Why, it is evident he is some bad sort of enchanter, whom it would be well to rid the earth of. If you were to take this stiletto and put it into his breast when he is asleep, we might all come down there and be happy together."

"Oh, I could never do that!"

"Ah, you are so selfish you want to keep all for yourself. If you had any spirit in you, you would burst open that locked door, where you may depend the best of the treasure is concealed, and then put this stiletto into the old enchanter, and call us all down to live with you."

It was in vain she protested she could not be so ungrateful and cruel; they over-persuaded her with their arguments, and frightened her so with their reproaches that she went back resolved to do their bidding.

The next morning she called up all her courage and pushed open the closed door. Inside were a number of beautiful maidens weaving glittering raiment.

"What are you doing?" asked the chicory-gatherer.

"Making raiment for the bride of the Dark King against her espousals," replied the maidens.

A little further on was a goldsmith and all his men working at all sorts of splendid ornaments filled with pearls and diamonds and rubies.

"What are you doing?" asked the girl.

"Making ornaments for the bride of the Dark King against her espousals," replied the goldsmiths.

A little further on was a little old hunchback sitting cross-legged, and patching an old torn coat with a heap of other worn-out clothes lying about him.

"What are you doing?" asked the maiden.

"Mending the rags for the girl to go away in who was to have been the bride of the Dark King," replied the little old hunchback.

Beyond the room where this was going on was a passage, and at the end of this a door, which she also pushed open. It gave entrance to a room where, on a bed, the Dark King lay asleep.

"This is the time to apply the stiletto my sisters gave me," thought the maiden. "I shall never have so good a chance again. They said he was a horrid old enchanter; let me see if he looks like one."

So saying she took one of the tapers from a golden bracket and held it near his face. It was true enough; his skin was black, his hair was grizzly and rough, his features crabbed and forbidding.

"They're right, there's no doubt. It were better the earth were rid of him, as they say," she said within herself; and, steeling herself with this reflection, she plunged the knife into his breast.

But as she wielded the weapon with the right hand, the left, in which she held the lighted taper, wavered, and some of the scalding wax fell on the forehead of the Dark King. The dropping of the wax woke him; and when he saw the blood flowing from his breast, and perceived what she had done, he said sadly,

"Why have you done this? I meant well by you and really loved you, and thought if I fulfilled all you desire, you would in time have loved me. But it is over now. You must leave this place, and go back to be again what you were before."

Then he called servants, and bade them dress her again in her poor chicory-gatherer's dress, and send her up to earth again; and it was done. But as they were about to lead her away, he said again,

"Yet one thing I will do. Take these three hairs; and if ever you are in dire distress and peril of life with none to help, burn them, and I will come to deliver you."

Then they took her back to the dining-hall, where the staircase was seen as at the first, and when they touched the ceiling, it opened, and they pushed her through the opening, and she found herself in the place where she had been picking chicory on the day that she first found the Dark King's palace.

Only as they were leading her along, she had considered that it might be dangerous for her, a young girl, to be wandering about the face of the country alone, and she had, therefore, begged the servants to give her a man's clothes instead of her own; and they gave her the worn-out clothes that she had seen the little old hunchback sitting cross-legged to mend.

When she found herself on the chicory-bed it was in the cold of the early morning, and she set off walking towards her parents' cottage. It was about midday when she arrived, and all the family were taking their meal. Poor as it was, it looked very tempting to her who had tasted nothing all the morning.

"Who are you?" cried the mother, as she came up to the door.

"I'm your own child, your youngest daughter. Don't you know me?" cried the forlorn girl in alarm.

"A likely joke!" laughed out the mother; "my daughter comes to see me in a gilded coach with prancing horses!"

"Had you asked for a bit of bread in the honest character of a beggar," pursued the father, "poor as I am, I would never have refused your weary, woebegone looks; but to attempt to deceive with such a falsehood is not to be tolerated;" and he rose up, and drove the poor child away.

Protests were vain, for no one recognized her under her disguise.

Mournful and hopeless, she wandered away. On, on, on, she went, till at last she came to a palace in a great city, and in the stables were a number of grooms and their helpers rubbing down horses.

"Wouldn't there be a place for me among all these boys?" asked the little chicory-gatherer, plaintively. "I, too, could learn to rub down a horse if you taught me."

"Well, you don't look hardly strong enough to rub down a horse, my lad," answered the head-groom; "but you seem a civil-spoken sort of chap, so you may come in; I dare say we can find some sort of work for you."

So she went into the stable-yard, and helped the grooms of the palace.

But every day the queen stood at a window of the palace where she could watch the fair stable-boy, and at last she sent and called the head-groom, and said to him, "What are you doing with that new boy in the stable-yard?"

The head-groom said, "Please Your Majesty he came and begged for work, and we took him to help."

Then the queen said, "He is not fit for that sort of work, send him to me."

So the chicory-gatherer was sent up to the queen, and the queen gave her the post of master of the palace, and appointed a fine suite of apartments and a dress becoming the rank, and was never happy unless she had this new master of the palace with her.

Now the king was gone to the wars, and had been a long time absent. One day the queen said to the master of the palace that very likely the king would not come back, so that it would be better they should marry.

Then the poor chicory-gatherer was sadly afraid that if the queen discovered that she was a woman she would lose her fine place at the palace, and become a poor beggar again without a home; so she said nothing of this, but only reasoned with the queen that it was better to wait and see if the king did not come home. But as she continued saying this, and at the same time never showed any wish that the king might not come back, or that the marriage might take place, the queen grew sorely offended, and swore she would be avenged.

Not long after, the king really did come back, covered with glory, from the wars. Now was the time for the queen to take her revenge.

Choosing her opportunity, therefore, at the moment when the king was rejoicing that he had been permitted to come back to her again, with hypocritical tears she said,

"It is no small mercy, indeed, that Your Majesty has found me again here as I am, for it had well-nigh been a very different case."

The king was instantly filled with burning indignation, and asked her further what her words meant.

"They mean," replied the queen, "that the master of the palace, on whom I had bestowed the office only because he seemed so simple, as you too must say he looks, presumed on my favour, and would have me marry him, urging that peradventure the king, who had been so long absent at the wars, might never return."

The king started to his feet at the words, placing his hand upon his sword in token of his wrath; but the queen went on:

"And when he found that I would not listen to his suit, he dared to assume a tone of command, and would have compelled me to consent; so that I had to call forth all my courage, and determination, and dignity, to keep him back; and had the King's Majesty not been directed back to the palace as soon as he was, who knows where it might have ended!"

It needed no more. The king ordered the master of the palace to be instantly thrown into prison, and appointed the next day for him to be beheaded.

The chicory-gatherer was ready enough now to protest that she was a woman. But it helped nothing; they only laughed. And who could stand against the word of the queen?

Next day, accordingly, the scaffold was raised, and the master of the palace was brought forth to be beheaded, the king and the queen, and all the court, being present.

When the chicory-gatherer, therefore, found herself in dire need and peril of life, she took out one of the hairs the Dark King had given her, and burnt it in the flame of a torch. Instantly there was a distant roaring sound as of a tramp of troops and the roll of drums. Everyone started at the sound, and the executioner stayed his hand.

Then the maiden burnt the second hair, and instantly a vast army surrounded the whole place; round the palace they marched and up to the scaffold, and so to the very throne of the king. The king had now something to think of besides giving the signal for the execution, and the headsman stayed his hand.

Then the maiden burnt the third hair, and instantly the Dark King himself appeared upon the scene, clothed in shining armour, and fearful in majesty and might. And he said to the king,

"Who are you that you have given over my wife to the executioner?"

And the king said,

"Who is thy wife that I should give her to the executioner?"

The Dark King, taking the master of the palace by the hand, said,

"This is my wife. Touch her who dares!"

Then the king knew that it had been true when the master of the palace had alleged that she was not guilty of the charge the queen had brought against her, being a woman; and seeing clearly what had been the malice of the queen, he ordered the executioner to behead her instead, but the chicory-gatherer he gave up to the Dark King.

Then the Dark King said to the chicory-gatherer,

"I came at your bidding to defend you, and I said you were my wife to save your life; but whether you will be my wife or not depends on you. It is for you to say whether you will or not."

Then the maiden answered,

"You have been all goodness to me; ungrateful indeed should I be did I not, as I now do, say 'yes.'"

As soon as she said, "yes," the earth shook, and she was no longer standing on a scaffold, but before an altar in a splendid cathedral, surrounded by a populous and flourishing city. By her side stood the Black King, but he was now a most beautiful prince; for with all his kingdom he had been under enchantment, and the condition of his release had been that a fair maiden should give her free consent to marry him.

La Candeliera

THEY SAY THERE WAS ONCE a king who wanted to make his beautiful young daughter marry an old, ugly king. Every time the king talked to his daughter about this marriage, she

cried and begged him to spare her; but he only went on urging her the more, till at last she feared he would command her to consent, so that she might not disobey; therefore at last she said: "Before I marry this ugly old king to please you, you must do something to please me."

"Oh, anything you like I will do," replied he.

"Then you must order for me," she replied, "a splendid candelabrum, ten feet high, having a thick stem bigger than a man, and covered all over with all kinds of ornaments and devices in gold."

"That shall be done," said the king; and he sent for the chief goldsmith of the court, and told him to make such a candelabrum; and, as he was very desirous that the marriage should be celebrated without delay, he urged him to make the candelabrum with all dispatch.

In a very short space of time the goldsmith brought home the candelabrum, made according to the princess's description, and the king ordered it to be taken into his daughter's apartment. The princess expressed herself quite pleased with it, and the king was satisfied that the marriage would now shortly take place.

Late in the evening, however, the princess called her chamberlain to her, and said to him: "This great awkward candlestick is not the sort of thing I wanted; it does not please me at all. Tomorrow morning you may take it and sell it, for I cannot bear the sight of it. You may keep the price it sells for, whatever it is; but you had better take it away early, before my father gets up."

The chamberlain was very pleased to get so great a perquisite, and got up very early to carry it away. The princess, however, had got up earlier, and had placed herself inside the candlestick; so that she was carried out of the palace by the chamberlain, and thus she escaped the marriage she dreaded so much with the ugly old king.

The chamberlain, judging that the king would be very angry if he heard of his selling the splendid candelabrum he had just had made, did not venture to expose it for sale within the borders of his dominions, but carried it to the capital of the neighbouring sovereign. Here he set it up in the marketplace, and cried, "Who'll buy my candelabrum? Who'll buy my fine candelabrum?" When all the people saw what a costly candelabrum it was, no one would offer for it. At last it got bruited about till it reached the ears of the son of the king of that country that there was a man standing in the market-place, offering to sell the most splendid candelabrum that ever was seen; so he went out to look at it himself.

No sooner had the prince seen it than he determined that he must have it; so he bought it for the price of three hundred scudi, and sent his servants to take it up into his apartment. After that, he went about his affairs as usual. In the evening, however, he said to his body-servant, "As I am going to the play tonight, and shall be home late, take my supper up into my own room." And the servant did as he told him.

When the prince came home from the play, he was very much surprised to find his supper eaten and all the dishes and glasses disarranged.

"What is the meaning of this?" he exclaimed, calling his servant to him in a great fury. "Is this the way you prepare supper for me?"

"I don't know what to say, Your Royal Highness," stammered the man; "I saw the supper properly laid myself. How it got into this condition is more than I can say. With the leave of Your Highness, I will order the table to be relaid."

But the prince was too angry to allow anything of the sort, and he went supperless to bed.

The next night the same thing happened, and the prince in his displeasure threatened to discharge his servant. The night after, however, his curiosity being greatly excited as he thought over the circumstance, he called his servant, and said: "Lay the supper before I go out, and I will lock the room and take the key in my pocket, and we will see if anyone gets in then."

But, though this is what he said out loud, he determined to stay hidden within the room; and this is what he did. He had not remained there hidden very long when, lo and behold, the candelabrum, on which he had never bestowed a thought since the moment he bought it, opened, and there walked out the most beautiful princess he had ever seen, who sat down at the table, and began to sup with hearty appetite.

"Welcome, welcome, fair princess!" exclaimed the astonished prince. "You have heard me from within your hiding-place speaking with indignation because my meal had been disturbed. How little did I imagine such an honour had been done me as that it should have served you!" And he sat down beside her, and they finished the meal together. When it was over, the princess went away into her candelabrum again; and the next night the prince said to his servant: "In case anyone eats my supper while I am out, you had better bring up a double portion." The next day he had not his supper only, but all his meals, brought into his apartment; nor did he ever leave it at all now, so happy was he in the society of the princess.

Then the king and queen began to question about him, saying: "What has bereft our son of his senses, seeing that now he no more follows the due occupations of his years, but sits all day apart in his room?"

Then they called him to them and said: "It is not well that you should sit thus all day long in your private apartments alone. It is time that you should bethink yourself of taking a wife."

But the prince answered, "No other wife will I have but the candelabrum."

When his parents heard him say this they said: "Now there is no doubt that he is mad;" and they spoke no more about his marrying.

But one day, the queen-mother, coming into his apartment suddenly, found the door of the candelabrum open, and the princess sitting talking with the prince. Then she, too, was struck with her beauty, and said: "If this is what you were thinking of when you said you would marry the candelabrum, it was well judged." And she took the princess by the hand and led her to the presence of the king. The king, too, praised her beauty, and she was given to the prince to be his wife.

And the king her father, when he heard of the alliance, he too was right glad, and said he esteemed it far above that of the ugly old king he wanted her to have married at the first.

The Pilgrims

🎵

THERE WAS A HUSBAND AND WIFE, who had been married two or three years, and had no children. At last, they made a vow to S. Giacomo di Galizia that if they only had two

children, one boy and one girl, even if no more than that, they would be so grateful that they would go on a pilgrimage to his shrine, all the way to Galizia.

In due time two children were born to them, a boy and a girl, who were twins; and they were full of gladness and rejoicing, and devoted themselves to the care of their children, but they forgot all about their vow. When many years were passed, and the children were, it maybe, fifteen or sixteen years old, they dreamed a dream, both husband and wife in one night, that St. James appeared, and said:

"You made a vow to visit my shrine if you had two children. Two children have been born to you, and you have not kept your vow; most certainly evil will overtake you for your broken word. Behold, time is given you; but if now you fulfil not your vow, both your children will die."

In the morning the wife told the dream to the husband, and the husband told the dream to the wife, and they said to each other, "This is no common dream; we must look to it." So they bought pilgrims' dresses, and went to "Galizia," the husband, and wife, and the son; but concerning the daughter they said, "The maiden is of too tender years for this journey, let her stay with her nurse;" and they left her in the charge of the nurse and the parish priest. But that priest was a bad man – for it will happen that a priest may be bad sometimes; and, instead of leading her right, he wanted her to do many bad things, and when she would not listen to him, he wrote false letters to her parents about her, and gave a report of her conduct to shock her parents. When the brother saw these letters of the priest concerning his sister, he was indignant with her, and, without waiting for his parents' advice, went back home quickly, and killed her with his dagger, and threw her body into a ditch. But he went back to the shrine of St. James to live in penance.

Not long had her body lain in the ditch when a king's son came by hunting, and the dogs scented the blood of a Christian lying in the ditch, and bayed over it till the huntsmen came and took out the body; when they saw it was the body of a fair maiden, yet warm, they showed it to the prince, and the prince, when he saw the maiden, loved her, and took her to a convent to be healed of her wound, and afterwards married her; and when his father died, he was king and she became a queen.

But her father and mother, hearing only that her brother had killed her and thrown her body in the ditch, and supposing she was dead, said one to the other, "Why should we go back home, seeing that our daughter is dead? What have we to go home for? There is nothing but sorrow for us there." So they remained at the shrine of St. James, and built a hospice for poor pilgrims, and tended them.

Meantime the daughter, who had become a queen, she also had two children, a boy and a girl, and her husband rejoiced in them and in her. But troubled times came, and her husband had to go forth to battle, and while she was left without him in the palace, the viceroy came to her and wanted her to do wrong, and when she would not listen to him, he took her two children and killed them before her eyes. "What do I here," said she, "seeing my two children are dead?" And she took the bodies of her children and went forth. When she had wandered long by solitary places, she came one day to a mountain, and at the foot of the mountain sat a dwarf, and the dwarf had compassion when he saw how she was worn with crying, and he said to her, "Go up the mountain and be consoled." Thus she went up the mountain till she saw a majestic woman, with an infant in her arms; and this was the Madonna, you must know.

When she saw a woman like herself, with a child too, for all that she looked so bright and majestic, she was consoled; and she poured all her story into her ear. "And I would go to S. Giacomo di Galizia to ask that my husband's love may be restored to me, for I know the viceroy will calumniate me to him; but how can I leave these children?" Then the lady said, "Leave your children with me, and they shall be with my child, and go you to Galizia as you have said, and be consoled." So she put on pilgrim's weeds, and went to Galizia.

Meantime the king came back from battle, and the viceroy told him evil about the queen; and his mother, who also believed the viceroy, said, "Did I not tell you a woman picked up is never good for anything?" But the king was grieved, for he had loved the queen dearly, and he took a pilgrim's dress and went to Galizia, to the shrine of S. Giacomo, to pray that she might be forgiven. Then the viceroy, he too was seized with compunction, and, unknown to the king, he too became a pilgrim, and went to do penance at the same shrine.

Thus it happened that they all met together, without knowing each other, in the hospice that that husband and wife had built at Galizia; and when they had paid their devotions at the shrine, and all sat together in the hospice in the evening, all told some tale of what he had seen and what he had heard. But there sat one who told nothing. Then said the king to this one, "And you, good man, why do you tell no story?" for he knew not that it was the queen, nor that it was even a woman.

Thus appealed to, however, she rose and told a tale of how there had been a husband and wife who had made a vow that if they had children, they would go on a pilgrimage to S. Giacomo di Galizia; "and," said she, "they were just two people such as you might be," and she pointed to the two who were founders of the hospice. And that when they were absent, and left their daughter behind, the parish priest calumniated her, so that her brother came back and stabbed her, and threw her body in a ditch. "And he was just such a young man, strong and ardent, as you may have been," and she pointed to the son of the founders. "But that maiden was not dead," she went on, "and a king found her, and married her, and she had two children, and lived happily with him till he went to the wars, then the viceroy calumniated her till she ran away out of the palace; and the viceroy was just such a one, strong and dark, as you may be," and she pointed to the viceroy, who sat trembling in a corner; "and when the king came back, he told him evil of her; but that king was noble and pious as you may be," and she pointed to the king, "and in his heart he believed no evil of his wife, but went to S. Giacomo di Galizia to pray that the truth might be made plain."

As she spoke, one after another they all arose, and said, "How comes this peasant to know all the story of my life; and who has sent him to declare it here?" And they were all strangely moved, and called upon the peasant to tell them who had shown him these things. But the supposed peasant answered, "My old grandfather, as we sat on the hearth together." "That cannot be," said they, "for to every one of us you have told his own life; and now you must tell us more, for we will not rest till we have righted her who has thus suffered." When she found them so earnest and so determined to do right, she said further, "That queen am I!" And she took off her hood, and they knew her, and all fell round and embraced her. Then said the king, "And on this viceroy, on whose account you have suffered so sadly, what vengeance will you have on him?" But she said, "I will have no vengeance; but now that he has come to the shrine of Galizia, God will forgive him; and may he find peace!"

Thus all were restored and united; and when she had embraced her parents and her brother, and spent some days with them, she went home with her husband and reigned in his kingdom.

St. Theodora

WHEN SANTA THEODORA was young she was married, and lived very happily with her husband, for they were both very fond of each other.

But there was a count who saw her and fell in love with her, and tried his utmost to get an opportunity of telling her his affection, but she was so prudent that he could not approach her. So what did he do? He went to a bad old woman and told her that he would give her ever so much money if she would get him the opportunity of meeting her. The old wretch accepted the commission willingly, and put all her bad arts in requisition to make Theodora forget her duty. For a long time Theodora refused to listen to her and sent her away, but she went on finding excuses to come to her, and again and again urged her persuasions and excited her curiosity so that finally she consented that he might just come and see her, and the witch woman assured her that was all he asked. But what he wanted was the opportunity of speaking his own story into her ear, and when that was given him he pushed his suit so successfully that it wasn't only once he came, but many times.

Yet it was not a very long time before a day came when Theodora saw how wrong she had been, and then, seized with compunction, she determined to go away and hide herself where she would never be heard of more. Before her husband came home she cut off all her hair, and putting on a coarse dress she went to a Capuchin monastery and asked admission.

"What is your name?" asked the Superior.

"Theodore," she replied.

"You seem too young for our severe rule," he continued; "you seem a mere boy;" but she expressed such sincere sentiments of contrition as showed him she was worthy to embrace their life of penance.

The Devil was very much vexed to see what a perfect penitent she made, and he stirred up the other monks to suspect her of all manner of things; but they could find no fault against her, nor did they ever suspect that she was a woman.

One day when she was sent with another brother to beg for the convent a storm overtook them in a wood, and they were obliged to seek the shelter of a cottage there was on the borders of the wood where they were belated. "There is room in the stable for one of you," said the peasant who lived there; "but that other one who looks so young and so delicate" (he meant Theodora) "must sleep indoors, and the only place is the loft where my daughter sleeps; but it can't be helped." Theodora, therefore, slept in the loft and the monk in the stable, and in the morning when the weather was fair they went back to their convent. Months passed away, and the incident was almost forgotten, when one day the peasant came to the monastery and rang the bell in a great fury, and he laid down at the entrance a bundle in which was a baby. "That young monk of yours is the father of this child," he said, "and you ought to turn him out of the convent." Then the Superior sent for "Theodore," and repeated what the peasant had said.

"Surely God has sent me this new penance because the life I lead here is not severe enough," she said. "He has sent me this further punishment that all the community should think me guilty." Therefore she would not justify herself, but accepted the accusation and took the baby and went away. Her only way of living now was to get a night's lodging how she could, and come every day to the convent gate with the child and live on the dole that was distributed there to the poor. What a life for her who had been brought up delicately in her own palace!

She was not allowed to rest, however, even so, for people took offence because she was permitted to remain so near the monastery, and the monks had to send her away. So she went to seek the shelter of a wood, and to labour to find the means of living for herself and the child in the roots and herbs she could pick up. But one of the monks one day found her there, and saw her so emaciated that he told the Superior, and he let her come back to receive the dole.

At last she died, and when they came to bury her they found she had in one hand a written paper so tightly clasped that no one had the strength to unclose it; and there she lay on her bier in the church looking so sad and worn, yet as sweetly fair as she had looked in life, and with the written paper tightly grasped in her closed hand.

Now when her husband found that she had left his palace the night she went away he left no means untried to discover where she was; and when he had made enquiries and sent everywhere, and could learn no tidings whatever, he put on pilgrim's weeds and went out to seek for her everywhere himself.

It so happened that he came into the city where she died just as she was thus laid on her bier in the church. In spite of her male attire he knew her; in the midst of his grief he noticed the written paper she held. To *his* touch her hand opened instantly, and in the scroll was found recorded all she had done and all she had suffered.

The Beautiful Englishwoman

THERE WAS A beautiful Englishwoman here once, beautiful and rich as the sun. Heads without number were turned by her: but she would have nothing to say to anyone who wanted to marry her. Some defect she found in all. She was very accomplished, as well as rich and beautiful, and she drew a picture, and said, "When one comes who is like this I will marry him; but no one else." Some time after a friend came to her, and said:

"There is So-and-so, he is exactly like the portrait you have drawn, and is dying to see you."

"Is he *really* like it?" she enquired.

"To me he seems exactly like it; and I don't see he has any defect at all, except that he has one tooth a little green."

"Then I won't have anything to say to him."

"But, if he is exactly like the portrait you have drawn?"

"He can't be, or he wouldn't have any defect."

"But he *is* exactly like it, and so you must see him; if it's only for curiosity."

"Well, for curiosity, then, I'll see him; but don't let him build any hopes upon it."

The friend arranged that they should meet at a ball, and the one was as well pleased as the other; but not wishing to seem to yield too soon, she said:

"Do you know, I don't like that green tooth you've got."

And he, not to appear too easy either, answered:

"And, do you know, I don't like that patch you have on your face."

The next time they met, neither he had a green tooth, nor had she a patch; for, you know, a patch can be put on and taken off at pleasure, and this happened a long, long while ago, in the days when they wore such things.

She then said:

"If you've put in a false tooth I'll have nothing to say to you."

"No," answered he; "you have taken off your patch; and I've taken off my green tooth."

"How could you do that?" she asked.

"Oh! it was only a leaf I put on to see if you were really as particular as you seemed to be."

As they were desperately in love with each other, the next thing was to arrange the marriage secretly. His father had a great title, and would never have consented to his marrying her, because she had none. But she had money enough for both; so they contrived a secret marriage. And then they bought a villa some way off, and lived there.

For thirteen years they lived devoted to each other, and full of happiness; and two children were born to them, a boy and a girl. It was only after thirteen years that the father discovered where the son was, and when he did, he sent for an assassin, and giving him plenty of money, told him to go and by some device or other to bring him to him and get through the affair. The assassin took a carriage and dressed like a man of some importance, and said that some chief man or other in the Government had sent for him to speak to him. The husband suspected nothing, and went with him. As it was night he could not see which way they drove, and thus he delivered his son to his father, who kept him shut up in his palace.

The assassin went back to the villa, and by giving each of the servants fifty scudi apiece, got access to the wife, and murdered her, and then took the children to the grandfather's palace.

"Papa, that man killed Mama," said the little boy, as soon as he saw his father.

The husband seized the man, and made him confess it.

"Then now you must kill him who hired you to do it," he exclaimed. "As you have done the one, you must do the other. He who ordered my wife to be killed is no father to me."

So the assassin went in and killed the father, but when he came out the husband was ready for him, and he said:

"Now your turn has come," and he shot him dead.

The Satyr

T HERE WAS ONCE a great king who had one only little daughter, and this daughter was always entreating him to take her out hunting.

"It is not proper for little girls to go out hunting," he used to say; but it was no use. She went on begging all the same, and at last her importunity gained the day, and he took her with him. But in the forest she got separated from him and lost herself, and he, full of the ardour of the chase, forgot the care of her, and, when he came to think of her, she could no more be found.

She wandered about the forest crying for her father, but her father came not; and instead of her father a *selvaggio* found her, and fell in love with her, and took her to his den and married her, and she had two children.

When ten years had passed, and there were no tidings of her, the queen, her mother, died of a broken heart.

But the *selvaggio* loved her dearly, and did everything in his power to give her pleasure. When he found she could not eat the raw game which he brought her, he would go into the towns and steal cooked food and bring it to her, and when he could not get that he would go ever so far to find fruits and roots. Everything he did to please her, but it was no use, she could not love him.

At last, however, after so many years were passed, he thought she was at least used to the way of life with him, and he no longer watched her so closely. One day when he was gone to a long distance she wandered on to a cliff that overhung the sea, and looked till she saw a ship, then she called to it and made signs to it to come and pick her up.

The captain took compassion on her distress, and made for the land, and took her on board and wrapped her in a cloak, and she told him who she was and he promised to take her home. He gave her a white kerchief to put on her head and another to hold in her hand.

They had not got far out to sea when the *selvaggio* found out what had happened, and came running to the same cliff where she had stood, and made signs entreating her to come back; but she shook the handkerchief she held in token of refusal.

Then what did he do? He ran back to the den and fetched one of the children and held it up, appealing to her mother's instincts; but she always continued waving the handkerchief in token of refusal. When he saw that this prevailed not, he ran back to the den and fetched the other child, and held them both up to plead with her to come back. But she always, and always, went on waving the handkerchief in token of refusal. Then what did he do? He took out his knife and plunged it into the one child, as signifying that if she did not come back he would kill the other also. But even for that she was not moved, but went on waving the handkerchief in token of refusal. Then with his knife he killed the other child, for he had no hope left; but she could not go back to that life with him, and went on waving the handkerchief in token of refusal.

Then with his claw he tore open his breast, and tore out his heart, and died for the love he bore her.

But the sailors took her home, and they were richly rewarded, and there was great rejoicing.

Amadea

AMADEA WAS A BEAUTIFUL QUEEN who fell in love with a king not of her own country; he loved her too, and married her, and took her home. But the king her father, and the prince her brother, were very wroth that she should go away with the stranger.

When Amadea heard that her brother was preparing to prevent her going away with her husband, she turned upon him and killed him, and then cut his body in pieces, and threw the mangled limbs in her father's way, to show him what he might expect if he followed after her too. And when she found that he was not deterred by the sight, she turned and killed him in like manner.

Only fancy what a woman she must have been!

When her husband, who had liked her before, saw this, he began to be afraid of her; nevertheless, they lived for some time happily together, and had two beautiful children. But after that again, her husband's love cooled towards her when he thought of the horrors she had committed, and he took their two children and went away and left her.

After a time Amadea not only found out where he was, but found out that she had a rival. Then she made her way to the place, and demanded to see her rival; but knowing of what she was capable, this her husband would by no means allow. Then she prepared a most beautiful necklace of pearls, and sent it as a present to her rival. But she had poisoned it by her arts, for she was a sort of witch, and when her rival put it on she died.

Meantime she had sent a message to her husband, saying, "If I may not come to your court, at least let me see my children for one hour, and then I will go away, and molest you no more for ever."

"*That* I will grant you," was his answer; and the children were brought to her.

When she saw her children, she wept, and embraced them, and wept again, and said:

"Now, my children, I must kill you."

"And why must you kill us?" asked the little boy.

"Because of the too great love I bear you," she replied, and drew out her dagger.

At that instant her husband came into the room, and she stabbed the children before his eyes. After that she stabbed herself, and he died of grief.

The Lenten Preacher

A FRIAR CAME TO PREACH the Lenten sermons in a country place. The wife of a rich peasant sat under the pulpit, and thought all the time what a nice-looking man he was, instead of listening to his exhortations to penance.

When the sermon was over she went home and took out half a dozen nice fine pocket-handkerchiefs, and sent them to him by her maid, with a very civil note to beg him to come and see her.

As the maid was going out, the husband met her.

"Where are you going?" said he.

The maid, who did not at all like her errand, promised if he would not be angry with her, and would not let her mistress know it, she would tell him all.

The husband promised to hold her harmless, and she gave him the handkerchiefs and the note.

"Come here," said the husband; and he took her into his room and wrote a note as if from the friar, saying he was much obliged by her presents, and would like to see the lady very much, but that it was impossible they could meet, so she must not think of it. This note the maid took back to her mistress as if from the friar.

A few days after this the husband gave out that he would have to go to a fair, and would be away two or three days. Immediately the wife took a pound of the best snuff and sent it as a present to the friar by the same maid with another note, saying the husband was going away on such an evening, and if he then came to see her at an hour after the Ave he would find the door open. This also the maid took to her master; the husband took the snuff and wrote an answer, as if from the friar, to say he would keep the appointment. In the evening he said goodbye to his wife, and went away. But he went to the butcher and bought a stout beef sinew, and at the hour appointed for the friar, he came back dressed as a friar, and beat her with the beef sinew till she was half dead. Then he went down in the kitchen and sent the servant up to heal her, and went away for three days. When he came back the wife was still doubled up, and suffering from the beating.

"What is the matter?" he said, sympathisingly.

"Oh! I fell down the cellar stairs."

"What do you mean by leaving your mistress to go down to the cellar?" he cried out to the servant, with great solicitude. "How can you allow her to do such things? What's the use of you?"

"Don't scold the servant," answered the wife; "it wasn't her fault. I shall be all right soon." And she made as light of her ailment as she could, to keep him from asking her any more questions. But he was discreet enough to say no more.

Only when she was well again he sent to the friar and asked him to come home to dine with them.

"My wife is subject to odd fancies sometimes," he said, as they walked home. "If she should do anything extravagant, don't you mind; I shall be there to call her to order."

Then he told the servant to bring in the soup and the boiled meat without waiting for orders, but to keep the grill back till he came to the kitchen door to call her.

At the time for the grill, therefore, he got up from table to go and call her, and thus left his wife and the friar alone together. They were no sooner alone than she got up, and calling him a horrid friar, gave him a sound drubbing. The husband came back in time to prevent mischief, and to make excuses; and finding she was cured of her affection, said no more of the affair.

The Root

THERE WAS A RICH COUNT who married an extravagant wife. As he had plenty of money he let her spend whatever she liked. But he had no idea what a woman could spend, and very much surprised was he when he found that dressmakers, and milliners, and hairdressers and shoemakers had made such a hole in his fortune that there was very little left. He saw it was high time to look after it, and he ventured to tender some words of remonstrance; but the moment he began to speak about it she went into hysterics. There was such a dreadful scene that he feared to approach the subject again, but the matter became so serious that at last he was obliged to do so. The least allusion, however, brought on another fit of hysterics.

What was he to do? To go on at this extravagant rate was impossible; equally impossible was it to endure the terrible scenes which ensued when he attempted to make her more careful.

At last he went to a doctor whom he knew, and asked him if he could give him any remedy for hysterics, telling him the whole story of what he wanted it for.

"Oh, yes!" replied the doctor; "I have an infallible cure. It is a certain root which must be applied very sharply to the back of the neck. If it doesn't succeed with the first half-dozen applications, you must go on till it does. It never fails in the end." So saying, he gave him a stout root, as thick as a walking stick, with a knobbed end.

Strong with the promised remedy, the husband went home, and sent word to all the dressmakers, milliners, hairdressers and shoemakers that he would pay for nothing more except what he ordered himself. Indeed he met the shoemaker on the step of the door, who had just come to take the measure for a pair of velvet slippers.

"Don't bring them," he said; "she has seven or eight pairs already, and that is quite enough."

Then he went up to his wife, and told her what he had done. Such a scene of hysterics as he had never imagined before awaited him now, but he, full of confidence in his remedy, took no notice further than to go up to her and apply the root very smartly to the back of her neck as he had been directed.

"But to me it seems that was all one with beating her with a stick," exclaimed another old woman who was sitting in the room knitting.

"Of course! That's just the fun of it!" replied the narrator. "And the beauty of it was that he was so simple that he thought it was some virtue in the root that was to effect the cure."

The hysterics stopped, and he ran off to the doctor to thank him for the capital remedy. The wife ran off, too, and went to her friends crying with terrible complaints that her husband would not allow her a single thing to put on, and, moreover, had even been beating her.

When the Count got back from the doctor, he found the father and half the family there ready to abuse him for making his wife go about with nothing on, and beating her into the bargain.

"It is all a mistake," said the Count. "I will allow her everything that is right, only I will order myself what I pay for; and, as to beating her, I only applied this root which I got from the doctor to cure hysterics; nothing more."

"Oh! it's a case of hysterics, is it?" said the father; "then it is all quite right," and he and the rest went away; and the Count and his wife got on very well after that, and he never had to make use of the doctor's root again.

The Bad-Tempered Queen

THEY SAY THERE WAS a queen who was so bad-tempered that no one who could help it would come near her. All the servants ran away when she came out of her apartment, for fear she should scold and maltreat them; all the people ran away when she drove out, for fear she should vex them with some tyrannical order.

As she was rich and beautiful, and ruled over vast dominions, many princes – who in their distant kingdoms had heard nothing of her failing – came to sue for her hand, but she sent them all away and would have nothing to say to any of them. She used to say she did not want to have anyone to be her master; she had rather live and govern by herself, and have everything her own way.

As time went on, however, the council of state grew dissatisfied with this resolution. They insisted that she must marry, that there might be a family of princes to carry on the succession to the throne without dispute. When the queen found that she could not help it she agreed she would marry; but she was determined she would not marry any of the princes who had come to court her, because, as they were equal to herself in birth and state, they would want to rule over her and expect obedience from her. She declared she would marry no one but a certain duke, who, as she had observed in the council and in the state banquets and balls, was always very quiet and hardly ever spoke at all. She thought he would make a nice quiet manageable sort of husband, and she would have him if she must have one at all.

The duke was as silent as usual when he was spoken to about it; but as he made no objection he was reckoned to have consented, and the marriage was duly solemnised.

As soon as the marriage was over the queen went on making her arrangements and ordering matters in the palace just as if nothing had happened and she were still her own mistress. In particular she issued invitations for the grandest ball she had ever given, asking to it all the ministers and their families, and all the nobility of the kingdom.

The husband said nothing to all this. Only a few hours before the time appointed for the banquet he called to the queen, saying: "Put on your travelling dress, and make haste; the carriage will be round directly."

"I'm not going to put on my travelling dress," answered the queen scornfully; "I am just seeing about my evening dress for the banquet this evening."

"If you are not ready in your travelling dress in five minutes, when the carriage comes round, it will be worse for you. Mind I have warned you."

And he looked so determined that she quailed before him.

"How can we be going into the country when I have invited half the kingdom to a banquet?" exclaimed the queen.

"*I* have invited no one," answered the husband quietly. "Don't stand hesitating when I tell you to do a thing; go and get ready directly! We are going into the country!" he added in his most positive voice, and, though she shed many secret tears over the loss of the banquet, she ventured to oppose nothing more to his orders, but went up and dressed, and when the carriage came round she was nearly ready. In about five minutes she came down.

"I won't say anything this time about your keeping me waiting," he said when she appeared; "but mind it does not happen again, or you will be sorry for it."

The queen had a favourite little dog, which she fondled and talked to all the way, to show she was offended with her husband and independent of his conversation.

Watching an opportunity when she was silent, the husband said to the little dog, "Jump on to my lap."

"He's not going to obey you," said the queen contemptuously; "he's *my* dog!"

"I keep no one about me who does not obey me," said her husband quietly; and he took out his pistol and shot the dog through the head.

The queen began to understand that the husband she had chosen was not a person to be trifled with, nor did she venture even to utter a complaint.

When they arrived at the villa, as the queen was going to her apartment to undress, her husband called her to him into his room and bade her pull off his boots.

The queen's first impulse was to utter a haughty refusal; but by this time she had learnt that, as she would certainly have to give in to him in the end, it was better to do his bidding with a good grace at the first. So she said nothing, but knelt down and pulled off his boots.

When she had done this he got up and said: "Now sit down in this armchair and I will take off your shoes; for my way is that one should help the other. If you behave to me as a wife should, you need never fear but that I shall behave to you as a husband should."

By the time their visit to the country was at an end, and when they returned to the capital, everybody found their naughty queen had become the most angelic being imaginable.

The Good Grace of the Hunchback

A MOTHER AND DAUGHTER lived alone in a cottage. The mother was old and came to die; the daughter was turned out of house and home. An ugly hunchback, who was a tailor, came by and said:

"What is your name, my pretty girl?"

"They call me la Buona Grazia," answered the girl.

"Well, la Buona Grazia, I've got twenty scudi a month, will you come with me and be my wife?"

The girl was starving, and didn't know where to set her foot, so she thought she could not afford to refuse; but she went along with a very bad grace, for she did not feel at all happy at the idea of marrying the ugly old hunchback.

When the hunchback saw how unhappy she was, he thought, "This will never do. She's too young and too pretty to care for me. I must keep her locked up, and then when she sees no one else at all, she will at last be glad even of my company." So he went all the errands himself, and never let her go out except to Mass, and then he took her to the church, and watched her all the time, and brought her back himself. The windows he whitened all over, so that she couldn't see out into the street, and there he kept her with the door locked on her, and she was very miserable.

So it went on for three years. But there was a dirty little window of a lumber room which, as it only gave a look out on to the court, he had not whitened. As she happened to look out here one day a stranger stood leaning on the balcony of the court, for part of the house was an inn, and he had just arrived.

"What are you looking for, my pretty girl?" said the stranger.

"O! nothing particular; only I'm locked up here, and I just looked out for a change."

"Locked up! Who has locked you up?" asked the stranger.

"An old hunchback, who's going to marry me," said the girl, almost crying.

"You don't seem much pleased at the idea of being married," answered the stranger.

"It is not likely that I should, to such a husband!" returned the girl.

"Would you like to get away from him?" asked the stranger.

"Shouldn't I!" heartily exclaimed the girl; "but it's impossible to manage that, as I'm locked in," she added sorrowfully.

"It's not so difficult as you think," rejoined the stranger. "Most likely there's some picture or other on your wall."

"Oh, yes! A great big one with the fair Giuditta just ready with her pouch to put Lofferno's head in," answered the girl.

"All right. You make a big hole behind the picture on your side, and when I hear by the sound where you are, I'll make one on mine. And when our two holes meet, you can come through."

"Yes, that's a capital plan; but the hunchback will soon come after me."

"Never mind, I will see to that; let's make the hole first?"

"Very well, I rely upon you, and will set to work immediately."

"Tell me first how I am to call you?"

"They always call me la Buona Grazia."

"A very nice name. Goodbye, and we'll set to work."

La Buona Grazia ran and unhooked the picture, and set to work to make a hole with all the available tools she could find; and the stranger, as soon as he had ascertained by the noise where she was at work, set to also. It turned out to be only a partition, and not a regular wall, and the hole was soon cut.

"What fun!" said the girl, as she jumped through. "Oh, how nice to be free! But," she added, "I can't travel with you in these poor clothes."

"No," said the stranger. "I'll have a travelling dress made for you, by the hunchback himself."

"Oh, take care!" cried the girl, earnestly.

"Don't be afraid," answered the stranger; "and above all don't look frightened."

Then he sent his servant to call the hunchback, and when he came he said:

"I want a travelling dress made directly for my wife here, so please take her measure."

The hunchback started when he saw who it was he had to measure.

"Why, she's exactly like my Buona Grazia!" exclaimed he.

"Very likely. I have always observed there was a sort of likeness between the inhabitants of a town. She too is a Roman, though I am a stranger. But make haste and take the measure, I didn't call you here to make remarks."

The hunchback got frightened at the stranger's authoritative tone, and took the measure without saying any more; and the stranger then gave him something to go and have a breakfast at the *caffè* to give the girl time to get back and set the picture in its place again.

When he came up into the room all looked right, and nothing seemed to have been moved.

"I've got to work hard today," said the hunchback, "to get a travelling dress ready for the wife of a gentleman staying in the inn, who is exactly like you."

"Are they going to travel, then?" asked la Buona Grazia.

"Yes, the gentleman said they should start as soon as the dress is done."

"Oh, do let me see them drive off!" said la Buona Grazia, coaxingly. "I should so like to see a lady who looked like me wearing a dress you had made."

"Nonsense, nonsense!" said the hunchback; "get on with your work."

And she did get on with her work, and stitched away, for she was anxious enough to help him to get the dress done; but she went on teasing him all the while to let her go to the window to see the gentleman and the lady, "who looked so like her," drive off, that at last the hunchback consented for that day only to take the whiting off the windows and let her look out.

The travelling dress was finished and taken home; and while the hunchback was taking it up by the stairs, la Buona Grazia was getting in by the hole behind the picture; but she had first made a great doll, and dressed it just like herself, and stuck it in the window. The *gobbo*, who stood down below to see the gentry drive off, looked up and saw her, as he thought, at the window, and made signs for her not to stay there too long.

Presently the stranger and his lady came down; the hunchback was standing before the carriage door, as I have said, and two stablemen were standing by also.

"You give me your good grace?" asked the stranger.

"Yes, yes!" readily responded the hunchback, delighted to find a rich gentleman so civil to him.

"You say it sincerely, with all your heart?" again asked the stranger.

"Yes, yes, yes! with all my heart," answered the hunchback.

"Then give me your hand upon it."

And the hunchback, more and more delighted, put out his hand, the two stablemen standing by looking on attentively all the time.

As soon as the carriage had driven away, the hunchback's first care was to look up at the window to see if the girl had gone in; but the doll was still there.

"Go in! Go in!" he cried, waving his hand. But the figure remained unmoved. Indignant, he took a stick and ran up to punish the girl for her disobedience, and when the blows fell thick and fast and no cries came, he discovered the trick that had been played.

Without loss of time he ran off to the Court and laid a complaint before the judge, demanding that soldiers should be called out and sent after the fugitives; but the stablemen had their orders, and were there before him, and deposed that they were witnesses to his having given "his good grace" up to the gentleman "with all his heart," and given him his hand upon the bargain.

"You see you have given her up of your own accord; there is nothing to be done!" said the judge. So he got no redress.

The Princess and the Gentleman

THERE WAS A PRINCESS whose mother had died of vexation because she was in love with a simple gentleman of the chamber, and would not hear of marrying anyone else, nor would she look at any prince who came to sue for her hand.

The king, not only vexed at her perversity, but still more at the loss of his wife, determined to devise a punishment to cure them both. He had two suites of apartments walled up, therefore; in one he had the princess imprisoned, and in the other the gentleman of the chamber with whom she was in love. The latter, he commanded, should see no one, thinking thereby to weary him out; the former he allowed only to see such persons as he should appoint, these persons being the princes one or other of whom he wished her to marry; for he thought that in her weariness at being so shut up, she would welcome the hand of anyone who would be her deliverer. It was not so, however. When the cook came in to the princess with her dinner, she begged him to give her a chicken that had been killed several days, and kept till it had a bad smell.

When her father now sent any prince to visit her she said, "It is no use my father sending you here, the reason why I cannot marry anyone is that I have a great defect; my breath smells so bad that it is not pleasant for anyone to live with me."

As the bad smell from the chicken was readily to be perceived in the room, they all believed her words and went away. There was one, indeed, who was so much pleased with her seeming candour that he thought he would excuse her defect, but on a second visit the smell of the dead chicken drove him away too.

The cooks in the kitchen talked together after the manner of cooks, and thus the cook who waited on the princess told what had happened to the cook who waited on the other prisoner, and thus it came round to his ears also, what the princess had done for love of him. Her stratagem then suggested another to him. Accordingly he sent to crave urgently an audience of the king.

When the king came in to him he said: "Sire, closely as I have been confined and guarded, yet something of what goes on in the outer world has reached my ears, and the fact which has the greatest interest for me has naturally been told to me. I now learn that the reason why your daughter has refused the suit of all the princes is not as we thought, her love for me, but a certain personal defect, which in politeness I will not name more particularly. But that being so, my desire to marry her is, of course, cured like that of others; so if Your Majesty will give me my liberty I will go away to a far country, and Your Majesty would never hear of me anymore."

The king was delighted to get rid of him, for he believed that if he were at a distance the great obstacle to his daughter's happiness would be removed. As he knew nothing about the chicken, he thought that all the suitors had believed the princess's representations upon her simple word; and as he very well knew she had no defect, he thought the time would come when some prince should please her, whom she also should please. Therefore, he very willingly gave the gentleman his liberty, and bade him godspeed on his journey.

The gentleman, however, before setting out, went to his friend the cook, and, giving him three hundred scudi, begged him to house him for a few nights, while he dug out an underground passage between the garden and the apartment where the princess was imprisoned. In the garden was a handsome terrace, all set out with life-sized statues; under one of these the gentleman worked his way, till he had reached the princess's chamber.

"You here!" exclaimed the princess in great astonishment, as soon as he had made his way through.

"Yes; I have come to fetch you," he replied.

She did not wait for a second injunction to escape from prison, but gathering all the money and jewels she had at command, she followed him through the underground way he had made.

As soon as they had reached the free air, the gentleman replaced the statue, and no one could guess by which way they had passed. Then they went to a church to be married, and, after that, to a city a long way off, as the gentleman had promised the king he would.

For a long time they lived very happily on the money and jewels each had brought from home; but, by and by, these came to an end, and neither durst write for more, for fear of betraying where they were. So at last, having no means of living, they engaged themselves to a rich lady who had a large mansion; the one as butler, and the other as nurse. Here they were well content to live at peace; and the lady was well content to have two such faithful and intelligent dependants, and they might have lived here till the end of their lives, but for a coincidence which strangely disconcerted them, as you shall hear, as well as what came of it.

One day there came to visit the lady, their mistress, a nobleman belonging to the king's court. At dinnertime the princess had to come to table along with the little daughter of the house, of whom she had the charge. Great was her terror when she recognized in the guest of the day one so familiar to herself and so near the sovereign. In conformity with the lowliness of the station she had assumed, she could escape actually talking to him, and she did her best to withdraw herself from his notice. She half hoped she had succeeded, when suddenly the butler had to come into the room to communicate an important dispatch which had just arrived, to the mistress of the house. The princess could not restrain an anxious glance at the stranger, to see if he betrayed any sign of recognition; but he was used to courts, and therefore to dissemble; nor could she satisfy herself that he had discovered either of them. It was so likely that he should, however, that she was filled with fear, and he was no sooner gone than she held a long consultation with her husband as to what course they should pursue.

In the end, the difficulty of finding other employment decided them to remain, for the probability that they would be tracked seemed remote. After all, they reasoned, was it likely that the nobleman should think it worthwhile to observe two persons occupying such humble posts with sufficient attention to see who they were or who they were not?

The king meantime had been searching everywhere for his daughter, not being able by any means to divine how she could have escaped. Then one morning, all this time after, the nobleman came down upon him with the news:

"I have found the princess. She is living as nurse to the Duchessa such a one, and her husband is the butler."

The king could not rest a moment after he had heard the news; his travelling carriage was ordered round, and away he drove. It was just dinnertime when he arrived at the Duchessa's palace. If the princess had been terrified before, at being called to sit at table with a nobleman of the court, judge how much greater was her alarm when she saw her father himself seated at the board!

Great as had been his indignation, however, the joy of again meeting his child after the long separation blotted out all his anger, and after embracing her tenderly, he placed her by his side at the table. It was only when he came to take leave and realized that she really belonged to another that his ire broke forth again. At this point the Duchessa put in a word. She highly extolled the excellent qualities of her butler, and declared he had been so skillful in the administration of her affairs that he deserved to have a kingdom committed to him. In short, she softened the king's heart so completely that she brought him to own that, as he had now grown very old and feeble, he could not do better than recognize him for his son-in-law, and associate him with himself in the government.

And so he did, and they all lived happily.

What Happened in the Room of a Hotel

THEY SAY THERE WAS a Countess who was very fond of her husband, and her husband was very fond of her; and they vowed nothing should ever make the one think ill of the other.

One day the brother of the Countess, who had been long away at the wars, and whom the Count had never seen, came back to see her just while the Count was out.

"Now we'll have some fun," said the Countess. "We'll watch till my husband is coming home, and then as he comes into the room you just be kissing me; he will be so astonished to see a stranger kissing me, he will not know what to make of it. Then in five minutes we will tell him who you really are, and it will make a good laugh."

The brother thought it would be a good joke, and they did as she had said.

It happened, however, that by accident the Count did not that day as usual come into his wife's room, but passing along the terrace in front of it, he saw, as she had arranged, one who was a stranger to him kissing her.

Then he went into his room, and calling his confidential servant he told him what had happened, and adding, "You will never see me anymore," went his way.

The Countess waited on and on for her husband to come in, full of impatience to have her joke out. But when she found he did not come at all, she went into his room to seek him there. There she found the servant, who told her what the Count had said, and the desperate resolution he had taken.

"What have I done!" exclaimed the terrified Countess. "Is it possible that I am to be punished thus for a harmless joke!"

Then, without saying anything to anyone she wrapped her travelling cloak about her, and set out to seek her husband.

The Count had walked on till he could walk no farther, and then he had gone into an inn, where he hired a room for a week; but he went wandering about the woods in misery and despair, and only came in at an hour of night.

The Countess also walked on till she could walk no farther, and thus she came to the same inn; but as she had only a woman's strength the same journey took her a much longer time, and it was the afternoon of the next day when she arrived. She too asked for a room, but the host assured her with many expressions of regret that he had not a single room vacant. The Countess pleaded her weariness; the man reiterated his inability to serve her.

"Give me only a room to rest a little while in," she begged; "just a couple of hours, and then I will start again and journey farther."

Really compassionating her in her fatigue, the man now said:

"If you will be satisfied with that much, I can give you a room for a couple of hours; but no more."

She was fain to be satisfied with that, as she could get no more, and the host showed her into her husband's room, which he would not want till "an hour of night."

By accident, however, the Count came in that night an hour earlier, and very much surprised he was to find a lady in his room. The Countess, equally surprised to see a stranger enter, pulled her veil over her face, so that they did not recognize each other.

"I am sorry to disturb you, madam, but this room, I must inform you, I have engaged," said the Count; but sorrow had so altered his voice that the Countess did not know it again.

"I hope you will spare me," replied the Countess. "They gave me this room to rest in for two hours, and I have come so long a way that I really need the rest."

"I can hardly believe that a lady of gentle condition can have come a very long way, all alone and on foot, for there is no carriage in the yard; so I can only consider this a frivolous pretext," replied the Count, for sorrow had embittered him.

"Indeed it is too true though," continued the Countess. "I came all the way from such a place (and she named his own town) without stopping for one moment's rest."

"Indeed!" said the Count, his interest roused at the mention of his own town; "and pray what need had you to use such haste to get away from that good town?"

"I had no need to haste to leave the place," replied the Countess, hurt at the implied suspicion that she was running away for shame. "I hasted to arrive at another place."

"And that other place was…?" persisted the Count, who felt that her intrusion on his privacy gave him a right to cross-question her.

The Countess was puzzled how to reply. She had no idea what place she was making for.

"*That* I don't know," she said at last, with no little embarrassment.

"You will permit me to say that you seem to have no adequate reason to allege for this unwarrantable occupation of my room; and what little you tell me certainly in no way inclines me to take a favourable view of the affair."

The Countess was once more stung by the manner in which he seemed to view her journey, and feeling bound to clear herself, she replied:

"If you only knew what my journey is about, you would not speak so!" and she burst into a flood of tears.

Softened by her distress, the Count said in a kinder tone:

"Had you been pleased to confide that to me at first, maybe I had not spoken so; but till you tell me what it is, what opinion can I form?"

"This is it," answered the Countess, still sobbing. "Yesterday I was the happiest woman on the face of the earth, living in love and confidence with the best husband with whom woman was ever blessed. So strong was my confidence that I hesitated not to trifle with this great happiness. My brother came home from the wars, a stranger to my husband. 'Let him see you kiss me,' I said, 'it will seem so strange that we will make him laugh heartily afterwards.' He saw him kiss me, but waited for no explanation. He went away without a word, as indeed (fool that I was) I well deserved, and I journey on till I overtake him."

The Count had risen to his feet, and had torn the veil from her face.

"It can be no other but my own!" he exclaimed, in a voice from which sorrow being banished his own tones sounded forth, and clasped her in his arms.

Religion & Magic

THE DIVERSITY OF supernatural creatures and the permeable borders between Catholicism and pre-Christian forms of magic are pervasive themes in Busk's volume. The Roman Rapunzel at the start of this section is held captive not by a witch, as in the Grimms' more famous version, but by an 'Orca' – a bewitched and powerful evil beast popular in Italian folklore. The two lovers are then aided in their escape by a fairy with the appearance of 'a little old woman'. The usually benevolent Roman fairies are not ethereal beings like their nineteenth-century British counterparts, but rather powerful enchantresses who may appear quite ordinary.

A pedagogically inclined fairy in this section has a queen and a tripe seller trade places for a while, so that each may better appreciate her own lot. Other benevolent supernatural creatures include numerous saints – none more generous with miracles than the beloved Philip Neri – and, of course, the Madonna, who first appears in one of the legends about the time when Jesus was still on earth that are so popular in European folklore. In this tale the Madonna is an enchantress. She curses a field of lupins so that, as they wither away and fall flat to the ground, she can ensure her baby's safety; eventually, she blesses the lupins back into life. On the opposite side of these benevolent creatures is the Devil. In one tale he comes to Earth, gets married and is so pestered by his wife that he prefers to go back to Hell, while in another he tries in vain to break up a happy couple. Like the Orca in the first tale, this Roman Devil is singularly ineffectual.

Filagranata

ONCE UPON A TIME there was a poor woman who had a great fancy for eating parsley. To her it was the greatest luxury, and as she had no garden of her own, and no money to spend on anything not an absolute necessity of life, she had to go about poaching in other people's gardens to satisfy her fancy.

Near her cottage was the garden of a great palace, and in this garden grew plenty of fine parsley; but the garden was surrounded by a wall, and to get at it she had to carry a ladder with her to get up by, and, as soon as she had reached the top of the wall, to let it down on the other side to get down to the parsley-bed. There was such a quantity of parsley growing here that she thought it would never be missed, and this made her bold, so that she went over every day and took as much as ever she liked.

But the garden belonged to a witch, who lived in the palace, and, though she did not often walk in this part of the garden, she knew by her supernatural powers that someone was eating her parsley; so she came near the place one day, and lay in wait till the poor woman came. As soon, therefore, as she came, and began eating the parsley, the witch at once pounced down, and asked her, in her gruff voice, what she was doing there. Though dreadfully frightened, the poor woman thought it best to own the whole truth; so she confessed that she came down by the ladder, adding that she had not taken anything except the parsley, and begged forgiveness.

"I know nothing about forgiveness," replied the witch. "You have eaten my parsley, and must take the consequences; and the consequences are these: I must be godmother to your first child, be it boy or girl; and as soon as it is grown to be of an age to dress itself without help, it must belong to me."

When, accordingly, the poor woman's first child was born, the witch came, as she had declared she would, to be its godmother. It was a fine little girl, and she gave it the name of Filagranata; after that she went away again, and the poor woman saw her no more till her little girl was grown up old enough to dress herself, and then she came and fetched her away inexorably; nor could the poor mother, with all her tears and entreaties, prevail on her to make any exchange for her child.

So Filagranata was taken to the witch's palace to live, and was put in a room in a little tower by herself, where she had to feed the pigeons. Filagranata grew fond of her pigeons, and did not at all complain of her work, yet, without knowing why, she began to grow quite sad and melancholy as time went by; it was because she had no one to play with, no one to talk to, except the witch, who was no very delightful companion. The witch came every day, once in the day, to see that she was attending properly to her work, and as there was no door or staircase to the tower – this was on purpose that she might not escape – the witch used to say when she came under the tower:

> *Filagranata, so fair, so fair,*
> *Unloose thy tresses of golden hair:*
> *I, thy old godmother, am here;*

and as she said these words, Filagranata had to let down her beautiful long hair through the window, and by it the witch climbed up into her chamber to her. This she did every day.

Now, it happened that about this time a king's son was travelling that way searching for a beautiful wife; for you know it is the custom for princes to go searching all over the world to find a maiden fit to be a prince's wife; at least they say so.

Well, this prince, travelling along, came by the witch's palace where Filagranata was lodged. And it happened that he came that way just as the witch was singing her ditty. If he was horrified at the sight of the witch, he was in proportion enchanted when Filagranata came to the window. So struck was he with the sight of her beauty, and modesty, and gentleness, that he stopped his horse that he might watch her as long as she stayed at the window, and thus became a spectator of the witch's wonderful way of getting into the tower.

The prince's mind was soon made up to gain a nearer view of Filagranata, and with this purpose he rode round and round the tower seeking some mode of ingress in vain, till at last, driven to desperation, he made up his mind that he must enter by the same strange means as the witch herself. Thinking that the old creature had her abode there, and that she would probably go out for some business in the morning, and return at about the same hour as on the present occasion, he rode away, commanding his impatience as well as he could, and came back the next day a little earlier.

Though he could hardly hope quite to imitate the hag's rough and tremulous voice so as to deceive Filagranata into thinking it was really the witch, he yet made the attempt and repeated the words he had heard:

> *Filagranata, thou maiden fair,*
> *Loose thy tresses of golden hair:*
> *I, thy old godmother, am here.*

Filagranata, surprised at the soft modulation of voice, such as she had never heard before, ran quickly to the window with a look of pleasure and astonishment which gave her face a more winning expression than ever.

The prince looked up, all admiration and expectation; and the thought quickly ran through Filagranata's head: "I have been taught to loose my hair whenever those words are said; why should not I loose it to draw up such a pleasant-looking cavalier, as well as for the ugly old hag?" And, without waiting for a second thought, she untied the ribbon that bound her tresses and let them fall upon the prince. The prince was equally quick in taking advantage of the occasion, and, pressing his knees firmly into his horse's flanks, so that it might not remain below to betray him, drew himself up, together with his steed, just as he had seen the witch do.

Filagranata, half frightened at what she had done the moment the deed was accomplished, had not a word to say, but blushed and hung her head. The prince, on the other hand, had so many words to pour out, expressive of his admiration for her, his indignation at her captivity, and his desire to be allowed to be her deliverer, that the moments flew quickly by, and it was only when Filagranata found herself drawn to the window by the power of the witch's magic words that they remembered the dangerous situation in which they stood.

Another might have increased the peril by cries of despair, or lost precious time in useless lamentations; but Filagranata showed a presence of mind worthy of a prince's wife by catching up a wand of the witch, with which she had seen her do wonderful things. With this she gave the prince a little tap, which immediately changed him into a pomegranate, and then another to the horse, which transformed him into an orange. These she set by on the shelf, and then proceeded to draw up the witch after the usual manner.

The old hag was not slow in perceiving there was something unusual in Filagranata's room.

"What a stink of Christians! What a stink of Christians!" she kept exclaiming, as she poked her nose into every hole and corner. Yet she failed to find anything to reprehend; for as for the beautiful ripe pomegranate and the golden orange on the shelf, the Devil himself could not have thought there was anything wrong with them. Thus baffled, she was obliged to finish her inspection of the state of the pigeons, and end her visit in the usual way.

As soon as she was gone Filagranata knew she was free till the next day, and so once more, with a tap of the wand, restored the horse and his rider to their natural shapes.

"And this is how your life passes every day! Is it possible?" exclaimed the prince. "No, I cannot leave you here. You may be sure my good horse will be proud to bear your little weight; you have only to mount behind me, and I will take you home to my kingdom, and you shall live in the palace with my mother, and be my queen."

It is not to be supposed but that Filagranata very much preferred the idea of going with the handsome young prince who had shown so devoted an appreciation of her, and being his queen, to remaining shut up in the doorless tower and being the witch's menial; so she offered no opposition, and the prince put her on to his good horse behind him, and away they rode.

On, on, on, they rode for a long, long way, until they came at last to a wood; but for all the good horse's speed, the witch, who was not long in perceiving their escape and setting out in pursuit, was well nigh overtaking them. Just then they saw a little old woman standing by the way, making signs and calling to them to arrest their course. How great soever was their anxiety to get on, so urgent was her appeal to them to stop and listen to her that they yielded to her entreaties. Nor were they losers by their kindness, for the little old woman was a fairy, and she had stopped them, not on her own account, but to give them the means of escaping from the witch.

To the prince she said: "Take these three gifts, and when the witch comes very near throw down first the mason's trowel; and when she nearly overtakes you again throw down the comb; and when she nearly comes upon you again after that, throw down this jar of oil. After that she won't trouble you anymore." And to Filagranata she whispered some words, and then let them go.

But the witch was now close behind, and the prince made haste to throw down the mason's trowel. Instantly there rose up a high stone wall between them, which it took the witch some time to climb over. Nevertheless, by her supernatural powers she was not long in making up for the lost time, and had soon overtaken the best speed of the good horse. Then the prince threw down the comb, and immediately there rose up between them a strong hedge of thorns, which it took the witch some time to make her way through, and that only with her body bleeding all over from the thorns. Nevertheless, by her supernatural powers she was not long in making up for the lost time, and had soon overtaken the best speed of the good horse. Then the prince threw down the jar of oil, and the oil spread and spread till it had overflowed the whole countryside; and as wherever you step in a pool of oil the foot only slides back, the witch could never get out of that, so the prince and Filagranata rode on in all safety towards the prince's palace.

"And now tell me what it was the old woman in the wood whispered to you," said the prince, as soon as they saw their safety sufficiently secured to breathe freely.

"It was this," answered Filagranata; "that I was to tell you that when you arrive at your own home you must kiss no one – no one at all, not your father, or mother, or sisters, or anyone – till after our marriage. Because if you do you will forget all about your love for me, and all you have told me you think of me, and all the faithfulness you have promised me, and we shall become as strangers again to each other."

"How dreadful!" said the prince. "Oh, you may be sure I will kiss no one if *that* is to be the consequence; so be quite easy. It will be rather odd, to be sure, to return from such a long journey and kiss none of them at home, not even my own mother; but I suppose if I tell them how it is they won't mind. So be quite easy about that."

Thus they rode on in love and confidence, and the good horse soon brought them home.

On the steps of the palace the chancellor of the kingdom came out to meet them, and saluted Filagranata as the chosen bride the prince was to bring home; he informed him that the king his father had died during his absence, and that he was now sovereign of the realm. Then he led him in to the queen-mother, to whom he told all his adventures, and explained why he must not kiss her till after his marriage.

The queen-mother was so pleased with the beauty, and modesty, and gentleness of Filagranata, that she gave up her son's kiss without repining, and before they retired to rest that night it was announced to the people that the prince had returned home to be their king, and the day was proclaimed when the feast for his marriage was to take place.

Then all in the palace went to their sleeping-chambers. But the prince, as it had been his wont from his childhood upwards, went into his mother's room to kiss her after she was asleep, and when he saw her placid brow on the pillow, with the soft white hair parted on either side of it, and the eyes which were wont to gaze on him with so much love, resting in sleep, he could not forbear from pressing his lips on her forehead and giving the wonted kiss.

Instantly there passed from his mind all that had taken place since he last stood there to take leave of the queen-mother before he started on his journey. His visit to the witch's palace, his flight from it, the life-perils by the way, and, what is more, the image of Filagranata herself – all passed from his mind like a vision of the night, and when he woke up and they told him he was king, it was as if he heard it for the first time, and when they brought Filagranata to him it was as though he knew her not nor saw her.

"But," he said, "if I am king there must be a queen to share my throne;" and as a reigning sovereign could not go over the world to seek a wife, he sent and fetched him a princess meet to be the king's wife, and appointed the betrothal. The queen-mother, who loved Filagranata, was sad, and yet nothing that she could say could bring back to his mind the least remembrance of all he had promised her and felt towards her.

But Filagranata knew that the prince had kissed his mother, and this was why the spell was on him; so she said to her mother-in-law: "You get me much fine-sifted flour and a large bag of sweetmeats, and I will try if I cannot yet set this matter straight." So the queen-mother ordered that there should be placed in her room much sifted flour and a large bag of sweetmeats. And Filagranata, when she had shut close the door, set to work and made paste of the flour, and of the paste she moulded two pigeons, and filled them inside with the comfits.

Then at the banquet of the betrothal she asked the queen-mother to have her two pigeons placed on the table; and she did so, one at each end. But as soon as all the company were seated, before anyone was helped, the two pigeons which Filagranata had made began to talk to each other across the whole length of the table: and everybody stood still with wonder to listen to what the pigeons of paste said to each other.

"Do you remember," said the first pigeon, "or is it possible that you have really forgotten, when I was in that doorless tower of the witch's palace, and you came under the window and imitated her voice, saying,

> *Filagranata, thou maiden fair,*
> *Loose thy tresses of golden hair:*
> *I, thy old godmother, am here,*

till I drew you up?"

And the other pigeon answered:

"Si, signora, I remember it now."

And as the young king heard the second pigeon say "Si, signora, I remember it now," he, too, remembered having been in a doorless tower, and having sung such a verse.

"Do you remember," continued the first pigeon, "how happy we were together after I drew you up into that little room where I was confined, and you swore if I would come with you we should always be together and never be separated from each other anymore at all?"

And the second pigeon replied:

"Ah yes! I remember it now."

And as the second pigeon said, "Ah yes! I remember it now," there rose up in the young king's mind the memory of a fair sweet face on which he had once gazed with loving eyes, and of a maiden to whom he had sworn lifelong devotion.

But the first pigeon continued:

"Do you remember, or have you quite forgotten, how we fled away together, and how frightened we were when the witch pursued us, and how we clung to each other, and vowed, if she overtook us to kill us, we would die in each other's arms, till a fairy met us and gave us the means to escape, and forbade you to kiss anyone, even your own mother, till after our marriage?"

And the second pigeon answered:

"Yes, ah yes! I remember it now."

And when the second pigeon said, "Yes, ah yes! I remember it now," the whole of the past came back to his mind, and with it all his love for Filagranata. So he rose up and would have stroked the pigeons which had brought it all to his mind, but when he touched them they melted away, and the sweetmeats were scattered all over the table, and the guests picked them up. But the prince ran in haste to fetch Filagranata, and he brought her and placed her by his side in the banquet-hall. But the second bride was sent back, with presents, to her own people.

"And so it all came right at last," pursued the narrator. "Lackaday! that there are no fairies now to make things all happen right. There are plenty of people who seem to have the devil in them for doing you a mischief, but there are no fairies to set things straight again, alas."

When Jesus Christ Wandered on Earth

1

ONE DAY THE MADONNA was carrying the Bambino through a lupin-field, and the stalks of the lupins rustled so that she thought it was a robber coming to kill the Santo Bambino. She turned, and sent a malediction over the lupin-field, and immediately the lupins all withered away and fell flat and dry on the ground, so that she could see there was no one hidden there. When she saw there was no one hidden there, she sent a benediction over the lupin-field, and the lupins all stood up straight again, fair and flourishing, and with tenfold greater produce than they had at the first.

2

One day when Jesus Christ was grown up, and went about preaching, He came to a certain village and knocked at the first door, and said, "Give me a lodging." But the master of the house shut the door in his face, saying, "Here is nothing for you." He came to the next house, and received the same answer; and the next, and the next, no one in all the village would take Him in. Weary and footsore, He came to the cottage of a poor little old woman, who lived all alone on the outskirts, and knocked there. "Who is there?" asked the old woman. "The Master with the Apostles," answered Jesus Christ. The old woman opened the door, and let them all in. "Have you no fire?" asked Jesus Christ. "No fire have I," answered the old woman. Then Jesus Christ blessed the hearth, and there came a pile of wood on it, and a fire was soon made. "Have you nothing to give us to eat?" asked Jesus Christ. "Nothing worth offering you," answered the old woman; "here is a little fish" (it was a little fish, that, not so long as my hand) "and some crusts of bread, which they gave me at the eating-shop in charity just now, and that's all I have;" and she set both on the table. "Have you no wine?" again asked Jesus Christ. "Only this flask of wine and water they gave me there, too;" and she set it before Him.

Then Jesus Christ blessed all the things, and handed them round the table, and they all dined off them, and at the end there remained just the same as at the beginning. When they had finished, He said to the old woman, "This fire, with the bread, and the fish, and the wine, will always remain to you, and never diminish as long as you live. And now follow Me a little way."

The Master went on before with His Apostles, and the old woman followed after, a little way behind. And behold, as they walked along, all the houses of that inhospitable village fell down one after the other, and all the inhabitants were buried under them. Only the cottage of the old woman was left standing. When the judgment was complete, Jesus Christ said to her, "Now, return home."

As she turned to go, St. Peter said to her, "Ask for the salvation of your soul." And she went and asked it of Jesus Christ, and He replied, "Let it be granted you!"

3

One day as He was going into the Temple, He saw two men quarrelling before the door: a young man and an old man. The young man wanted to go in first, and the old man was vindicating the honour of his grey hairs.

"What is the matter?" asked Jesus Christ; and they showed Him wherefore they strove.

Jesus Christ said to the young man, "If you are desirous to go in first, you must accept the state to which honour belongs," and He touched him, and he became an old man, bowed in gait, feeble and grey-haired, while to the old man He gave the compensation for the insult he had received by investing him with the youth of the other.

4

In the days when Jesus Christ roamed the earth, He found Himself one day with His disciples in the Campagna, far from anything like home.

The only shelter in sight was a cottage of wretched aspect. Jesus Christ knocked at the door.

"Who is there?" said a tremulous voice from within.

"The Master with the disciples," answered Jesus Christ. The man didn't know what He meant; nevertheless, the tone was too gentle to inspire fear, so he opened, and let them all in.

"Have you no fire to give us?" asked Jesus Christ.

"I'm only a poor beggar. I never have any fire," said the man.

"But these poor things," said Jesus Christ, "are stiff with cold and weariness; they must have a fire."

Then Jesus Christ stood on the hearth, and blessed it, and there came a great blazing fire of heaped-up wood. When the beggar saw it, he fell on his knees in astonishment.

"Have you no food to set before us?" asked Jesus Christ.

"I have one loaf of Indian corn, which is at your service," answered the beggar.

"One loaf is not enough," answered Jesus Christ; "have you nothing else at all?"

"Nothing at all about the place that can be eaten," answered the beggar. "Leastwise, I have one ewe, which is at your service."

"That will do," answered Jesus Christ; and he sent St. Peter to help the man to prepare it for dressing.

"Here is the mutton," said the beggar; "but I cannot cook it, because I have no lard."

"Look!" said Jesus Christ.

The beggar looked on the hearth, and saw everything that was necessary ready for use.

"Now, then, bring the wine and the bread," said Jesus Christ, when the meat was nearly ready.

"There is the only loaf I have," said the beggar, setting the polenta loaf on the table; "but, as for wine, I never see such a thing."

"Is there none in the cellar?" asked Jesus Christ.

"In the cellar are only a dozen empty old broken wine-jars that have been there these hundred years; they are well covered with mould." Jesus Christ told St. Peter to go down and see, and when he went down with the beggar, there was a whole ovenful of fresh-baked bread boiling hot, and beyond, in the cellar, the jars, instead of being broken and musty, were all standing whole and upright, and filled with excellent wine.

"See how you told us falsely," said St. Peter, to tease him.

"Upon my word, it was even as I said, before you came."

"Then it is the Master who has done these wonderful things," answered St. Peter. "Praise Him!"

Now the meat was cooked and ready, and they all sat down to table; but Jesus Christ took a bowl and placed it in the midst of the table and said, "Let all the bones be put into this bowl;" and when they had finished he took the bones and threw them out of the window, and said, "Behold, I give you a hundred for one." After that they all laid them down and slept.

In the morning when they opened the door to go, behold there were a hundred sheep grazing before the door.

"These sheep are yours," said Jesus Christ; "moreover, as long as you live, neither the bread in the oven nor the wine in the cellar shall fail;" and He passed out and the disciples after Him.

But St. Peter remained behind, and said to the man who had entertained them, "The Master has rewarded you generously, but He has one greater gift yet which He will give you if you ask Him."

"What is it? Tell me, what is it?" said the beggar.

"The salvation of your soul," answered St. Peter.

"Signore! Signore! add to all Thou hast given this further, the salvation of my soul," cried the man.

"Let it be granted thee," answered the Lord, and passed on His way.

5

Another day Jesus Christ and His disciples dined at a tavern.

"What's to pay?" said Jesus Christ, when they had finished their meal.

"Nothing at all," answered the host.

But the host had a little hunchback son, who said to him, "I know some have found it answer to give these people food instead of making them pay for it; but suppose they forget to give us anything, we shall be worse off than if we had been paid in the regular way. I will tell you what I'll do now, so as to have a hold over them. I'll take one of our silver spoons and put it in the bag that one of them carries, and accuse them of stealing it."

Now St. Peter was a great eater, and when anything was left over from a good meal he was wont to put it by in a bag against a day when they had nothing. Into this bag therefore the hunchback put the silver spoon.

When they had gone on a little way the young hunchback ran after them and said to Jesus Christ,—

"Signore! one of these with you has stolen a spoon from us."

"You are mistaken, friend; there is not one of them who would do such a thing."

"Yes," persevered the hunchback; "it is *that* one who took it," and he pointed to St. Peter.

"I!" said St. Peter, getting very angry. "How dare you to say such a thing of me!"

But Jesus Christ made him a sign that he should keep silence.

"We will go back to your house and help you to look for what you have lost, for that none of us have taken the spoon is most certain," He said; and He went back with the hunchback.

"There is nowhere to search," answered the hunchback, "but in that man's bag; I know it is there, because I saw him take it."

"Then there's my bag inside out," said St. Peter, as he cast the contents upon the floor. Of course the silver spoon fell clattering upon the bricks.

"There!" said the hunchback, insolently. "Didn't I tell you it was there? You said it wasn't!"

St. Peter was so angry he could not trust himself to speak; but Jesus Christ answered for him:

"Nay, I said not it was not there, but that none of these had taken it. And now we will see who it was put it there." With that He motioned to them all to stand back, while He, standing in the midst and raising his eyes to Heaven, said solemnly,

"Let whoso put it in the bag be turned to stone!"

Even as He spoke the hunchback was turned into stone.

6

There was another tavern, however, where the host was a different sort of man, and not only *said* he would take nothing when Jesus Christ and His disciples dined there, but really would never take anything; nor was it that by any miracle he had received advantages of another sort, but out of the respect and affection he bore the Master he deemed himself sufficiently paid by the honour of being allowed to minister to Him.

One day when Jesus Christ and His disciples were going away on a journey, St. Peter went to this host and said, "You have been very liberal to us all this time: if you were to ask for some gift, now, you would be sure to get it."

"I don't know that there is anything that I want," said the host. "I have a thriving trade, which you see not only supplies all my wants, but leaves me the means of being liberal also; I have no wife to provide for, and no children to leave an inheritance to: so what should I ask for? There is one thing, to be sure, I should like. My only amusement is playing at cards: if He would give me the faculty of always winning, I should like that; it isn't that I care for what one wins, it is that it is nice to win. Do you think I might ask *that*?"

"I don't know," said St. Peter, gravely. "Still you might ask; He is very kind."

The host did ask, and Jesus Christ granted his desire. When St. Peter saw how easily He granted it, he said, 'If I were you, I should ask something more.'

"I really don't know what else I have to ask," replied the host, "unless it be that I have a fig-tree which bears excellent figs, but I never can get one of them for myself; they are always stolen before I get them. I wish He would order that whoever goes up to steal them might get stuck to the tree till I tell him he may come down."

"Well," said St. Peter, "it is an odd sort of thing to ask, but you might try; He is very kind."

The host did ask, and Jesus Christ granted his request. When St. Peter saw that He granted it so easily, he said, "If I were you I should ask something more."

"Do you really think I might?" answered the host. "There is one thing I have wanted to ask all along, only I didn't dare. But you encourage me, and He seems to take a pleasure in giving. I have always had a great wish to live four hundred years."

"That is certainly a great deal to ask," said St. Peter, "but you might try; He is very kind."

The host did ask, and Jesus Christ granted his petition, and then went His way with His disciples. St. Peter remained last, and said to the host, "Now run after him, and ask for the salvation of your soul." ("St. Peter always told them all to ask that," added the narrator in a confidential tone.)

"Oh, I can't ask anything more, I have asked so much," said the host.

"But that is just the best thing of all, and what He grants the most willingly," insisted St. Peter.

"Really?" said the host; and he ran after Jesus Christ, and said, "Lord! who hast so largely shown me Thy bounty, grant me further the salvation of my soul."

"Let it be granted!" said Jesus Christ; and continued His journey.

All the things the host had asked he received, and life passed away very pleasantly, but still even four hundred years come to an end at last, and with the end of it came Death.

"What! is that you, Mrs. Death, come already?" said the host.

"Why, it's time I should come, I think; it's not often I leave people in peace for four hundred years."

"All right, but don't be in a hurry. I have such a fancy for the figs of that fig-tree of mine there. I wish you would just have the kindness to go up and pluck a good provision of them to take with me, and by that time I'll be ready to go with you."

"I've no objection to oblige you so far," said Mrs. Death; "only you must mind and be quite ready by the time I do come back."

"Never fear," said the host; and Mrs. Death climbed up the fig-tree.

"Now stick there!" said the host, and for all her struggling Mrs. Death could by no means extricate herself any more.

"I can't stay here, so take off your spell; I have my business to attend to," said she.

"So have I," answered the host; "and if you want to go about your business, you must promise me, on your honour, you will leave me to attend to mine."

"I can't do it, my man! What are you asking? It's more than my place is worth. Every man alive has to pass through my hands. I can't let any of them off."

"Well, at all events, leave me alone another four hundred years, and then I'll come with you. If you'll promise that, I'll let you out of the fig-tree."

"I don't mind another four hundred years, if you so particularly wish for them; but mind you give me your word of honour you come then, without giving me all this trouble again."

"Yes! and here's my hand upon it," said the host, as he handed Mrs. Death down from the fig-tree.

And so he went on to live another four hundred years. ("For you know in those times men lived to a very great age," was the running gloss of the narrator.)

The end of the second four hundred years came too, and then Mrs. Death appeared again. "Remember your promise," she said, "and don't try any trick on me this time."

"Oh, yes! I always keep my word," said the host, and without more ado he went along with her.

As she was carrying him up to Paradise, they passed the way which led down to Hell, and at the opening sat the Devil, receiving souls which his ministers brought to him from all parts. He was marshalling them into ranks, and ticketing them ready to send off in batches to the distinct place for each.

"You seem to have got plenty of souls there, Mr. Devil," said the host. "Suppose we sit down and play for them?"

"I've no objection," said the Devil. "Your soul against one of these. If I win, you go with them; if you win, one of them goes with you."

"That's it," said the host, and picking out a nice-looking soul, he set him for the Devil's stake.

Of course the host won, and the nice-looking soul was passed round to his side of the table.

"Shall we have another game?" said the host, quite cock-a-hoop.

The Devil hesitated for a moment, but finally he yielded. The host picked out a soul that took his fancy, for the Devil's stake, and they sat down to play again, with the same result.

So they went on and on till the host had won fifteen thousand souls of the Devil. "Come," said Death when they had got as far as this, "I really can't wait any longer. I never had to do with anyone who took up so much time as you. Come along!"

So the host bowed excuses to the Devil for having had all the luck, and went cheerfully the way Mrs. Death led, with all his fifteen thousand souls behind him. Thus they arrived at the gate of Paradise. There wasn't so much business going on there as at the other place, and they had to rig before anyone appeared to open the door.

"Who's there?" said St. Peter.

"He of the four hundred years!"

"And what is all that rabble behind?" asked St. Peter.

"Souls that I have won of the Devil for Paradise," answered the host.

"Oh, that won't do at all, here!" said St. Peter.

"Be kind enough to carry the message up to your Master," responded the host.

St. Peter went up to Jesus Christ. "Here is he to whom you gave four hundred years of life," he said; "and he has brought fifteen thousand other souls, who have no title at all to Paradise, with him."

"Tell him he may come in himself," said Jesus Christ, "but he has nothing to do to meddle with the others."

"Tell Him to be pleased to remember that when He came to my eating-shop I never made any difficulty how many soever He brought with Him, and if He had brought an army I should have said nothing," answered the host; and St. Peter took up that message too.

"That is true! That is right!" answered Jesus Christ. "Let them all in! Let them all in!"

7: Pret' Olivo

When Jesus Christ was on earth, He lodged one night at a priest's house, and when He went away in the morning He offered to give His host, in reward for his hospitality, whatever he asked. What Pret' Olivo (for that was his host's name) asked for was that he should live a hundred years, and that when Death came to fetch him he should be able to give her what orders he pleased, and that she must obey him.

"Let it be granted!" said Jesus Christ.

A hundred years passed away, and then, one morning early, Death came.

"Pret' Olivo! Pret' Olivo!" cried Death. "Are you ready? I'm come for you at last."

"Let me say my mass first," said Pret' Olivo; "that's all."

"Well, I don't mind that," answered Death; "only mind it isn't a long one, because I've got so many people to fetch today."

"A mass is a mass," answered Pret' Olivo; "it will be neither longer nor shorter."

As he went out, however, he told his servant to heap up a lot of wood on the hearth and set fire to it. Death went to sit down on a bench in the far corner of the chimney, and by-and-by the wood blazed up and she couldn't get away anymore. In vain she called to the servant to come and moderate the fire. "Master told me to heap it up, not to moderate it," answered the servant; and so there was no help. Death continued calling in desperation, and nobody came. It was impossible with her dry bones to pass the blaze, so there she had to stay.

"Oh, dear! oh, dear! What can I do?" she kept saying. "All this time everybody is stopped dying! Pret' Olivo! Pret' Olivo! Come here."

At last Pret' Olivo came in.

"What do you mean by keeping me here like this?" said Death; "I told you I had so much to do."

"Oh, you want to go, do you?" said Pret' Olivo, quietly.

"Of course I do. Tell someone to clear away those burning logs, and let me out."

"Will you promise me to leave me alone for another hundred years if I do?"

"Yes, yes; anything you like. I shall be very glad to keep away from this place for a hundred years."

Then he let her go, and she set off running with those long thin legs of hers.

The second hundred years came to an end.

"Are you ready, Pret' Olivo?" said Death one morning, putting her head in at the door.

"Pretty nearly," answered Pret' Olivo. "Meantime, just take that basket, and gather me a couple of figs to eat before I go."

As she went away he said, "Stick to the tree" (but not so that she could hear it); for you remember he had power given him to make her do what he liked. She had therefore to stick to the tree.

"Well, Lady Death, are you never going to bring those figs?" cried Pret' Olivo after a time.

"How can I bring them, when you know I can't get down from this tree? Instead of making game of me, come and take me down."

"Will you leave me alone another hundred years if I do?"

"Yes, yes; anything you like. Only make haste and let me go."

The third hundred years came to an end, and Death appeared again. "Are you ready this time, Pret' Olivo?" she cried out as she approached.

"Yes, this time I'll come with you," answered Pret' Olivo. Then he vested himself in the Church vestments, and put a cope on, and took a pack of cards in his hand, and said to Death, "Now take me to the gate of Hell, for I want to play a game of cards with the Devil."

"Nonsense!" answered Death. "I'm not going to waste my time like that. I've got orders to take you to Paradise, and to Paradise you must go."

"You know you've got orders to obey whatever I tell you," answered Pret' Olivo; and Death knew that was true, so she lost no more time in disputing, but took him all the way round by the gate of Hell.

At the gate of Hell they knocked.

"Who's there?" said the Devil.

"Pret' Olivo," replied Death.

"Out with you, ugly priest!" said the Devil. "I'm surprised at you, Death, making game of me like that; you know that's not the sort of ware for my market."

"Silence, and open the door, ugly Pluto! I'm not come to stay. I only want to have a game of cards with you. Here's my soul for stake on my side, against the last comer on your side," interposed Pret' Olivo.

Pret' Olivo won the game, and hung the soul on to his cope.

"We must have another game," said the Devil.

"With all my heart!" replied Pret' Olivo; and he won another soul. Another and another he won, and his cope was covered all over with the souls clinging to it.

Meantime, Death thought it was going on rather too long, so she looked through the keyhole, and, finding they were just beginning another game, she cried out loudly;

"It's no use playing anymore, for I'm not going to be bothered to carry all those souls all the way up to Heaven – a likely matter, indeed!"

But Pret' Olivo went on playing without taking any notice of her; and he hung them on to his beretta, till at last you could hardly see him at all for the number of souls he had clinging to him. There was no place for any more, so at last he stopped playing.

"I'm not going to take all those other souls," said Death when he came out; "I've only got orders to take you."

"Then take me," answered Pret' Olivo.

Death saw that the souls were all hung on so that she could not take him without taking all the rest; so away she went with the lot of them, without disputing any more.

At last they arrived at the Gate of Paradise. St. Peter opened the door when they knocked; but when he saw who was there he shut the door again.

"Make haste!" said Death; "I've no time to waste."

"Why did you waste your time in bringing up souls that were not properly consigned to you?" answered St. Peter.

"It wasn't I brought them, it was Pret' Olivo. And your Master charged me I was to do whatever he told me."

"My Master! Oh, then, I'm out of it," said St. Peter. "Only wait a minute, while I just go and ask Him whether it is so." St. Peter ran to ask; and receiving an affirmative answer, came back and opened the gate, and they all got in.

8: Domine Quoe Vadis

"You know, of course, about St. Peter, when they put him in the prisons here; he found a way of escaping through the 'catacomboli', and just as he had got out into the open road again he met Jesus Christ coming towards him carrying His cross. And St. Peter asked Him what he was doing going into the 'catacomboli'. But Jesus Christ answered, 'I am not going into the "catacomboli" to stay; I am going back by the way you came to be crucified over again, since you refuse to die for the flock.' Then St. Peter turned and went all the way back, and was crucified with his head downwards, for he said he was not worthy to die in the same way as his Master."

"Lord Jesus Christ and St. Peter went in the morning out.
As Our Lady went on before she said (turning about),
'Ah, dear Lord! whither must we go in and out?
We must over hill and dale (roundabout).
May God guard the while my flock (devout).
Let not St. Peter go his keys without;
But take them and lock up the wild dogs' snout,
That they no bone of them all may flout.'"

Nun Beatrice

℧

NUN BEATRICE HAD NOT altogether the true spirit of a religious: she was somewhat given to vanity; though but for this she was a good nun, and full of excellent dispositions. She held the office of portress; and, as she determined to go away out of her convent and return into the world, this seemed to afford her a favourable opportunity for carrying out her design. Accordingly, one day when the house was very quiet, and there seemed no danger of being observed, having previously

contrived to secrete some secular clothes such as passed through her hands to keep in store for giving to the poor, she let herself out and went away.

In the parlour was a kneeling-desk with a picture of Our Lady hanging over it, where she had been wont to kneel and hold converse with Our Lady in prayer whenever she had a moment to spare. On this desk she laid the keys before she went, thinking it was a safe place for the Superior to find them; and she commended them to the care of Our Lady, whose picture hung above, and said, "Keep thou the keys, and let no harm come to this good house and my dear sisters."

As she said the words Our Lady looked at her with a glance of reproach, enough to have melted her heart and made her return to a better mood had she seen it; but she was too full of her own thoughts and the excitement of her undertaking to notice anything. No sooner was she gone out, however, than Our Lady, walking out of the canvas, assumed the dress that she had laid aside, and, tying the keys to her girdle, assumed the office of portress.

With the habit of the portress Our Lady also assumed her semblance; so that no one noticed the exchange, except that all remarked how humble, how modest, how edifying Beatrice had become.

After a time the nuns began to say it was a pity so perfect a nun should be left in so subordinate a position, and they made her therefore Mistress of the Novices. This office she exercised with as great perfection, according to its requirements, as she had the other; and so sweetly did she train the young nuns entrusted to her direction that all the novices became saints.

Beatrice meantime had gone to live in the world as a secular; and though she often repented of what she had done, she had not the courage to go back and tell all. She prayed for courage, but she went on delaying. While she was in this mind it so happened one day that the factor of the convent came to the house where she was living. What strange and moving memories of her peaceful home filled her mind as she saw his well-known form, though he did not recognize her in her secular dress! What an opportunity too, she thought, to learn what was the feeling of the community towards her, and what had been said of her escape!

"I hope all your nuns are well," she said. "I used to live in their neighbourhood once, and there was one of them I used to know, Suora Beatrice. How is she now?"

"Sister Beatrice!" said the factor. "She is the model of perfection, the example of the whole house. Everybody is ready to worship her. With all respect to the Church, which never canonizes the living, no one doubts she is a saint indeed."

"It cannot be the same," answered Beatrice. "The one I knew was anything but a saint, though I loved her well, and should like to have news of her." And she hardly knew how to conceal the astonishment with which she was seized at hearing him speak thus; for the event on which she expected him to enlarge at once was the extraordinary fact of her escape. But he pursued in the same quiet way as before.

"Oh yes, it must be the same. There has never been but one of the name since I have known the convent. She was portress some time ago; but latterly she has been made Mistress of the Novices."

There was nothing more to be learnt from him; so she pursued her enquiries no further. But he had no sooner had start enough to put him at a safe distance than she set out to go to the convent and see this Sister Beatrice who so strangely represented her.

Arrived at the convent door, she asked to see Sister Beatrice, and in a very few minutes the Mistress of the Novices entered the parlour.

The presence of the new Mistress of the Novices filled Beatrice with an awe she could not account for; and, without waiting to ask herself why, she fell on her knees before her.

"It is well you have come back, my child," said Our Lady; "resume your dress, which I have worn for you; go in to the convent again, and do penance, and keep up the good name I have earned for you."

With that Our Lady returned to the canvas; Beatrice resumed her habit, and strove so earnestly to form herself by the model of perfection Our Lady had set while wearing it that in a few months she became a saint.

The Queen and the Tripe-Seller

🎵

T HEY SAY THERE WAS a queen who had such a bad temper that she made everybody about her miserable. Whatever her husband might do to please her, she was always discontented, and as for her maids she was always slapping their faces.

There was a fairy who saw all this, and she said to herself, "This must not be allowed to go on;" so she went and called another fairy, and said, "What shall we do to teach this naughty queen to behave herself?" and they could not imagine what to do with her; so they agreed to think it over, and meet again another day.

When they met again, the first fairy said to the other, "Well, have you found any plan for correcting this naughty queen?"

"Yes," replied the second fairy; "I have found an excellent plan. I have been up and all over the whole town, and in a dirty little back lane I have found a tripe-seller as like to this queen as two peas."

"Excellent!" exclaimed the first fairy. "I see what you mean to do. One of us will take some of the queen's clothes and dress up the tripe-seller, and the other will take some of the tripe-seller's clothes and dress up the queen in them, and then we will exchange them till the queen learns better manners."

"That's the plan," replied the second fairy. "You have said it exactly. When shall we begin?"

"This very night," said the first fairy.

"Agreed!" said the second fairy; and that very night, while everyone else was gone quietly to bed they went, one into the palace and fetched some of the queen's clothes, and, bringing them to the tripe-seller's room, placed them by the side of her bed; and the other went to the tripe-seller's room and fetched her clothes, and took them and put them by the side of the queen's bed. They also woke them very early, and when each got up she put on the things that were by the side of the bed, thinking they were the things she had left there the night before. Thus the queen was dressed like a tripe-seller, and the tripe-seller like a queen.

Then one fairy took the queen, dressed like a tripe-seller, and put her down in the tripe-seller's shop, and the other fairy took the tripe-seller, dressed like a queen, and placed her in the palace, and both of them did their work so swiftly that neither the queen nor the tripe-seller perceived the flight at all.

The queen was very much astonished at finding herself in a tripe-shop, and began staring about, wondering how she got there.

"Here! Don't stand gaping about like that!" cried the tripe-man, who was a very hot-tempered fellow; "Why, you haven't boiled the coffee!"

"Boiled the coffee!" repeated the queen, hardly apprehending what he meant.

"Yes; you haven't boiled the coffee!" said the tripe-man. "Don't repeat my words, but do your work!" and he took her by the shoulders, put the coffee-pot in her hand, and stood over her looking so fierce that she was frightened into doing what she had never done or seen done in all her life before.

Presently the coffee began to boil over.

"There! Don't waste all the coffee like that!" cried the tripe-man, and he got up and gave her a slap, which made the tears come in her eyes.

"Don't blubber!" said the tripe-man; "but bring the coffee here and pour it out."

The queen did as she was told; but when she began to drink it, though she had made it herself, it was so nasty she didn't know how to drink it. It was very different stuff from what she got at the palace; but the tripe-man had his eye on her, and she didn't dare not to drink it.

"A halfp'th of cat's-meat!" sang out a small boy in the shop.

"Why don't you go and serve the customer?" said the tripe-man, knocking the cup out of the queen's hand.

Fearing another slap, she rose hastily to give the boy what he wanted, but not knowing one thing in the shop from another, she gave him a large piece of the best tripe fit for a prince.

"Oh, what fine tripe today!" cried the small boy, and ran away as fast as he could.

It was in vain the tripe-man hallooed after him, he was in too great a hurry to secure his prize to think of returning.

"Look what you've done!" cried the tripe-man, giving the queen another slap; "you've given that boy for a penny a bunch of tripe worth a shilling." Luckily, other customers came in and diverted the man's attention.

Presently all the tripe hanging up had been sold, and more customers kept coming in.

"What has come to you today?" roared the tripe-man, as the queen stood not knowing what to do with herself. "Do you mean to say you haven't washed that other lot of tripe?" And this time he gave her a kick.

To escape his fury, the queen turned to do her best with washing the other tripe, but she did it so awkwardly that she got a volley of abuse and blows too.

Then came dinnertime, and nothing prepared, or even bought to prepare, for dinner. Another stormy scene ensued at the discovery, and the tripe-man went to dine at the inn, leaving her to go without any dinner at all, in punishment for having neglected to prepare it.

While he was gone she helped all the customers to the wrong things, and, when he came home, got another scolding and more blows for her stupidity. And all through the afternoon it was the same story.

But the tripe-seller, when she found herself all in a palace, with half a dozen maids waiting to attend her, was equally bewildered. When they kept asking her if there was nothing she pleased to want, she kept answering, "No thank you," in such a gentle tone, the maids began to think that a reign of peace had come to them at last.

By and by, when the ladies came, instead of saying, as the queen had been wont, "What an ugly dress you have got; go and take it off!" she said, "How nice you look; how tasteful your dress is!"

Afterwards the king came in, bringing her a rare nosegay. Instead of throwing it on one side to vex him, as the queen had been wont, she showed so much delight, and expressed her thanks so many times, that he was quite overcome.

The change that had come over the queen soon became the talk of the whole palace, and everyone congratulated himself on an improvement which made them all happy. The king was no less pleased than all the rest, and for the first time for many years he said he would drive out with the queen; for on account of her bad temper he had long given up driving with her. So the carriage came round with four prancing horses, and an escort of cavalry to ride before and behind it. The tripe-seller hardly could believe she was to drive in this splendid carriage, but the king handed her in before she knew where she was. Then, as he was so pleased with her gentle and grateful ways, he further asked her to say which way she would like to drive.

The tripe-seller, partly because she was too much frightened to think of any other place, and partly because she thought it would be nice to drive in state through her own neighbourhood, named the broader street out of which turned the lane in which she lived, for the royal carriage could hardly have turned down the lane itself. The king repeated the order, and away drove the royal cortège.

The circumstance of the king and queen driving out together was sufficient to excite the attention of the whole population, and wherever they passed the people crowded into the streets; thus a volley of shouts and comments ran before the carriage towards the lane of the tripe-man. The tripe-man was at the moment engaged in administering a severe chastisement to the queen for her latest mistake, and the roar of the people's voices afforded a happy pretext for breaking away from him.

She ran with the rest to the opening of the lane just as the royal carriage was passing.

"My husband! my husband!" she screamed as the king drove by, and plaintive as was her voice, and different from her usual imperious tone, he heard it and turned his head towards her.

"My husband! my royal husband!" pleaded the humbled queen.

The king, in amazement, stopped the carriage and gazed from the queen in the gutter to the tripe-seller in royal array by his side, unable to solve the problem.

"This is certainly my wife!" he said at last, as he extended his hand to the queen. "Who then can you be?" he added, addressing the tripe-seller.

"I will tell the truth," replied the good tripe-seller. "I am no queen; I am the poor wife of the tripe-seller down the lane there; but how I came into the palace is more than I can say."

"And how come you here?" said the king, addressing the real queen.

"That, neither can I tell; I thought you had sent me hither to punish me for my bad temper; but if you will only take me back I will never be bad-tempered again; only take me away from this dreadful tripe-man, who has been beating me all day."

Then the king made answer: "Of course you must come back with me, for you are my wife. But," he said to the tripe-seller; "what shall I do with you? After you have been living in luxury in the palace, you will feel it hard to go back to sell tripe."

"It's true I have not many luxuries at home," answered the tripe-seller; "but yet I had rather be with my husband than in any palace in the world;" and she descended from the carriage, while the queen got in.

"Stop!" said the king. "This day's transformation, howsoever it was brought about, has been a good day, and you have been so well behaved, and so truth-spoken, I don't like your going back to be beaten by the tripe-man."

"Oh, never mind that," said the good wife; "he never beats me unless I do something very stupid. And, after all, he's my husband, and that's enough for me."

"Well, if you're satisfied, I won't interfere any further," said the king; "except to give you some mark of my royal favour."

So he bestowed on the tripe-man and his wife a beautiful villa, with a nice casino outside the gates, on condition that he never beat her anymore.

The tripe-man was so pleased with the gifts which had come to him through his wife's good conduct that he kept his word, and was always thereafter very kind to her. And the queen was so frightened at the thought that she might find herself suddenly transformed into a tripe-seller again that she kept a strict guard over her temper, and became the delight of her husband and the whole court.

The Penance of San Giuliano

🎵

"CAN YOU TELL ME the story of San Giovanni Bocca d'oro?"
"Of course I know about San Giovanni Bocca d'oro, that is, I know he was a great penitent, but I couldn't remember anything, not to tell you about him. But I know about another great penitent. Do you know about the Penitence of San Giuliano? That is a story you'll like if you don't know it already; but it's not a favola, mind."

"I know there are seven or eight saints at least of the name of Julian, but I don't know the acts of them all; so pray tell me your story."

"Here it is then.

"San Giuliano was the only son of his parents, who lived at Albano. In his youth he was rather wild, and gave his parents some anxiety; but what gave them more anxiety still on his account was that an astrologer had predicted that when he grew up he should kill both his parents.

"'It is not only for our lives,' said the parents, 'that we should be concerned – that is no such great matter; but we must put him out of the way of committing so great a crime.'

"Therefore they gave him a horse, and his portion of money, and told him to ride forth and make himself a home in another place. So San Giuliano went forth; and thirty years passed, and his parents heard no more of him. Thirty years is a long time; many things pass out of mind in thirty years. Thus the astrologer's prediction passed out of their minds; but what never passes out of the mind of a mother is the love of her child, and the mother of San Giuliano yearned to see him after thirty years as though he had gone away but yesterday.

"One day when they were walking in the woods about Albano they saw a little boy come and climb into a tree and take a bird's nest; and presently, after the little boy was gone away with the nest, the parent birds came back and fluttered all about, and uttered piercing cries for the loss of their young.

"'See!' said San Giuliano's mother, taking occasion by this example, 'how these unreasoning creatures care for the loss of their young, and we live away from our only son and are content.'

"'By no means are we content,' replied the father; 'let us therefore rise now and go seek him.'

"So they put on pilgrims' weeds, and wandered forth to seek their son. On and on they went till they came to a place, a city called Galizia; and there, as they walk along weary, they meet a gentle lady, who looks upon them mildly and compassionately, and says, 'Whence do you come, poor pilgrims? What a long way you must have travelled!'

"And they, cheered by her mode of address and sympathy, make answer, 'We have wandered over mountains and plains. We come from the mountain town of Albano. We go about seeking our son Giuliano.'

"'Giuliano!' exclaimed the lady, 'is the name of my husband. Just now he is out hunting, but come in with me and receive my hospitality for love of his name.' She took them home and washed their feet, and refreshed them, and set food before them, and ultimately gave them her own bed to sleep in.

"But the Devil came to Giuliano out hunting, and tempted him with jealous thoughts about his wife, and tormented him with all manner of calumnious insinuations, so that his mind was filled with fury. Coming home hunting-knife in hand, he rushed into the bedroom, and seeing two forms in bed, without waiting to know who they were, he plunged his knife into them, and killed them.

"Thus, without knowing it, he had killed both his father and his mother.

"Coming out of the room he met his wife, who came to seek him to welcome him.

"'What, you here!' he cried. 'Who then are those in the bed, whom I have killed?'

"'Killed!' replied the wife. 'They were a pilgrim couple to whom I gave hospitality for love of you, because they wandered seeking a son named Giuliano.' Then Giuliano knew what he had done, and was seized with penitence for his hasty yielding to suspicion and anger. So stricken with sorrow was he, he was as one dead, nor could anyone move him to speak. Then his wife came to him and said, 'We will do penance together; we will lay aside ease and riches, and will devote ourselves to the poor and needy.'

"And he embraced her and said, 'It is well spoken.'

"Near where they lived was a rapid river, and no bridge, and many were drowned in attempting to cross it, and many had a weary way to walk to find a bridge. Said Giuliano, 'We will build a bridge over the river.' And many pilgrims came to Galizia who had not where to rest. Said Giuliano, 'We will build a hospice for poor pilgrims, where they may be received and be tended according to their needs, till God forgives me.'

"So they set forth, Giuliano and his wife, to go to Rome to find workmen. But as they went, a troop met them, and came round them, and said to them, 'Where are you going?'

"'We go to Rome,' answered Giuliano, 'to find workmen to build a bridge.'

"'We are your men, we are your men; for we have built many bridges ere now.'

"Then Giuliano took them back with him, and all in two days they built the bridge.

"'How can this be?' said Giuliano's wife; 'here is something that is not right,' for she was so holy that she discerned the Evil One was in it.

"'Be sure, Giuliano,' she said, 'there is some snare here. Take, therefore, a cheese, hard and round, and roll it along the bridge, and send our dog after it; if they get across, well and good.'

"Giuliano, always prone to accept his wife's prudent counsel, did as she bade him, and rolled the cheese along the bridge, and sent the dog after it; and, see! no sooner were they in the middle of the bridge than the bridge sank in; and they knew that the Devil had built it, and that it was no bridge for Christians to go over.

"Then said Giuliano, 'God has not forgiven me yet. Now, let us build the hospice.'

"They set out, therefore, to go to Rome to find workmen to build the hospice; and when the troop of demons came round them, saying, 'We are your workmen, we are your workmen!' they paid them no heed, but went on to Rome, and fetched workmen thence, and the hospice was built; and all the pilgrims who came they received, and gave them hospitality, and the whole house was full of pilgrims.

"Then, when the house was full, quite full of pilgrims, there came an old man, and begged admission. 'Good man,' said Giuliano's wife, 'it grieves my heart to say so, but there is not a bed, nor so much as an empty corner left;' and the old man said:

"'If ye cannot receive me, it is because ye have done so much charity to me already; therefore take this staff:' so he gave them his pilgrim's staff, and went his way.

"But it was Jesus Christ who came in the semblance of that old man; and when Giuliano took the staff, behold three flowers blossomed on it, and he said:

"'See! God has forgiven me!'"

St. Margaret of Cortona

S T. MARGARET WASN'T always a saint, you must know: in her youth she was very much the reverse. She had a very cruel stepmother, who worried her to death, and gave her work she was unequal to do.

One day her stepmother had sent her out to tie up bundles of hay. As she was so engaged a Count came by, and he stopped to look at her, for she was rarely beautiful.

"What hard work for such pretty little hands," he began by saying; and after many tender words had been exchanged he proposed that she should go home with him, where her life would be the reverse of the suffering existence she had now to endure.

Margaret consented at once, for her stepmother, besides working her hard, had neglected to form her to proper sentiments of virtue.

The Count took her to his villa at a place called Monte Porciana, a good way from Cortona. Here her life was indeed a contrast to what it had been at home at Cortona. Instead of having to work, she had plenty of servants to wait upon her; her dress and her food were all in the greatest luxury, and she was supplied with everything she wished for. Sometimes as she went to the theatre, decked out in her gay attire, and knowing that she was a scandal to all, she would say in mirth and wantonness, "Who knows whether one day I may not be stuck up there on high in the churches, like some of those saints? As strange things have happened ere now!" But she only said it in wantonness. So she went on enjoying life, and when their son was born there was nothing more she desired.

In the midst of this gay existence, word was brought her one evening that the Count, who had gone out that morning full of health and spirits to the hunt, had been overtaken and assassinated, and as all had been afraid to pursue the murderers, they knew not where his body was.

Margaret was thrown into a frenzy at the news; her fine clothing and her rich fare gave her little pleasure now. All amusement and frivolity were put out of sight; and she sat on her sofa and stared before her, for she had no heart to turn to anything that could distract her thoughts from her great loss. Then one day – it might have been three days after – a favourite dog belonging to the Count came limping and whining up to her. Margaret rose immediately; she knew that the dog would take her to the Count's body, and she rose up and motioned to him to go: and the dog, all glad to return to his master, ran on before. All the household were too much afraid of the assassins to venture in their way, so Margaret went forth alone. It was a long rough way; but the dog ran on, and Margaret kept on as well as her broken strength would admit. At last they came to a brake where the dog stopped, and now whined no longer but howled piteously.

Margaret knew that they had reached the object of their search, and it was indeed here the assassins had hidden the body. Moving away with her own hands the leaves and branches with which they had covered it over, the fearful sight of her lover's mangled body lay before her. The condition into which the wounds and the lapse of time had brought it was more than she could bear to look at, and she swooned away on the spot.

When she came to herself all the course of her thoughts was changed. She saw what her life had been; the sense of the scandal she had given was more to her even than her own distracting grief. As the most terrible penance she could think of, she resolved to go back to her stepmother and endure her hard treatment, sharpened by the invectives with which she knew it would now be seasoned.

Taking with her her son, she went to her, therefore, and with the greatest submission of manner entreated to be re-admitted. But not even this would the stepmother grant her, but drove her away from the door. She then turned to her father, but he was bound to say the same as his wife. She now saw there was one misery worse than harsh treatment, and that was penury – starvation, not only for herself, but her child.

Little she cared what became of her, but for the child something must be done. What did she do? She went and put on a sackcloth dress, tied about the waist with a rope, and she went to the church at the high mass time; and when mass was over she stood on the altar step, and told all the people she was Margaret of Cortona, who had given so much scandal, and now was come to show her contrition for it.

Her sufferings had gone up before God. As she spoke her confession so humbly before all the people, the Count's mother rose from her seat, and, coming up to her, threw her handkerchief over her head – for she was bareheaded – and led her away to her home.

She would only accept her hospitality on condition of being allowed to live in a little room apart, with no more furniture than a nun's cell. Here she lived twelve years of penance, till her boy was old enough to choose his state in life. He elected to be a Dominican, and afterwards became a Preacher of the Apostolic Palace; and she entered a Franciscan convent, where she spent ten more years of penance, till God took her to Himself.

She cut off all her long hair when she went to live in her cell at the house of the Count's mother, that she might not again be an occasion of sin to anyone. And after that, when she found she was still a subject of human admiration, she cut off her lips, that no one might admire her again.

Padre Filippo

THERE WAS IN Padre Filippo's time a cardinal who was
Prefect of the provisions, who let everything go wrong
and attended to nothing, and the poor were all suffering
because provisions got so dear.

Padre Filippo went to the Pope – Papa Medici it was – and told him how
badly off the poor were; so the Pope called the Cardinal to account, and
went on making him attend to it till Padre Filippo told him that things
were on a better footing.

But the Cardinal came to Padre Filippo and said:

"Why do you vex me by going and making mischief to the Pope?"

But Padre Filippo, instead of being frightened at his anger, rose up
and said:

"Come here and I will show you what is the fate of those who oppress
and neglect the poor. Come here Eminentissimo, and look," and he took
him to the window and asked him what he saw.

The Cardinal looked, and he saw a great fire of Hell, and the souls
writhing in it. The Cardinal said no more and went away, but not long
after he gave up being a cardinal and became a simple brother under
Padre Filippo.

Some of their stories of him are jocose. There was a young
married lady who was a friend of the Order, and had done
it much good. She was very much afraid of the idea of her
confinement as the time approached and said she could never
endure it. Padre Filippo knew how good she was and felt great
compassion for her.

"Never mind, my child," said the "good Philip"; "I will take all your
pain on myself."

Time passed away, and one night the community was very much
surprised to hear "good Philip" raving and shouting with pain; he who
voluntarily submitted to every penance without a word, and whom they

had often seen so patient in illness. That same night the lady's child was born and she felt no pain at all.

Early next morning she sent to tell him that her child was born, and to ask how he was.

"Tell her I am getting a little better now," said "good Philip," "but I never suffered anything like it before. Next time, mind, she must manage her affairs for herself. For never will *I* interfere with anything of *that* sort again."

Another who had no child was very anxious to have one, and came to Padre Filippo to ask him to pray for her that she might have one. Padre Filippo promised to pray for her; but instead of a child there was only a shapeless thing. She sent for Padre Filippo once more, therefore, and said:

"There! that's all your prayers have brought!"

"Oh never mind!" said Padre Filippo; and he took it and shaped it (the narrator twisted up a large towel and showed how he formed first one leg then the other, then the arms, then the head, as if she had seen him do it). Then he knelt down by the side and prayed while he told them to keep silence, and it opened its eyes and cried, and the mother was content.

There was a man who was dying, and would not have a priest near him. He said he had so many sins on him it was impossible God could forgive him, so it was no use bothering himself about confessing. His wife and his children begged and entreated him to let them send for a priest, but he would not listen to them.

So they sent for Padre Filippo, and as he was a friend he said:

"If he comes as a visitor he may come in, but not as a priest."

"Good Philip" sat down by his side and said:

"A visitor may ask a question. Why won't you let me come as a priest?"

The sick man gave the same answer as before.

"Now you're quite mistaken," said "good Philip", "and I'll show you something."

Then he called for paper and pen and wrote a note.

"Padre Eterne!" he wrote. "Can a man's sins be forgiven?" and he folded it, and away it went of itself right up to heaven.

An hour later, as they were all sitting there, another note came back all by itself, written in shining letters of gold, and it said:

"Padre Eterno forgives and receives everyone who is penitent."

The sick man resisted no longer after that; he made his confession and received the sacrament, and died consoled in "good Philip"'s' arms.

Padre Filippo was walking one day through the streets of Rome when he saw a great crowd very much excited. "What's the matter?" asked "good Philip."

"There's a man in that house up there beating his wife fit to kill her, and for nothing at all, for she's an angel of goodness. Nothing at all, but because she's so ugly."

Padre Filippo waited till the husband was tired of beating her and had gone out, and all the crowd had dispersed. Then he went up to the room where the poor woman lived, and knocked at the door. "Who's there?" said the woman.

"Padre Filippo!" answered "good Philip," and the woman opened quickly enough when she heard it was Padre Filippo who knocked.

But "good Philip" himself started back with horror when he saw her, she was so ugly. However, he said nothing, but made the sign of the cross over her, and prayed, and immediately she became as beautiful as she had been ugly; but she knew nothing, of course, of the change.

"Your husband won't beat you anymore," said "good Philip", as he turned to go; "only if he asks you who has been here send him to me."

When the husband came home and found his wife had become so beautiful, he kissed her, and was beside himself for joy; and she could not imagine what had made him so different towards her. "Who has been here?" he asked.

"Only Padre Filippo," answered the wife; "and he said that if you asked I was to tell you to go to him;" the husband ran off to him to thank him, and to say how sorry he was for having beaten her.

But there lived opposite a woman who was also in everything the opposite of this one. She was very handsome, but as bad in conduct as the other was good. However, when she saw the ugly wife become so handsome, she said to herself, "If 'good Philip' would only make me a little handsomer than I am, it would be a good thing for me;" and she went to Padre Filippo and asked him to make her handsomer.

Padre Filippo looked at her, and he knew what sort of woman she was, and he raised his hand and made the sign of the cross over her, and prayed, and she became ugly; uglier even than the other woman had been!

"Why have you treated me differently from the other woman?" exclaimed the woman, for she had brought a glass with her to be able to contemplate the improvement she expected him to make in her appearance.

"Because beauty was of use to her in her state of life," answered Padre Filippo. "But you have only used the beauty God gave you as an occasion of sin; therefore a stumbling-block have I now removed out of your way."

And he said well, didn't he?

One Easter there came to him a young man of good family to confession, and Padre Filippo knew that everyone had tried in vain to make him give up his mistress, and that to argue with him about it was quite useless. So he tried another tack. "I know it is such a habit with you to go to see her you *can't* give it up, so I'm not going to ask you to. You shall go and see her as often as you like, only will you do something to please me?"

The young man was very fond of "good Philip", and there was nothing he would have not done for him except to give up his mistress; so as he knew that was not in question, he answered "yes" very readily.

"You promise me to do what I say, punctually?" asked the saint.

"Oh, yes, Father, punctually."

"Very well, then; all I ask is that though you go to her as often as you like, you just pass by this way and come up and pull my bell every time you go; nothing more than that."

The young man did not think it was a very hard injunction, but when it came to performing it he felt its effect. At first he used to go three times a day, but he was so ashamed of ringing the saint's bell so often, that very soon he went no more than once a day. That dropped to two or three times a week, then once a week, and long before next Easter he had given her up and had become all his parents could wish him to be.

"There was another such case; just such another, only this man had a wife too, but he was so infatuated with the other, he would have it she loved him the better of the two."

"Yes; and the other was a miniature-painter," broke in corroboratively a kind of charwoman who had come in to tidy the place while we were talking.

"Yes, she was a miniature-painter," continued the narrator; "but it's I who am telling the story.

"Padre Filippo said, 'How much do you allow her?'

"Twenty pauls a day," broke in the charwoman.

"Forty scudi a month," said the narrator positively.

"There's not much difference," interposed I, fearing I should lose the story between them. "Twenty pauls a day is sixty scudi a month. It doesn't matter."

"Well, then, Padre Filippo said," continued the narrator, "'Now just to try whether she cares so much about you, you give her thirty scudi a month.'"

"Fifteen pauls a day," interposed the charwoman.

"Thirty scudi a month!" reiterated the narrator.

"Never mind," said I. "Whatever it was, it was to be reduced."

"Yes; that's it," pursued the narrator; "and he made him go on and on diminishing it. She took it very well at first, suspecting he was trying her, and thinking he would make it up to her afterwards."

"But when she found he didn't," said the charwoman.

"She turned him out," said the narrator, putting her down with a frown. "He was so infatuated, however, that even now he was not satisfied, and said that in stopping the money he had been unfair, and she was in the right. So "good Philip", who was patience itself, said, 'Go and pay her up, and we'll try her another way. You go and kill a dog, and put it in a bag, and go to her with your hands covered with blood, and let her think you have got into trouble for hurting someone, and ask her to hide you.' So the man went and killed a dog."

"It was a cat he killed, because he couldn't find a dog handy," said the irrepressible charwoman.

"Nonsense; of course it was a dog," asseverated the narrator. "But when he went to her house and pretended to be in a bad way, and asked her to have pity on him, she only answered: 'Not I, indeed! I'm not going to get myself into a scrape with the law for *him!*' and drove him away. And he came and told Padre Filippo.

"'Now,' said "good Philip", 'go to your wife whom you have abandoned so long. Go to her with the same story, and see what she does for you.'

"The man took the dead dog in the bag, and ran to the lodging where his wife was, and knocked stealthily at her door. 'It is I,' he whispered.

"'Come in, husband,' exclaimed the wife, throwing open the door.

"'Stop! Hush! Take care! Don't touch me!' said the husband. 'There's blood upon me. Save me! Hide me! Put me somewhere!'

"'It's so long since you've been here, no one will think of coming after you here, so you will be quite safe. Sit down and be composed,' said the wife soothingly; and she poured him out wine to drink.

"But the police were nearer than he fancied. He had thought to finish up the affair in five minutes by explaining all to her. But 'the other,' not satisfied with refusing him shelter, had gone and set the police on his track; and here they were after him.

"The wife's quick ears heard them on the stairs. 'Get into this cupboard quick, and leave me to manage them,' she said.

"The husband safely stowed away, she opened the door without hesitation, as if she had nothing to hide. 'How can you think he is here?' she said when they asked for him. 'Ask any of the neighbours how long it is since he has been here.'

"'Oh, three years,', 'four years,' 'five,' said various voices of people who had come round at hearing the police arrive.

"'You see you must have come to the wrong place,' she said. And the husband smiled as he heard her standing out for him so bravely.

"Her determined manner had satisfied the police; and they were just turning to go when one of them saw tell-tale spots of blood on the floor that had dropped from the dead dog. The track was followed to the cupboard, and the man dragged to prison. It was in vain that he assured them he had killed nothing but a dog.

"'Ha! that will be the faithful dog of the murdered man,' said the police. 'We shan't be long before we find the body of the man himself!'

"The wife was distracted at finding her husband, who had but so lately come back to her, was to be taken away again; and he could discern how real was her distress.

"'Go to Padre Filippo, and he will set all right,' said the husband as they carried him away. The woman went to Padre Filippo, and he explained all, amid the laughter of the Court. But the husband went back to his wife, and never left her anymore after that."

"Ah, there's plenty to be said about Padre Filippo," said the charwoman; and I should have liked to put her under examination, but that it would have been a breach of hospitality, as the other evidently did not like the interruption; so I was obliged to be satisfied with the testimony she had already afforded of the popularity of the saint. "Ha, good Padre Filippo, he was content to eat 'black bread' like us"; and she took a hunch out of her pocket to show me (it was only like our "brown bread").

"There was no lack where he was. Once I know, with half a rubbio of corn, he made enough to last all the community ten years," she, however, ran on to say before she could be dismissed.

One day Padre Filippo was going over Ponte S. Angelo, when he met two little boys who seemed to attract his notice. "Forty-two years hence you will be made a cardinal," he said to one, as he gave him a friendly tap with his walking-stick. "And that other one," he added, turning to his companion, "will be dead in two years."

And so it came true exactly.

There was another peasant who, when he came into Rome on a Sunday morning, always went to the church where St. Philip was. "You quite weary one with your continual preaching about the Blessed Sacrament. I'm so tired of hearing about it that I declare to you I don't care so much about it as my mule does about a sack of corn." Padre Filippo preferred convincing people in some practical way to going into angry discussions with them; so he did not say very much in answer to the countryman's remarks, but asked him the name of his village. Not long after he went down to this village to preach; and had a pretty little altar erected on a hill-side, and set up the Blessed Sacrament in Exposition. Then he went and found out the same countryman, and said, "Now bring a sack of corn near where the altar is, and let's see what the mule does." The countryman placed a sack of corn near the altar, and drove the mule by to see what it would do.

The mule kicked aside the sack of corn, and fell down on its knees before the altar; and the man, seeing the token, went to confession to St. Philip, and never said anything profane anymore.

There were two other fellows who were more profane still, and who said one to the other, "They make such a fuss about Padre Filippo and his miracles, I warrant it's all nonsense. Let's watch till he passes, and one of us pretend to be dead and see if he finds it out."

So said so done. "What is your companion lying on the ground for?" said St. Philip as he passed. "He's dead, Father," replied the other. "Dead, is he?" said Padre Filippo; "then you must go for a bier for him." He had no sooner passed on than the man burst out laughing, expecting his companion to join his mirth. But his companion didn't move. "Why don't you get up?" he said, and gave him a kick; but he made no sign. When he bent down to look at him he found he was really dead; and he had to go for the bier.

S. Giuseppe Labre

"**THERE WAS Giuseppe Labre too, and many wonderful things he did; he was a great saint, as all the people in the Monti knew. I don't know if they've put all about him in books yet; if so, you may have read it; but I can't read.**"

"I know a Life of him has been published; but tell me what you have heard about him all the same."

Giuseppe Labre, you know, passed much of his time in meditation in the Coliseum; the arch behind the picture of the Second Station, that's where he used to be all day, and where he slept most nights, too. There was a butcher in the Via de' Serpenti who knew him, and kept a little room for him, where he made him come and sleep when the nights were bad and cold, or stormy. These people were very good to him, and, though not well off themselves, were ready to give him a great deal more than he in his love for poverty would consent to accept.

One great affliction this butcher had; his wife was bedridden with an incurable disorder. One night there was a terrible storm, it was a burning hot night in summer, and Giuseppe Labre came to sleep at the butcher's. He was lying on his bed in the little room, which was up a step or two higher than the butcher's own room, where his wife lay, just as it might be where that cupboard is there. Presently the butcher's wife heard him call her, saying,

"Sora Angela, bring me a cup of water for the love of God!"

"My friend, you know how gladly I would do anything to help you, but my husband is not come up, and I have no one to send, and you know I cannot move."

Nevertheless Giuseppe called again, "Sora Angela, bring me a cup of water for the love of God!"

"Don't call so, good friend," replied she; "it distresses me; you know how gladly I would come if I could only move."

Yet still the third time Giuseppe Labre said,

"Sora Angela, hear me! Bring me a cup of water for the love of God!" And he spoke the words so authoritatively that the good woman felt as if she was bound to obey him, she made the effort to rise, and – can you believe it! – she got up as if there was nothing the matter with her; and from that time forwards she was cured.

There was a poor cobbler who always had a kind word for Giuseppe too. One day Giuseppe Labre came to him, and said he wanted him to lend him a pair of shoes as he was going on a pilgrimage to Loreto. The cobbler knew what a way it was from Rome to Loreto, and that there would not be much left of a pair of shoes after they had done the way there and back. Had Labre asked him to *give* them, his regard for him would have prompted him to assent however ill he could afford it; but to talk of lending shoes to walk to Loreto and back seemed like making game of him, and he didn't like it. Nevertheless he couldn't find it in his heart to refuse, and he gave him a pretty tidy pair which he had patched up strong to sell, but without expecting ever to see them again.

Giuseppe Labre took the shoes and went to Loreto, and when he came back his first call was at the cobbler's shed; and sure enough he brought the shoes none the worse for all the wear they had had. So perfectly uninjured were they that the cobbler would have thought they were another pair had it not been that he recognized the patches of his own clumsy work.

Another more matter-of-fact account of this story was that he did not wear the shoes on the journey, as he did that barefoot, i.e. with wooden sandals, and only borrowed the shoes to be decent and reverent in visiting the Sanctuary. In this case the story was told me to illustrate his conscientiousness both in punctually returning the shoes and in taking so much care of his trust.

The Dead Man's Letter

THERE WAS a rich man, I cannot tell you how rich he was, who died and left all his great fortune to his son, palaces and houses, and farms and vineyards. The son entered into possession of all, and became a great man; but he never thought of having a mass said for the soul of his father, from whom he had received all.

There was also, about the same time, a poor man, who had hardly enough to keep body and soul together, and he went into a church to pray that he might have wherewithal to feed his children. So poor was he that he said within himself, "None poorer than I can there be." As he said that, his eye lighted on the box where alms were gathered, that masses might be offered for the souls in Purgatory. "Yes," he said, then, "these are poorer than I," and he felt in his pocket for his single *baiocco*, and he put it in the alms box for the holy souls.

As he came out, he saw a *painone* standing before the door, as if in waiting for him; but as he was well-dressed, and looked rich, the poor man knew he could have no acquaintance with him, and would have passed on.

"You have done me so much good, and now you don't speak to me," said the stranger.

"When did I thee much good?" said the poor man, bewildered.

"Even now," said the stranger; for in reality he was no *painone*, but one of the holy souls who had taken that form, and he alluded to the poor man's last coin, of which he had deprived himself in charity.

"I cannot think to what Your Excellency alludes," replied the poor man.

"Nevertheless it is true," returned the *painone*; "and now I will ask you to do me another favour. Will you take this letter to such and such a palace?" And he gave him the exact address. "When you get there, you must insist on giving it into the hands of the master of the house himself. Never mind how many times you are refused, do not go away till you have given it to the master himself."

"Never fear, Your Excellency," answered the poor man, "I'll deliver it right."

When he reached the palace, it was just as the *painone* had seemed to expect it would be. First the porter came forward with his cocked hat and his gilt knobbed stick, with the coloured cord twisted over it all the way down, and asked him whither he was going.

"To Count so-and-so," answered the poor man.

"All right! Give it here," said the splendid porter.

"By no means, my orders were to consign it to the Count himself."

"Go in and try," answered the porter. "But you may as well save yourself the stairs; they won't let such as you in to the Count."

"I must follow orders," said the poor man, and passed on.

At the door of the apartment a liveried servant came to open.

"What do you want up here? If you have brought anything, why didn't you leave it with the porter?"

"Because my orders are to give this letter into the Count's own hands," answered the poor man.

"A likely matter I shall call the Signor Conte out, and to such as you! Give here, and don't talk nonsense."

"No! Into the Count's own hands must I give it."

"Don't be afraid; I've lived here these thirty years, and no message for the Signor Conte ever went wrong that passed through my hands. Yours isn't more precious than the rest, I suppose."

"I know nothing about that, but I must follow orders."

"And so must I, and I know my place too well to call out the Signor Conte to the like of you."

The altercation brought out the valet.

"This fellow expects the Signor Conte to come to the door to take in his letters himself," said the lackey, laughing disdainfully. "What's to be done with the poor animal?"

"Give here, good man," said the valet, patronisingly not paying much heed to the remarks of the servant; "I am the Signor Conte's own body servant, and giving it to me is the same as giving it to himself."

"Maybe," answered the poor man, "but I'm too simple to understand how one man can be the same as another. My orders are to give it to the Count alone, and to the Count alone I must give it."

"Take it from him, and turn him out," said the valet, with supreme disdain, and the lackey was not slow to take advantage of the permission. The poor man, however, would not yield his trust, and the scuffle that ensued brought the Count himself out to learn the reason of so much noise.

The letter was now soon delivered. The Count started when he saw the handwriting, and was impelled to tear the letter open at once, so much did its appearance seem to surprise him.

"Who gave you the letter?" he exclaimed, in an excited manner, as soon as he had rapidly devoured its contents.

"I cannot tell, I never saw the person before," replied the poor man.

"Would you know him again?" enquired the Count.

"Oh, most undoubtedly!" answered the poor man; "he said such strange things to me that I looked hard at him."

"Then come this way," said the Count; and he led him into a large hall, round which were hung many portraits in frames. "Do you see one among these portraits that at all resembles him?" he said, when he had given him time to look round the walls.

"Yes, that is he!" said the poor man, unhesitatingly, pointing to the portrait of the Count's father, from whom he had inherited such great wealth, and for whom he had never given the alms of a single mass.

"Then there is no doubt it was himself," said the Count. "In this letter he tells me that you of your poverty have done for him what I with all my wealth have never done," he added in a tone of compunction. "For you have given alms for the repose of his soul, which I never have; therefore he bids me now take you and all your family into the palace to live with me, and to share all I have with you."

After that he made the man and all his family come to live in the palace, as his father directed, and he was abundantly provided for the rest of his life.

The Procession of Velletri

MARIA GRAZIA LIVED in a convent of nuns at Velletri, and did their errands for them. One night one of the nuns who was ill got much worse towards night, and the factor not being there, the Superior called up Maria Grazia and said to her, "Maria Grazia, Sister Maria, such a one is so very bad that I must get you to go and call the provost to her. I'm sorry to send you out so late, but I fear she won't last till morning."

Maria Grazia couldn't say nay to such an errand, and off she set by a clear moonlight to go to the house of the provost, which was a good step off and out of the town. All went well till Maria Grazia had left the houses behind her, but she was no sooner in the open country than she saw a great procession of white-robed priests and acolytes bearing torches coming towards her, chanting solemnly. "What a fine procession!" thought Maria Grazia; "I must hasten on to see it. But what can it be for at this time of night?"

Still she never doubted it was a real procession till she got quite close, and then, to her surprise, the procession parted in two to let her go through the midst, which a real procession would never have done.

You may believe that she was frightened as she passed right through the midst of those beings who must have belonged to the other world, dazed as she was with the unearthly light of the flaring torches; it seemed as if it would last for ever. But it did come to an end at last, and then she was so frightened she didn't know what to do. Her legs trembled too much to carry her on further from home, and if she turned back there would be that dreadful procession again. Curiosity prompted her to turn her head, in spite of her fears; and what gave her almost more alarm than seeing the procession was the fact that it was no longer to be seen. What could have become of it in the midst of the open field? Then the fear of the good nun dying without the sacraments through her faint-heartedness stirred her, but in vain she tried to pluck up courage. "Oh!" she thought, "if there were only someone going the same road, then I shouldn't mind!"

She had hardly formed the wish when she saw a peasant coming along over the very spot where the procession had passed out of sight. "Now it's all right," she said; for by the light of the moon he seemed a very respectable steady-looking peasant.

"What did you think of that procession, good man," said Maria Grazia; "for it must have passed close by you, too?"

The peasant continued coming towards her, but said nothing.

"Didn't it frighten you? It did me; and I don't think I could have moved from the spot if you hadn't come up. I've got to go to the provost's house, to fetch him to a dying nun; it's only a step off this road, will you mind walking with me till I get there?"

The peasant continued walking towards her, but answered nothing.

"Maybe you're afraid of me, as I was of the procession, that you don't speak," continued Maria Grazia; "but I am not a spirit. I am Maria Grazia, servant in such and such a convent at Velletri."

But still the peasant said nothing.

"What a very odd man!" thought Maria Grazia. "But as he seems to be going my way he'll answer the purpose of company whether he speaks or not." And she walked on without fear till she came to the provost's house, the peasant always keeping beside her but never speaking. Arrived at the provost's gate she turned round to salute and thank him, and he was nowhere to be seen. He too had disappeared! He too was a spirit!

When the archpriest came he had his nephew and his servant to go with him, and they carried torches of straw, for it seems in that part of the country they use straw torches; so she went back in good company.

And Maria Grazia told me that herself.

The Devil Who Took to Himself a Wife

L ISTEN, AND I WILL tell you what the devil did who took to himself a wife.

Ages and ages ago, in the days when the devil was loose – for now he is chained and can't go about like that anymore – the head devil called the others, and said, "Whichever of you proves himself the boldest and cleverest, I will give him his release, and set him free from Inferno."

So they all set to work and did all manner of wild and terrible things, and the one who pleased the head devil best was set free.

This devil being set free, went upon earth, and thought he would live like the children of men. So he took a wife, and, of course, he chose one who was handsome and fashionable, but he didn't think about anything else, and he soon found that she was no housewife, was never satisfied unless she was gadding out somewhere, would not take a word of reproof, and, what was more, she spent all his money.

Every day there were furious quarrels; it was bad enough while the money lasted – and he had brought a good provision with him

– but when the money came to an end it was much worse; he was ever reproaching her with extravagance, and she him with stinginess and deception.

At last he said to her one day, "It's no use making a piece of work; I'm quite tired of this sort of life; I shall go back to Hell, which is a much quieter place than a house where you are. But I don't mind doing you a good turn first. I'll go and possess myself of a certain queen. You dress up like a doctor, and say you will heal her, and all you will have to do will be to pretend to use some ointments for two or three days, on which I will go out of her. Then they will be so delighted with you for healing her that they will give you a lot of money, on which you can live for the rest of your days, and I will go back to Hell." But though he said this, it was only to get rid of her. As soon as he had provided her with the price for casting him out once, he meant to go and amuse himself on earth in other ways; he had no real intention of going back to Hell. Then he instructed her in the means by which she was to find out the queen of whom he was to possess himself, and went his way.

The wife, by following the direction he gave, soon found him, and, dressed as a doctor, effected the cure; that is, she made herself known to him in applying the ointments, and he went away as he had agreed.

When the king and the court saw what a wonderful cure had been effected, they gave the woman a sackful of scudi, but all the people went on talking of her success.

The devil meantime had possessed himself of another sovereign, a king this time, and everybody in the kingdom was very desirous to have him cured, and went enquiring everywhere for a remedy. Thus they heard of the fame of the last cure by the devil's wife. Then they immediately sent for her and insisted that she should cure this king too. But she, not sure whether he would go out a second time at her bidding, refused as long as she could; but they took her, and said, "Unless you cure him we shall kill you!"

"Then," she said, "you must shut me up alone with this king, and I will try what I can do."

So she was shut up alone with him.

"What! you here again!" said the devil as soon as he perceived her. "No; that won't do this time. I am very comfortable inside this old king, and I mean to stay here."

"But they threaten to kill me if I don't make you go; so what am I to do?" answered the wife.

"I can't help that," he replied; "you must get out of the scrape the best way you can."

At this she got in a passion, and, as she used to do in the days when they were living together, rated him so fiercely that at last he was fain to go to escape her scolding.

Once more she received a high price for the cure, and her fame got the more bruited abroad.

But the devil went into another queen, and possessed himself of her. The fame of the two cures had spread so far that the wife was soon called in to try her powers again.

"I really can't," she pleaded; but the people said:

"What you did for the other two you can do for this one; and, if you don't, we will cut off your head."

To save her head, therefore, she said, "Then you must shut me up in a room alone with the queen."

So she was shut up in the room with her.

"What! you here again!" exclaimed the devil as soon as he perceived her. "No; I positively won't go this time; I couldn't be better off than inside this old queen, and till you came I was perfectly happy."

"They threaten to take my head if I don't make you go; so what am I to do?"

"Then let them take your head, and let that be an end of it," replied the devil testily.

"You are a pretty husband, indeed, to say such a speech to a wife!" answered she in a high-pitched voice, which he knew was the foretaste of one of those terrible storms he could never resist.

Basta! she stormed so loud that she sickened him of her for good and all, and this time, to escape her, instead of possessing himself of any more kings and queens, he went straight off to Hell, and never came forth anymore for fear of meeting her.

The Happy Couple

♫

I **CAN TELL YOU a story, or two perhaps. What a number I used to know, to be sure! But what can I do? It is thirty years and more since anyone has asked me for them, and it's hard to put one's ideas together after such a time. You mustn't mind if I put the wrong part of the story before, and have to go backwards and forwards a little.**

I know there was one that ran thus:

There was a married couple who lived so happy and content and fond of each other, that they never had a word of dispute about anything the live-long day, but only thought of helping and pleasing each other.

The Devil saw this, and determined to set them by the ears; but how was he to do it? Such love and peace reigned in their home that he couldn't find any way into the place. After prowling and prowling about, and finding no means of entrance, what does he do? He went to an old woman – she must have been one of those who dabble with things they have no business to touch – and said to her:

"You must do this job for me!"

"That's no great matter," answered the old hag. "Give me ten scudi for my niece and a new pair of shoes for me, and I'll settle the matter."

"Here are the ten scudi," said the Devil; "it will be time enough to talk about the shoes when we see how you do the business."

The bad old woman set off accordingly with her niece and the ten scudi, instructing her by the way what she was to do.

This husband and wife lived in a place where there was a house on one side and a shop on the other, so that through a window in the house where they lived they could give an eye to anything that went on in the shop.

Choosing a moment when the man was alone in the shop, she sent the girl in with the ten scudi; and the girl, who had been told what to do, selected a dress, and a handkerchief, and a number of fine things, and paid her ten scudi. Then she proceeded leisurely to put them on, and to walk up and down the shop in them. Meantime the bad old woman went up to the wife:

"Poor woman!" she said. "Poor woman! Such a good woman as you are, and to have such a hypocrite of a husband!"

"My husband a hypocrite!" answered the wife. "What can you mean – he is the best man that ever was."

"Ah! he makes you think so, poor simple soul. But the truth is, he is very different from what you think."

So they went on conversing, and the bad old woman all the time watching what was going on in the shop till the right moment came. Just as the girl was flaunting about and showing herself off, she said:

"Look here, he has given all those things to that girl there."

And though the wife did not believe a word, curiosity prompted her to look, and there she saw the girl bowing herself out with as many thanks and adieus as if the poor man had really given her the things she had bought.

"Perhaps you will believe that!" observed the bad old woman.

"Indeed, I cannot help believing it," answered the wife, "but never otherwise should I have thought it; and I owe you a great deal for opening my eyes;" and she gave her a whole cheese. "I know what I shall do," she continued, as she sobbed over her lost peace of mind; "I shall show him I know his bad conduct by having no dinner ready for him when he comes up by and by."

"That's right," said the bad old woman. "Do so, and show him you are not going to be trampled on for the sake of a drab of a girl like that;" and she tied her cheese up in a handkerchief, and went her way.

Down she went now to the husband, and plied him with suspicions of his wife, similar to those she had suggested to her against him. The husband was even less willing to listen to her than the wife had been, and when at last he drove her away, she said:

"You think she's busy all the morning preparing your dinner; but instead of that, she's talking to those you wouldn't like her to talk with. And you see now if today she hasn't been at this game so long that she has forgotten your dinner altogether."

The husband turned a deaf ear, and continued attending to his shop; but when he went into the house and found no dinner ready, it seemed as if all that the bad old woman had said was come true.

He was too sad for words, so they didn't have much of a quarrel, but there could not but be a coldness after such an extraordinary event as a day without dinner.

The husband went back to his shop and mused. The wife sat alone in her room crying; presently the old hag came back to her.

"Well, did you tell him you had found him out?" she enquired.

"No! I hadn't courage to do that. And he was so patient about there being no dinner, that I felt quite sorry to have suspected him. Oh, you who have been so clever in pointing out my misery to me, can you not tell me some means of reconciliation?"

"Yes, there is one; but I don't know if you can manage it."

"Oh yes; I would do *anything!*"

"Then you must watch till he is quite sound asleep, and take a sharp razor and cut off three hairs from the undergrowth of his beard, quite close to the skin. If you do that it will all come right again."

"It seems a very odd remedy," said the wife; "but if you say it will do, I suppose it will, and thank you kindly for the advice;" and she gave her another cheese.

Then the witch went back to the husband.

"I suppose I was mistaken, and you found your dinner ready after all?" she said.

"No!" he replied; "you were right about there being no dinner; but I am certain there was some cause for there being none, other than what you say."

"What other cause should there be?" exclaimed the old woman.

"That I don't know," he replied. "But some other cause I am persuaded there must have been."

"Well, if you are so infatuated, I will give you another token that I am right," replied the old woman. "You don't deserve that I should save your life, but I am so good-natured, I can't help warning you. Tonight, I have reason to know, she intends to murder you. You just give some make-believe snoring, but mind you don't sleep, whatever you do; and you see if she doesn't take up one of your razors to stab you in the throat."

The good husband refused to believe a word, and drove her away. Nevertheless, when night came he felt not a little anxious; and if he had tried to sleep ever so much he could not, for he felt so excited. Then curiosity to see if the woman's words would come true overcame him, and he pretended to snore.

He had not been snoring thus long, when the wife took up the razor and came all trembling to the bedside, and lifted up his beard.

A cold sweat crept over the poor husband as she approached – not for fear of his life, which he could easily rescue, as he was awake – but because the proof seemed there that the old hag had spoken the truth. However, instead of taking it for granted it was so, and refusing to hear any justification – perhaps killing her on the spot, as she had hoped and expected – he calmly seized her arm, and said:

"Tell me, what are you going to do with that razor?"

The wife sank on her knees by his side, crying:

"I cannot expect you to believe me, but this is really how it was. An old woman came and told me you were making love to a young girl in the shop, and showed me how she was bowing and scraping to you. I was so vexed, that to show you my anger I got no dinner ready; but afterwards, I felt as if I should like to ask you all about it, to make sure there was no mistake: only after what I had done, I didn't know how to begin speaking to you again. Then I asked the old woman if she couldn't tell me some means of bringing things straight again; and she said, if I could cut off three hairs from the undergrowth of your beard, all would come right. But I can't expect you to believe it."

"Yes, I do," replied the husband. "The same old wretch came to me, and wanted me in like manner to believe all manner of evil things of you, but I refused to believe you could do anything wrong. So I had more confidence in you than you had in me. But still we were both very nearly making ourselves very foolish and very unhappy; so we will take a lesson never to doubt each other again."

And after that there never was a bad word between them anymore. When the Devil saw how the old woman had spoilt the affair, he took the pair of shoes he was to have given her, and tied them on to a long cane which he fastened on the top of a mountain, and there they dangled before her eyes, but she could never get at them.

Classical Tales

THE NARRATIVE CONTINUITY between some of the stories Busk collected in late nineteenth-century Rome and those dating back to the city's antiquity, preserved in a variety of ancient sources, is best revealed by 'Cupid and Psyche'. This tale of love and magic from Apuleius's second-century Latin novel *The Golden Ass* is presented here in a new translation.

'Cupid and Psyche' is widely regarded as the oldest fairy tale in the West, and one central to the birth of the literary fairy tale in Renaissance Europe. Rediscovered in manuscript form, it was one of the first books to be printed. 'Cupid and Psyche' is clearly the inspiration for 'The Dark King' and 'The Enchanted Rose Tree', both included in this edition.

Other links between the stories in Busk's book and those from Roman antiquity may be found in Valerius Maximus's report, in his first-century *Nine Books of Memorable Deeds and Sayings*, of a daughter breastfeeding her jailed parents to preserve their lives. Known as 'Caritas Romana', this was a popular motif in early modern art; a version of it appears in Busk's book as 'The King of Portugal'. Another related ancient text is Pliny the Younger's second-century letter to Sura; the best-known ancient Roman ghost story, it attests to a fascination with this topic from long before Busk's collection. The horrifying legend of 'Amadea' in Busk's collection clearly harks back to the ancient Greek story of Medea, included here in the version found in Berens' 1894 *Hand-book of Mythology*. Finally, the lively and adventure-filled story 'Jonathan and the Three Talismans', which appears in the medieval Latin compilation *Gesta Romanorum*, is related to many later European fairy tales, including the one that Busk titles 'Twelve Feet of Nose'.

Cupid and Psyche
(by Apuleius, translated by John Cirignano)

ONCE THERE WAS A KING and a queen who had three beautiful daughters. It was obvious to all how beautiful the two older sisters were, but the beauty of the youngest was so exceptional that it could not be put into words. People from near and far heard about this girl's wondrous beauty, but when they actually saw her, they were struck dumb by the extraordinary sight of her. They would bow and wave their arms in worship, as though they were honouring the goddess Venus herself....This strange transfer of divine honours to a mortal infuriated the real Venus, who had no patience for such disrespect....So she summoned Cupid – her reckless winged son, equipped with fire and arrows. She incited her undisciplined son to go to the city and find Psyche – for this was the girl's name. Venus pointed her out to him and retold the entire story of Psyche's beauty. Then she said to Cupid, "By the bonds of maternal love, by the sweet wounds of your arrows, by the hot and honey-sweet sensations of your flame, I ask you to exact vengeance for your mother, and punish that girl severely for her insolent beauty. Make her fall passionately in love with the lowest man alive – someone whom fortune has condemned to the most wretched circumstances and to dire poverty. Make her fall for a man so foul that no one on earth will be as miserable as she."

Meanwhile Psyche was reaping no benefit from her beauty. Everyone looked at her, everyone praised her, but no one – king or commoner – approached her as a suitor for marriage. Everyone marvelled at her goddess-like appearance, as if they were looking at a well-polished statue. The two older sisters, whose more moderate beauty was not widely talked about, were already married to kings. But Psyche sat at home unmarried and lonely, wounded in her mind, physically sick, and although she continued to be courteous to everyone, she despised her own beauty. Psyche's father was very unhappy about his youngest daughter. Fearing the envy and wrath of the gods, he consulted the oracle of Apollo, and with prayers and sacrifices, sought a husband for her. The god Apollo gave him this response:

> *"On the cliff of a high mountain, O king,*
> *set the girl dressed as for a funeral wedding.*
> *Not a son-in-law of mortals born,*
> *but a fierce, winged, snake-like evil form,*
> *that flies and fills the heavens with discord,*
> *weakening everyone with fire and sword,*
> *terrifying to each god, even high king Jupiter;*
> *dreaded by the underworld and its dark river."*

After hearing this prophecy, the miserable king went home and told his wife about the oracle. They wept and mourned constantly until the day of the prophecy arrived. The fatal wedding was prepared....Psyche was brought to a ledge of the towering mountain and left there alone. Everyone else weeping returned home....A little later a soft breeze of the west wind, Zephyr, ruffled Psyche's dress, and then lifted the frightened girl gently carrying her down from the top of the cliff, and laying her in the lap of a flowering field in the valley below. After resting in the dewy bed of grass, the burdens of Psyche's mind were lightened. She saw a grove filled with tall trees, and a spring with water as clear as glass. In the middle of the grove was a palace built with supernatural skill. You could tell as soon as you entered that you were looking at the bright accommodations of a god....The house was so majestic that it was a palace suitable for Jupiter himself. Psyche was delighted by the wonderful scene. She began to walk around more confidently. While exploring the other side of the house she found storehouses filled with treasures. Everything she could ever want was there. She was surprised that these treasures from around the world were not locked up or guarded in any way. While enjoying this scene, suddenly she heard a voice say, "Why are you amazed at this wealth, mistress? Everything here is yours. Go to the bedroom and rest. Afterwards you may ask for a bath, when you feel like it. We are your servants, whose voices you hear. We will take care of you. Royal feasts will be ready when you have refreshed your body."

Psyche then felt the blessedness of divine providence. Following the voice's advice, she slept, then bathed. Then she discovered a semicircular table full of refreshments. As soon as she sat down, invisible servants, directed by another spirit, brought sweet wines and a variety of foods to the table. Psyche could hear the voices of the servants, but she saw no one. After this rich feast, a voice began singing, accompanied by an invisible lyre player; then a chorus of voices started singing. When evening arrived and the festivities were over, Psyche went to sleep. In the middle of the night suddenly she was awakened by a gentle and loving voice. Since she was alone she was afraid for her virginity. All of a sudden a husband whom she could not see and did not know was there with her. He climbed into bed and made Psyche his wife. Before sunrise he quickly left. In the morning the voices were ready to care for the new bride and her wounded virginity. This same thing happened repeatedly for many nights. In time the visits became pleasing to Psyche, and the sound of the unknown voice comforted her in her loneliness.

Meanwhile Psyche's parents and two sisters were in a constant state of grief. The older sisters went to commiserate with their parents. Meanwhile at night, the husband, whom Psyche could hear and touch but could not see, said to her: "Sweetest Psyche, my dear wife, a very cruel misfortune is threatening you. You need to be aware of it and guard against it. Your sisters are disturbed by some rumours concerning your death, so they are going to the cliff to investigate. If you hear them crying, do not respond to them; you should not even look at them. If you do, you will cause me to suffer greatly, and you will bring about your own ruin." Psyche promised to do as her husband asked, but when night was over, and he slipped away, she collapsed and cried the entire day. She kept saying that her life was finished; that she was locked up, like a prisoner – yes, it was a happy prison, but one without human contact; that she was not able to help her own sisters; that she was not even allowed to see them. Weeping profusely, and without eating or bathing, Psyche went to bed. She was still crying when her husband arrived; he embraced her and said, "Is this what you promised me, my Psyche? Is this what I should expect from you? All day and all night you weep, and you don't even stop during our conjugal embraces. Go then; do as you wish. Obey your heart, even though it will cause great harm. Just remember my warning – though it may be too late by the time you realize the danger we are in." After begging to see her sisters to console them, and after threatening that she would die if she didn't, her husband was forced to consent. He even allowed Psyche to give her sisters as much gold or jewels as she wanted. Even so, he kept warning her, to the point of frightening her, insisting that she should never ask what her husband looks like, no matter what her wicked sisters say; otherwise, her impious curiosity would destroy her good fortune, and she would never again feel his embrace.

Psyche thanked her husband and said, "I would die a hundred times before harming our sweet marriage. I love you so passionately, whoever you are. I value you as I do my own spirit. Cupid himself couldn't compare with you. But please, I beg you, order your servant, Zephyr, to bring my sisters here." While giving him passionate and persuasive kisses and compelling caresses and soothing words, she added, "My honey, my husband, sweet soul of your Psyche...." Her husband surrendered to the power of this intimate whispering, and promised to do all that she asked. Then as day was approaching, he vanished suddenly from Psyche's embrace.

Meanwhile the older sisters hurried to the cliff to investigate the place where Psyche had been abandoned. They were weeping and beating their breasts. The rocks and cliffs echoed their voices. They kept calling their sister's name. Hearing their shrieks, Psyche rushed from her home to the cliff, and said, "Why are you tormenting yourselves with misery and lamentations? I am here, the one you are mourning. Stop your wailing, dry your cheeks, and embrace the sister whom you grieve." Psyche then summoned Zephyr, who immediately carried them safely away with a gentle breeze.

The three sisters were hugging and kissing and crying joyfully at their reunion. "Sisters, come to my home and restore your troubled souls." Psyche showed them the golden house in all its splendour. She introduced them to her family of servant voices. The sisters then took an extraordinary bath and ate splendid food. Amazed by the superabundance of riches, the older sisters began to envy Psyche. One sister kept asking who the master of this heavenly house was, who her husband was, what was he like…but Psyche did not break the promise made to her husband, and she did not reveal the secrets of her heart. Instead she invented a story saying that her husband was a young and handsome man with a dark woolly beard; that he often hunted in fields and mountains; then, before saying too much, she quickly ordered Zephyr to carry her sisters back to their homes, laden with gold and jewellery. When the older sisters arrived home, they were intensely resentful and filled with envy. They began screeching to each other: "See how depraved and savage and unfair Fortune is?! Is it okay with you that we sisters, each born of the same parents, would have such different fortunes? We who are older have been given away to foreign husbands – exiled as slave girls. Must we go on as though banished from home and country, while this one, the youngest, receives so much wealth, and a god for a husband?! She does not even know how to take advantage of such treasures! Did you see, sister, the quantity and quality of necklaces and clothes lying around the house, the sparkling jewels, and gold everywhere?! But if her husband is as handsome as she claims, she is now the most fortunate woman in the whole world. Her god-husband may even make her a goddess, if that intimacy and affection endure. By Hercules, the way she carries herself! Now she thinks she's a superior wife, as if she's already a goddess. She has servant voices, and gives commands to the winds. I, on the other hand, have a husband older than my father, balder than a pumpkin, and smaller than any boy. He has the entire household guarded with bars and chains."

The other sister continued, "I too have to put up with a husband who is curved and bent over from arthritis, and he very rarely satisfies my desires. I have to rub his twisted, bony fingers, wrecking these delicate hands of mine with stinking poultices, dirty rags, and bandages. I've taken on the role of a nurse, not a wife. Sister, would you put up with these things, like a slave?! I speak freely what I feel. By my word, I cannot stand it that such good fortune has fallen upon someone so unworthy. Remember how arrogantly she acted with us, how she boasted, and then reluctantly handed us these tiny amounts of wealth?! And as soon as she was annoyed by us, she ordered us to be blown back home! I am not a living breathing woman if I don't knock her down from such great wealth. And if my outrage has provoked you, as it should, we should make a plan. First of all, let's agree not to tell our parents or anyone else what we've witnessed; let's not let anyone know that Psyche is safe. It is enough that we have seen what we wish we hadn't; much less should we want to bring such good news about her to our parents and to everyone else. No one is happy whose riches no one knows about. She will find out that she has elder sisters who are not slaves! Now let's return to our husbands and to our poor but respectable households. We will come back and punish her pride when we have made a plan."

The two wicked sisters began to carry out their wicked plan. They hid the expensive gifts given to them by Psyche; they messed up their hair, scratched their faces, and renewed their fake mourning. They didn't spend much time with their parents – just enough to stir up their grief again. Then they hurried to their homes inflamed with madness and continued plotting the death, the murder in fact, of their innocent sister.

Meanwhile that same evening Psyche's husband, whom she did not really know, warned her again, "Do you see what great danger you are in? For the time being, Fortune is fighting at a distance, but if you do not oppose her, she will soon be battling close by. Those treacherous little she-wolves are setting a wicked trap. Their goal is to persuade you to find out what I look like. But as I have often told you, if you see me, you will no longer see me. So when those horrible witches return – and they will, I know they will, with their wicked minds – you should not speak with them. And if you cannot avoid speaking to them, because of the simplicity and gentleness of your mind, you should definitely not respond to anything about me, your husband. You must know that our family is growing; you are now carrying our child – who will be a divine child, if you keep our secrets, but a mortal, if you desecrate them."

Psyche shouted and clapped with joy; she was so excited at the thought of having a divine child, and honoured by the name of 'Mother.' She marvelled that this growth in her womb came about from such a brief encounter. Meanwhile those beastly foul furies, spewing venom, were sailing swiftly towards her. Again Psyche's husband warned, "It's the final day, a desperate situation, the enemy has already taken up arms and positioned the camp and directed the battle line and sounded the war trumpet; now with drawn swords, your nefarious sisters are going for your jugular. We are surrounded by so many disasters. Sweetest Psyche, have pity on yourself and on me. With self-control you can still free our home, your husband, yourself, and that little one of ours, from the ruin that threatens. When your sisters lean over the side of the cliff and call with deadly voices, like Sirens, do not listen, and do not look at those wicked women, whom you should no longer call sisters, since they have trampled on their blood ties with murderous hatred."

Psyche sobbed tearfully and replied, "For a long time now you've seen proof of my loyalty; I will again prove to you the strength of my mind. Just order Zephyr to do his duty, and in exchange for not being allowed to see your venerable shape, let me at least have a glimpse of my sisters. By the cinnamon smell of your flowing hair, by your smooth and tender cheeks that are like mine, by your chest glowing with warmth, in this little one, at least, may I come to know your face. May my pious and anxious prayers win you over, and may you embrace me and restore with joy the soul of Psyche, who is devoted to you. I ask nothing more of your appearance; the darkness of night does not keep me away from you. I hold you, my light." Enchanted by these words and soft embraces, the husband dried Psyche's tears with his own hair, and promised to do what she wanted. He then left, just before daylight.

Meanwhile the two sisters agreed on their plan. Instead of visiting their parents, they went straight from their ships to the cliff. Without waiting for confirmation that Zephyr was there, they leapt recklessly into the air. Even though he did not want to, Zephyr obeyed the royal command. He lifted up the sisters in his breeze and returned them safely to the ground. They marched directly into Psyche's house and embraced their prey. They disguised their deceit with flattery: "Psyche, you are not so small as before. You are now a mother! What a great gift you are carrying in your little belly! What joy will fill our entire home thanks to you! How happy we are! We will be gladdened by your golden infant. If your baby imitates the beauty of his parents, we expect a little Cupid will be born!" In this way they invaded Psyche's mind with false affection. She in turn offered refreshments to her sisters, who were tired from their journey. She offered them delicious food, including sausages, and then a bath; she ordered a cithara to play, and flute music; she also commanded a chorus to sing. Their minds were calmed by the sweet invisible notes.

But the sweet music did not put to rest the evil plot of the wicked sisters. Directing the conversation towards a snare of lies, they again questioned Psyche about her husband: how does he treat her, who are his parents, where did he grow up? Simple Psyche, forgetting her original story, invented a new version saying that her husband was from a neighbouring province, that he was middle aged with grey hair, that he made a lot of money in the trading business. Then abruptly she gave her sisters gifts and sent them back again on the wind transport. While returning home on the breath of Zephyr, the older sisters again took turns complaining: "Sister, what should we say about our foolish little sister's lies? When we first asked her, she told us her husband was young with a soft beard, now she says he's middle aged with bright white hair. Who becomes so old in such a short time? Either she is lying or else she doesn't know what her husband looks like. Whichever it is, she must be stripped of that wealth as soon as possible! If she hasn't seen the face of her husband, she must be married to a god, which also means she is pregnant with a god. I hope this isn't true. If she is going to be the mother of a divine child, I will hang myself immediately. Let's go back to our parents and agree to weave the lies we talked about earlier."

So inflamed, they disturbed their weary parents with an unexpected visit. Then in a hurry again the next morning the sisters went to the cliff, and with Zephyr's help flew back down to visit Psyche. Pretending to be worried and frightened they called out to her, "Sister, you seem very happy, but you don't know the serious danger you are in. We, your sisters, are sleepless with worry and concern for your safety; we are afraid of what you are really facing. We are your companions in this misfortune, and cannot hide the truth from you: you have been lying at night with a huge serpent – one that has many coils and is bloodthirsty and venomous. Remember the Delphic oracle that announced that you would marry a wild beast? Many locals and hunters saw the beast returning from a feeding, swimming in the shallows of a nearby river. Everyone says that he will shower you with gifts and feasts for a while, but when you are fully pregnant, he will devour you and your baby. You must decide now whether to cooperate with us, your dear sisters, who are concerned for your safety and want to save your life, or to allow yourself to be eaten by a very savage beast. If you prefer the loneliness of this countryside and the voices and the dangerous sexual encounters with a poisonous serpent, at least we will have done our duty." Hearing these disturbing words Psyche, with her simple and tender mind, was gripped with fear. Unable to contain herself, she told them all about her husband's warnings as well as her own promises to him. Trembling and pale she kept babbling about her situation and the depths of her disaster. Three times she repeated the following: "My dearest sisters, you are right to persist in your pious duty. I don't think those people you mention would invent a lie. It's true, I have never seen the face of my husband. I have no idea where he is from. I only hear his voice at night. I have a husband whose family is unknown to me, and who avoids all daylight. The people you spoke with, who say he is some kind of monster, must be right. He prevents me from thinking about what he looks like by frightening me. If you can bring help to your sister, please do. Don't spoil your earlier kindnesses by being careless now."

Now that the wicked sisters had opened the gates of Psyche's simple mind, they drew their swords and invaded her terrified thoughts. Finally, one of them said, "Our family ties compel us to keep you safe. We have been thinking about this for a long time. Here is your only path to safety: Next to the bed where you sleep, you must hide a very sharp razor, one that cuts easily. You should also have an oil-filled lamp hidden in a pot nearby. When he comes to bed, and when he's sleeping, and begins to breathe deeply, you'll slip out of bed – barefoot to soften your steps – then you'll light the lamp, and with the sharp razor in your right hand, with all your strength you'll cut the deadly serpent's neck. We will be waiting anxiously for you; as soon as you kill him and save yourself, we will join you, and take away all that wealth, and find a normal man for you to marry." The sisters, who were actually afraid to stay, rushed to the cliff, and were carried back by Zephyr. They boarded their ship and quickly made their escape.

Psyche was alone now and of course was very upset by what was going to happen. Her disturbed thoughts fluctuated like the sea. She had a plan, but had conflicting feelings about it: She hurried, hesitated, dared, feared, despaired, became angry, and finally, in her one body she both hated the beast and loved her husband. Then when evening was approaching, she prepared what was needed to carry out the wicked deed. Night arrived; her husband arrived. After a few of Venus's battles, he fell into a deep sleep. Psyche, usually weak in body and mind, was strengthened by the fierceness of her fate. She lit the lamp and grabbed the razor. Her boldness made her act in a manly fashion. But as soon as the lamp's light illuminated the secrets of her bed, she saw the most gentle and sweetest beast of all, Cupid himself, the beautiful god, beautifully resting. At this sight the lamp rejoiced and brightened, and the razor regretted its sacrilegious sharpness. Psyche was terrified. Trembling and feeling faint, she fell to her knees wanting to plunge the weapon into her own chest – which she would have done if the razor itself, deeply ashamed, had not fallen from her hands. Still weary and faint, she recovered her mind as she gazed at the beauty of Cupid's divine face. She looked at the delightful hair on his golden head, drunk with ambrosia; his milky white neck, dark red cheeks, tufts of hair bound gracefully – some hanging down in the front, some in the back. The light of the lamp faltered in the presence of his gorgeousness. On the shoulders of the god, dewy feathers gleamed; the outermost feathers trembled restlessly while he slept. His body was so smooth, so shiny that Venus his mother would be pleased. At the foot of the bed were his bow and quiver and arrows, gracious weapons of the great god. Curious, Psyche marvelled at her husband and examined his weapons. She took an arrow from his quiver, and tested its tip with her thumb, puncturing it. A second time she pricked her thumb more deeply, until little drops of rose-red blood moistened her fingertip. And so Psyche fell in love with Love. Burning with desire for Desire, she bent over and kissed him passionately. She worried about waking him. Even though she was excited to be in the presence of so great a good, her mind was troubled. Then the lamp, either because of disloyalty or because of noxious envy or because it was eager to touch such a body with a kiss, that lamp spilt a drop of hot oil onto the god's right shoulder. Bold and reckless lamp, vile assistant of love! You burnt the god of all fires! When a lover wants to prolong his desire at night, he first finds you.

When the god felt the burn of the oil, he jumped up and realized Psyche's disloyalty. He immediately flew away from the kisses of his unfortunate spouse. Psyche with both hands grabbed his right leg as he was rising, a pitiable sight; for a time she hung on through the cloudy sky until at last she fell to the ground. The god and lover left her there and perched on a nearby cypress tree. From the treetop, deeply upset, he addressed Psyche: "Oh most simple Psyche, I disobeyed the commands of my mother, Venus, who ordered me to make you fall in love with a miserable mortal, and doom you to the vilest marriage possible. Instead, I myself flew to you as a lover – it was foolish of me to do this, I know. I, the famous archer, pierced myself with my own weapon, and made you my wife. But you thought I was a beast whose head you were going to cut off, the very head that has your lover's eyes. I kept warning you to beware of this. Those deadly advisors of yours with their destructive plans will be punished right away! And you will be punished by my absence." After saying this, Cupid flew away high into the sky. When she saw him leave, Psyche fell to the ground, her mind in extreme agony. When her husband, now a stranger, was out of sight, she jumped headfirst into the nearby river. The river, out of respect for the god who could burn away its waters, pushed Psyche ashore with a gentle wave, leaving her on a grassy bank....

Cimon and Pero
(by Valerius Maximus, translated by Samuel Speed)

T HE PRAETOR HAD DELIVERED to the triumvir a free-born woman to be put to death in prison, after she had been convicted of some heinous crime. But the compassionate jailer did not strangle her right away. Rather, he continued to give her daughter liberty to visit her, after he had diligently searched that she brought no food with her, believing that in a little time the mother would be starved to death. But seeing her live many days without any alteration, he began to wonder by what means she kept herself alive; thereupon, watching the daughter more carefully, he observed her giving her breast to her mother, and abating her hunger with her own milk. The novelty of this wonderful sight was reported by him to the triumvir, by the triumvir to the praetor, and by the praetor to the panel of judges, who granted the woman her pardon. What will piety not devise in order to preserve a parent's life in prison – even such strange a means as this? For what could be more unusual, what more extraordinary, than a mother nourished by the breasts of her daughter? One would say that this was against the course of nature, except that nature commands us in the first place to love our parents.

The same may be said of the piety of Pero, who preserved her father Mycon, who had fallen into the same misfortune, and was in prison; she nourished him like a baby, in his extreme old age, with the milk of her breasts. Men's eyes are full of wonder, when they observe this act of piety represented in painting.

Letter LXXXIII to Sura
(by Pliny the Younger, translated by William Melmoth)

THE PRESENT RECESS from business we are now enjoying affords you leisure to give, and me to receive, instruction. I am extremely desirous therefore to know whether you believe in the existence of ghosts, and that they have a real form, and are a sort of divinity, or only the visionary impressions of a terrified imagination. What particularly inclines me to believe

in their existence is a story which I heard of Curtius Rufus.
When he was in low circumstances and unknown in the world,
he attended the governor of Africa into that province.

One evening, as he was walking in the public portico, there appeared
to him the figure of a woman, of unusual size and of beauty more than
human. And as he stood there, terrified and astonished, she told him
she was the tutelary power that presided over Africa, and was come to
inform him of the future events of his life: that he should go back to
Rome, to enjoy high honours there, and return to that province invested
with the proconsular dignity, and there should die. Every circumstance of
this prediction actually came to pass. It is said farther that upon his arrival
at Carthage, as he was coming out of the ship, the same figure met him
upon the shore. It is certain, at least, that being seized with a fit of illness,
though there were no symptoms in his case that led those about him to
despair, he instantly gave up all hope of recovery; judging, apparently, of
the truth of the future part of the prediction by what had already been
fulfilled, and of the approaching misfortune from his former prosperity.
Now the following story, which I am going to tell you just as I heard it, is
it not more terrible than the former, while quite as wonderful? There was
at Athens a large and roomy house, which had a bad name, so that no one
could live there. In the dead of the night a noise, resembling the clashing
of iron, was frequently heard, which, if you listened more attentively,
sounded like the rattling of chains, distant at first, but approaching nearer
by degrees: immediately afterwards a spectre appeared in the form of
an old man, of extremely emaciated and squalid appearance, with a long
beard and dishevelled, hair, rattling the chains on his feet and hands.

The distressed occupants meanwhile passed their wakeful nights under
the most dreadful terrors imaginable. This, as it broke their rest, ruined
their health, and brought on distempers, their terror grew upon them, and
death ensued. Even in the daytime, though the spirit did not appear, yet the
impression remained so strong upon their imaginations that it still seemed
before their eyes, and kept them in perpetual alarm.

Consequently the house was at length deserted, as being deemed
absolutely uninhabitable; so that it was now entirely abandoned to the ghost.

However, in hopes that some tenant might be found who was ignorant of this very alarming circumstance, a bill was put up, giving notice that it was either to be let or sold. It happened that Athenodorus the philosopher came to Athens at this time, and, reading the bill, enquired the price. The extraordinary cheapness raised his suspicion; nevertheless, when he heard the whole story, he was so far from being discouraged that he was more strongly inclined to hire it, and, in short, actually did so.

When it grew towards evening, he ordered a couch to be prepared for him in the front part of the house, and, after calling for a light, together with his pencil and tablets, directed all his people to retire. But that his mind might not, for want of employment, be open to the vain terrors of imaginary noises and spirits, he applied himself to writing with the utmost attention. The first part of the night passed in entire silence, as usual; at length a clanking of iron and rattling of chains was heard: however, he neither lifted up his eyes nor laid down his pen, but, in order to keep calm and collected, tried to pass the sounds off to himself as something else. The noise increased and advanced nearer, till it seemed at the door, and at last in the chamber. He looked up, saw, and recognized the ghost exactly as it had been described to him: it stood before him, beckoning with the finger, like a person who calls another. Athenodorus in reply made a sign with his hand that it should wait a little, and threw his eyes again upon his papers; the ghost then rattled its chains over the head of the philosopher, who looked up upon this, and seeing it beckoning as before, immediately arose, and, light in hand, followed it. The ghost slowly stalked along, as if encumbered with its chains, and, turning into the area of the house, suddenly vanished. Athenodorus, being thus deserted, made a mark with some grass and leaves on the spot where the spirit left him.

The next day he gave information to the magistrates, and advised them to order that spot to be dug up. This was accordingly done, and the skeleton of a man in chains was found there; for the body, having lain a considerable time in the ground, was putrefied and mouldered away from the fetters. The bones, being collected together, were publicly buried, and thus after the ghost was appeased by the proper ceremonies, the house was haunted no more. This story I believe upon the credit of others; what I am going to mention, I give you upon my own. I have a freedman named

Marcus, who is by no means illiterate. One night, as he and his younger brother were lying together, he fancied he saw somebody upon his bed, who took out a pair of scissors, and cut off the hair from the top part of his own head, and in the morning, it appeared his hair was actually cut, and the clippings lay scattered about the floor.

A short time after this, an event of a similar nature contributed to give credit to the former story. A young lad of my family was sleeping in his apartment with the rest of his companions, when two persons clad in white came in, as he says, through the windows, cut off his hair as he lay, and then returned the same way they entered. The next morning it was found that this boy had been served just as the other, and there was the hair again, spread about the room. Nothing remarkable indeed followed these events, unless perhaps that I escaped a prosecution, in which, if Domitian (during whose reign this happened) had lived some time longer, I should certainly have been involved. For after the death of that emperor, articles of impeachment against me were found in his scrutore, which had been exhibited by Carus. It may therefore be conjectured, since it is customary for persons under any public accusation to let their hair grow, this cutting off the hair of my servants was a sign I should escape the imminent danger that threatened me.

Let me desire you then to give this question your mature consideration. The subject deserves your examination; as, I trust, I am not myself altogether unworthy a participation in the abundance of your superior knowledge. And though you should, as usual, balance between two opinions, yet I hope you will lean more on one side than on the other, lest, whilst I consult you in order to have my doubt settled, you should dismiss me in the same suspense and indecision that occasioned you the present application. Farewell.

The Story of Medea

A LL THE MOST beautiful ladies of the court were present at this entertainment; but in the eyes of Jason none could compare with the king's daughter, the young and lovely Medea....A

confession of mutual attachment took place....Meanwhile Aëtes, having discovered the loss of his daughter...despatched a large fleet, under the command of his son Absyrtus, in pursuit of the fugitives....Medea now consulted Jason, and, with his consent, carried out the following stratagem. She sent a message to her brother Absyrtus, to the effect that she had been carried off against her will, and promised that if he would meet her, in the darkness of night, in the temple of Artemis, she would assist him in regaining possession of the Golden Fleece. Relying on the good faith of his sister, Absyrtus fell into the snare, and duly appeared at the appointed trysting-place; and whilst Medea kept her brother engaged in conversation, Jason rushed forwards and slew him.

Medea and Jason now fled to Corinth, where at length they found, for a time, peace and tranquillity, their happiness being completed by the birth of three children.

As time passed on, however, and Medea began to lose the beauty which had won the love of her husband, he grew weary of her, and became attracted by the youthful charms of Glauce, the beautiful daughter of Creon, king of Corinth. Jason had obtained her father's consent to their union, and the wedding-day was already fixed, before he disclosed to Medea the treachery which he meditated against her. He used all his persuasive powers in order to induce her to consent to his union with Glauce, assuring her that his affection had in no way diminished, but that for the sake of the advantages which would thereby accrue to their children, he had decided on forming this alliance with the royal house. Though justly enraged at his deceitful conduct, Medea dissembled her wrath, and, feigning to be satisfied with this explanation, sent, as a wedding-gift to her rival, a magnificent robe of cloth-of-gold. This robe was imbued with a deadly poison which penetrated to the flesh and bone of the wearer, and burned them as though with a consuming fire. Pleased with the beauty and costliness of the garment, the unsuspecting Glauce lost no time in donning it; but no sooner had she done so than the fell poison began to take effect. In vain she tried to tear the robe away; it defied all efforts to be removed, and after horrible and protracted sufferings, she expired.

Maddened at the loss of her husband's love Medea next put to death her three sons, and when Jason, thirsting for revenge, left the chamber of his dead bride, and flew to his own house in search of Medea, the ghastly spectacle of his murdered children met his view. He rushed frantically to seek the murderess, but nowhere could she be found. At length, hearing a sound above his head, he looked up, and beheld Medea gliding through the air in a golden chariot drawn by dragons.

In a fit of despair Jason threw himself on his own sword, and perished on the threshold of his desolate and deserted home.

Jonathan and the Three Talismans

DARIUS WAS A WISE and prudent king; he had three sons whom he loved much, and amongst whom he divided his possessions. To the eldest he gave his kingdom; to the second, his personal wealth; to the third, a ring, a necklace and a valuable carpet. These three gifts were charmed. The ring rendered anyone who wore it beloved, and obtained for him whatsoever he desired. The necklace, if worn on the breast, enabled the wearer to realize every wish; whilst the cloth had such virtue that whosoever sat upon it, and thought where he would be carried, found himself there almost before his thought was expressed. These three precious gifts the king conferred upon Jonathan, his youngest son, to aid him in his studies; but his mother retained them during the earlier years of his youth; after a time his mother delivered to him the ring.

"Jonathan," she said, "take the first of thy father's bequests – this ring; guard it as a treasure. So long as you wear it, everyone shall love you, and whatsoever you wish shall be obtained by you; of one thing beware – an artful woman."

Jonathan, with many thanks and protestations, took the ring. Its magic effects were soon evident. Everyone sought his society, and everyone loved him. Though he had neither silver nor gold, house nor fields, he had but to wish for them, and lo, one gave him fields, and another houses, a third gold, a fourth merchandise. Walking one day in the streets of Rome, he met a lady so beautiful to look at that he could not restrain himself from following her, and eventually he had no happiness but in her society. She loved Jonathan, and Jonathan loved her.

"Dearest," said the lady one day, as Jonathan was enjoying her society, "how comes it that you immediately obtain everything you but wish for, and yet the good king did not leave thee his wealth, or his power?"

"It is a secret, Subtilia; a secret that I may not reveal, lest it lose its value."

"And do you profess to love me, Jonathan, and yet keep from me the secret of your power, your wealth and your life?"

"Ask me not, dearest, for it may not be."

"Farewell, then, Jonathan – thou lovest me not – never more will I love thee again."

"Nay, Subtilia, but thou canst not prevent thyself loving me as long as I wear this ring."

"Ah, Jonathan, the secret, the secret! You wear a magic ring."

"Fool that I was," exclaimed Jonathan, "in my haste I forgot my discretion; well, you know my secret – be honest, and keep it yourself."

"You have not told me all the properties of the ring; I must know all if thou wouldst have it kept a secret."

Subtilia at length elicited the secret from her lover. The source of his power once known to her, the next object of her plans was to obtain that power for herself.

"Thou art very wrong, Jonathan," said she, looking up into his face, with her dark black eyes; "surely thou art wrong to wear so precious a jewel on thy finger; someday, in the hurry of your occupation, you will lose the ring, and then your power is gone."

"There is some sense in what you say, Subtilia," replied Jonathan; "yet where shall I place it in security?"

"Let me be its guardian, dearest," said Subtilia, with a look of deep affection. "No one will seek such a treasure of me; and whensoever you wish for it, it will be ready to your hand; among the rest of my jewels it will be perfectly secure."

Jonathan acceded to her request, and placed the ring in her possession. For a time all went well; the ring was safe, and ready to his use, and the lady's love did not decrease. One day, when he came to visit her as usual, he found Subtilia sitting on a couch, bathed in tears.

"Oh, my dear, dear lord!" exclaimed she, casting herself at his feet; "how can I dare to approach my lord?"

"Why this anxiety, this sorrow, Subtilia?" said Jonathan, as he raised her from the ground, and strove to kiss away her tears.

"Oh, my lord! pardon me – the ring," exclaimed Subtilia.

"Ah! the ring – what of the ring?"

"It is gone, my lord – stolen."

"Gone! how gone, woman?" rejoined Jonathan, in anger.

"Ah, my good lord; this morning I went to my jewel-box to take out such ornaments as might best please my lord, and lo, the ring was not there; and now where it is I know not."

"Farewell, Subtilia – I am ruined."

With these words Jonathan left the lady. It was all in vain that he searched everywhere for the ring; it was of but a common form, and he dared not to reveal its secret, as once known no one would dream of resigning such a treasure. In his distress he returned to his mother, and told her all his misfortunes.

"My son," said his lady mother, "did I not warn thee of this very danger? By the subtlety of this woman thou hast lost thy charmed jewel.

"Receive now thy father's second bequest – this necklace; so long as you wear this on your breast, every wish of yours shall be fulfilled; go in peace, and, once more, beware of female subtlety."

Overjoyed with his new acquisition, and unable to believe that Subtilia had deceived him about the loss of the ring, Jonathan returned to the city, and to the society of that fair but deceitful lady. For a time his secret remained within his own breast; at length, however, he yielded to the blandishments of his lady-love, and disclosed to her the source of his prosperity. Long and subtle were the means by which Subtilia gained the knowledge of the secret of the necklace, and longer and more subtle the plans by which she at last gained it to her own possession. This too was lost, as the ring; and Jonathan returned a second time to his mother.

"My son," said she, "these two times you have fallen a victim to female subtlety, the ring and the necklace are not lost; Subtilia has them both, and if you would succeed, you must regain them from her. Receive this, the third and last bequest of your royal father; seated on this carpet, you have but to wish to find yourself forthwith in whatever place you desire; go in peace, my son – for the third time, beware of female subtlety."

"I will be revenged on this faithless woman," muttered Jonathan, as he entered Subtilia's house bearing the last bequest of Darius. "Subtilia," he said, "come, see the third bequest of the good king: this splendid carpet – here sit down with me on it."

Subtilia was hardly seated on the carpet, ere Jonathan wished that they were in a desert place, far, far from the abode of man. His wish was hardly complete before they were both in a drear solitude, many hundreds of miles from a human abode, and where wild beasts and deadly serpents abounded.

"Subtilia!" exclaimed Jonathan, "thou art now in my power: restore the ring and the necklace, or die by the mouths of beasts, or the slow torture of famine; no human footstep ever treads these solitudes."

"We perish together, Jonathan."

"Delude not thyself so, false woman," rejoined Jonathan, in anger; "I have but to wish myself away, and find my wish accomplished; choose therefore – death, or the restoration of the ring and the necklace."

"I have his secret," muttered Subtilia to herself; and then, with a most piteous voice, "my dear lord, I pray thee give me time – but an hour, or even less – before I decide."

"As you wish; until the sun touches the top of yonder pine tree, consider your choice."

Whilst the time was passing away, the heat of the day seduced Jonathan into a slight sleep. Subtilia saw the advantage; slowly, and softly, she drew away the carpet from beneath him, and as, awakened by her last efforts, he would have regained the magic carpet, she wished herself again at Rome, and passed from his sight. He was alone in the desert, whilst she revelled in every luxury that could be obtained through the means of the three gifts of his royal father.

Jonathan meditated on his situation, and upbraided himself for his own foolishness: whither to bend his steps from that dreadful wilderness he knew not, but committing himself by prayer to God's especial protection, he followed a narrow path, and at length reached the banks of a large river. The river was not deep, and Jonathan essayed to pass it. Though the water was so hot that it burnt the flesh off his bones, he persevered, and at length reached the opposite bank. He essayed to taste of the stream, but it was sore bitter, and burned the roof of his mouth as he drank of it. Astonished at the properties of the river, Jonathan placed a small quantity of it in a glass vessel, and proceeded, with great pain, on his journey.

Hunger soon succeeded to thirst, and the solitary wanderer wist not how to assuage his bitter craving. As he wandered on, limping with pain, he suddenly cast his eyes on a fair and tempting tree, abounding in fruit of a rich and golden hue. Without one thought of thanks to God, Jonathan limped to the tree, and plucked eagerly of the fruit. The fair meal had hardly concluded, ere he was a leper from head to foot, the foul disease broke out over his body. Weeping and mourning for his misfortunes, he gathered of the hurtful fruit, and renewed his miserable wanderings.

Another hour of painful travel brought Jonathan to the bank of a troubled, turbid stream, whose depth appeared unfathomable, and whose waters were repugnant even to the thirsty man. Careless of his life, with one prayer to God, the wanderer stept into the river, unconscious of its depth. It was shallow, and offered little resistance to his passage, though its stream seemed to roll onward with headlong violence. His burnt flesh, too, came again in all its original purity. Jonathan reached the bank, and on his bended knees gave thanks to God for his great kindness in relieving him from his pains. Of this stream, also, he took a small vase full, as a treasured medicine.

Still the wanderer continued his journey, hungry and a leper. No tree on either side of him gave any promise of sustenance, and he despaired of sustaining his fast-fleeting strength. Anon he came to a low, crooked, cankerous-looking bush, with two or three withered, and apparently rotten, apples on one of its branches. Desperate with hunger, he seized one of the wretched fruits and ate it. His hunger was assuaged; his leprosy was departed from him. Strength, health and a free spirit seemed renewed in him, and plucking another of the withered fruits, he went on his way rejoicing.

By the virtue of that food he wandered on without feeling hunger; by the virtue of that water his flesh suffered not from his journey, and he knew not what fatigue was. After many days he neared the gates of a walled city, and made as though he would have entered.

"Ho! sir traveller," said the gatekeeper, "whence comest thou – what art thou – and whither goest thou?"

"From Rome, good porter – a physician—"

"Stay," interrupted the porter; "a physician – you are in good fortune – canst cure a leprosy?"

"I can but try my skill."

"If you succeed with this case your fortune is made, friend; our king is ill of a leprosy. Whoever will cure him will receive great rewards, but death if he fails."

"I will undertake the cure," replied Jonathan; "lead me to the king."

Jonathan entered the palace, and was led to the chamber of the king, where he lay on his couch, wasted with disease, and covered from head to foot with a leprosy of the most virulent kind.

"A physician, my lord the king," said the attendant, "who would try to cure your disease."

"What, another victim?" rejoined the royal leper; "does he know the alternative?"

"My lord," said Jonathan, "I am aware of the terms, and accept them freely; by God's help I will cure my lord, or perish in the attempt. I pray my lord the king to eat of this fruit."

"What, this withered, rotten apple?" exclaimed the king.

"Even this, my lord."

The king took the fruit of the second tree, and ate it as Jonathan advised. In a moment his leprosy began to disappear, and the pimples to sink and become hardly visible.

"Thou art, indeed, a physician," exclaimed the king; "the promised reward is thine."

"Stay, my lord," said Jonathan, "we must restore the flesh to its original state."

With these words, he touched every mark on the king's body with the water of the second river, and the flesh returned fair and white as before the leprosy.

"Blessed physician, thy reward is doubled; stay, I pray thee, in our country."

"Nay, my lord, I may not. I must seek my own land, and all I ask is that my lord will divide the half of my reward amongst the poor of this city."

Soon after this Jonathan sailed from this city for Rome; arrived there, he circulated a report that a great physician had arrived. Now it happened that Subtilia, in spite of all the talismans, lay grievously sick, and nigh unto death. The report of the arrival of the great physician comforted her, and she sent for Jonathan. He knew her again, but she knew him not, for he was greatly altered and disguised.

"Great master," said she, in a faint voice, "I die."

"Death, lady, comes ever to those who confess not their sins against God and man, and defraud their friends; if thou hast done this my help is vain, without confession and restoration."

Then did Subtilia confess all her treachery against Jonathan, and how she had deprived him by her subtlety of the three talismans, and left him to die in a desert place.

"Woman," said Jonathan, "thy ill-used lover yet lives, and is prosperous; the talismans must be restored to him – where be they?"

"In yonder chest; here, take the keys, restore them to Jonathan, and give me of your medicine."

"Take this fruit – drink of this water."

"Mercy, mercy!" exclaimed Subtilia, "I am a leper – the flesh is burning away from my bones – I die – I die."

"Subtilia, thou hast met with thy reward – thou diest – and Jonathan is thy physician."

With one fearful look at Jonathan, and one agonized scream, the wretched woman fell back a corpse, her diseased flesh already mouldering to destruction.

Jonathan regained his father's bequests, and returned to his mother; the whole kingdom rejoiced at his return. Until his life's end he remembered the lessons he had learnt in his prosperity and his poverty, and he lived and died in peace with God and with man.

"Your tale, of course, boasts of a moral?"

"Yes; a moral far from unreasonable. The Emperor Darius is typical of our Saviour, as is generally the case in these tales; and the queen-mother is the Church. The two sons are the men of this world; the third son typifies the good Christian. The lady, his great temptation and source of all his evils, is the flesh. She first obtains from him the ring of faith, and after that deprives him, by her devices, of the necklace of hope; and in spite of these warnings, steals from him, at last, the cloth of charity. The bitter water, that burneth away the flesh from the bones, is repentance, and the first fruit is heartfelt remorse; the second river is repentance before God, and the unpromising fruit represents the deeds of faith, prayer, self-denial and charity."

"You have left the leprous king and the ship still unexplained."

"The former is but a type of a sinful man, the other is intended to represent the Divine command, but the application seems forced and inappropriate."

"You have another link between the East and West in this tale," remarked Herbert. "The talisman of the magic cloth may be found in the 'Arabian Nights,' in the story of Prince Ahmed, and the Fairy Pari Banou."

"All the three talismans proclaim the Eastern origin of the story," remarked Lathom; "and besides this, its entire structure resembles the tale of Fortunatus, to which few have hesitated to assign an Eastern origin."

"Many of the incidents of your story are to be found in the old German nursery tale of The Dwarf and the Three Soldiers."

"Not unlikely; but the tale in question is so little known to me that I cannot trace the likeness."

"The tale, in a few words, is this," replied Thompson. "Three poor soldiers obtain from a dwarf three gifts: a cloak, a purse and a horse – one and all equally useful in promoting their worldly advantage. A crafty princess steals all these gifts, and the soldiers are once more poor. Driven by hunger, one of the three eats of an apple tree by the roadside, and forthwith his nose grows, not by inches, but by miles. The friendly dwarf, in pity of his misery, cures him by administering another kind of apple; and the nose shrinks as quickly as it had grown.

"Now comes the revenge on the princess. The old soldier offers some of the fatal apples for sale; the princess buys and eats; her nose grows without ceasing. Under pretence of curing her, the old soldier, disguised as a doctor, makes her nose grow more and more, and at length, having terrified her into restoring the dwarf's gifts, kindly gives her a piece of the second kind of apples, and cures her of the nasal protuberance."

"And now that we have concluded our criticisms," said Herbert, "let us give all due praise to the admirable instruction contained in this last narrative."

"May we not extend our praise to all the tales?"

"As critics, well intentioned towards the writers, and especially towards this translation, we must not set much store on our criticism. We need not, however, fear to give our own opinions, and therefore I agree with you that great praise may with reason be given to all the tales we have heard, and to no one more than that with which our last evening, I fear, must now conclude. One thing I would ask you, Lathom; you spoke of the want of the usual accessories in these old monks' stories. One or two slips have not escaped me; but unless you have reproduced many of the tales, the credit of great experience in writing fictions must be allowed to the authors of the Gesta."

"I do not mean to deny that I have rewritten many of these tales, and in some places introduced a little embroidery, but nowhere have I done more than re-set the old jewels, and put old pictures into new frames."

"This, then, is our last evening with the old storytellers," said Thompson; "tomorrow Herbert and I are off for a week of home, whilst you are left here to—"

"To re-set some more old jewels, should these, through your report, obtain favour and acceptance with my friends."

FLAME TREE PUBLISHING